Christie Barlow is the number one international bestselling author of twenty-three romantic comedies including the iconic Love Heart Lane Series, *A Home at Honeysuckle Farm* and *Kitty's Countryside Dream*. She lives in a ramshackle cottage in a quaint village in the heart of Staffordshire with her four children and two dogs.

Her writing career came as a lovely surprise when Christie decided to write a book to teach her children a valuable life lesson and show them that they are capable of achieving their dreams.

Christie writes about love, life, friendships and the importance of community spirit. She loves to hear from her readers and you can get in touch via X, Facebook and Instagram.

- facebook.com/ChristieJBarlow
- x.com/ChristieJBarlow
- bookbub.com/authors/christie-barlow
- instagram.com/christie_barlow

Also by Christie Barlow

The Love Heart Lane Series

Love Heart Lane

Foxglove Farm

Clover Cottage

Starcross Manor

The Lake House

Primrose Park

Heartcross Castle

The New Doctor at Peony Practice

New Beginnings at the Old Bakehouse

The Hidden Secrets of Bumblebee Cottage

A Summer Surprise at the Little Blue Boathouse

A Winter Wedding at Starcross Manor

The Library on Love Heart Lane

The Vintage Flower Van on Love Heart Lane

The Puffin Island Series

A Postcard from Puffin Island

The Lighthouse Daughters of Puffin Island

Standalones

Kitty's Countryside Dream

The Cosy Canal Boat Dream

A Home at Honeysuckle Farm

THE STORY SHOP

CHRISTIE BARLOW

One More Chapter
a division of HarperCollins*Publishers* Ltd
1 London Bridge Street
London SE1 9GF
www.harpercollins.co.uk
HarperCollins*Publishers*
Macken House, 39/40 Mayor Street Upper,
Dublin 1, D01 C9W8, Ireland

This paperback edition 2025

1

First published in Great Britain in ebook format
by HarperCollins*Publishers* 2025
Copyright © Christie Barlow 2025
Christie Barlow asserts the moral right to
be identified as the author of this work
A catalogue record of this book is available from the British Library

ISBN: 978-0-00-870805-4

This novel is entirely a work of fiction. The names, characters and incidents portrayed in it are the work of the author's imagination. Any resemblance to actual persons, living or dead, events or localities is entirely coincidental.

Printed and bound in the UK using 100% Renewable Electricity
by CPI Group (UK) Ltd

All rights reserved. No part of this publication may be reproduced, stored in a retrieval system, or transmitted, in any form or by any means, electronic, mechanical, photocopying, recording or otherwise, without the prior permission of the publishers.
Without limiting the exclusive rights of any author, contributor or the publisher of this publication, any unauthorised use of this publication to train generative artificial intelligence (AI) technologies is expressly prohibited. HarperCollins also exercise their rights under Article 4(3) of the Digital Single Market Directive 2019/790 and expressly reserve this publication from the text and data mining exception.

For Julie Wetherill
You're simply the best! An amazing friend, my go-to travel buddy, and the queen of making me belly laugh. Thank you for being there for all the adventures, the chats, and the gin (obviously). Life's better with you in it – this one's for you!

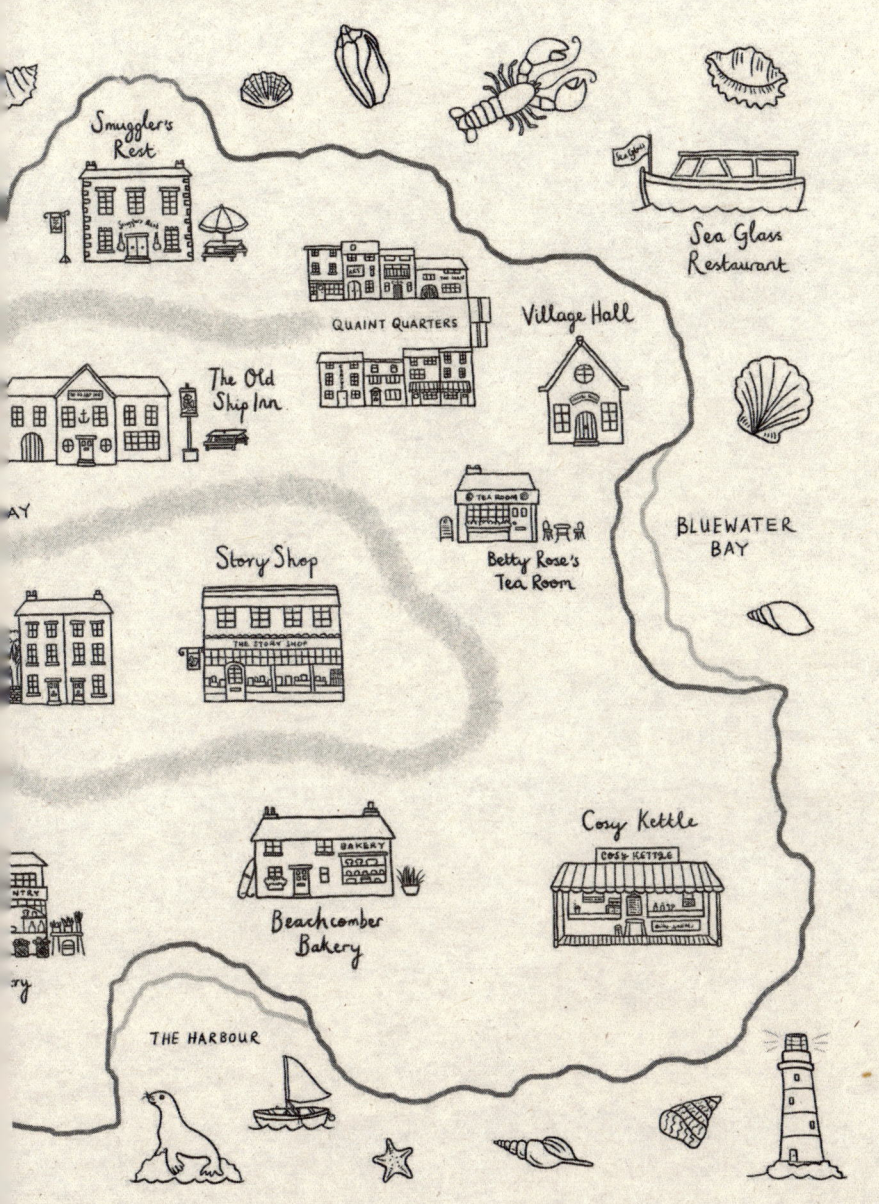

Prologue

AMELIA

Puffin Island, with its windswept cliffs and rugged coastline, had once been a place of belonging and stability for Amelia Brown. But now, with every inch of it carrying memories of her father, taken too soon in a tragic yacht accident, it was a place of sadness and grief. Ethan Brown had loved her with his whole heart, and nourished her love of the written word, first teaching her to read, then how to write with passion. But now he was gone, and Amelia was alone.

Her stomach churned as she ascended the narrow, creaking staircase leading to Edgar Carmichael's office. The old solicitor had been a fixture of Puffin Island for as long as anyone could remember, and his office, tucked above an antique shop on Anchor Way, was small and unassuming, and its faded sign hanging precariously from a rusty chain outside was the only hint that it was there. Despite its modest exterior, this was the hallowed ground where countless Puffin Island family legacies had been determined, and today it would see her own fate decided.

The smell of coffee hit Amelia as she stepped into the dimly lit room. Edgar's office was a time capsule, every surface adorned with signs of a life spent in quiet contemplation. Shelves sagged under the weight of thick legal volumes and dusty files from cases long closed. The large oak desk was the room's centrepiece, its surface covered with papers, but still meticulously organised. To the left of the desk, a small window allowed slivers of the afternoon light to seep in.

Edgar had been a friend of her father's for many years. Dressed in a worn but neat suit, he was in his late sixties, with salt-and-pepper hair that curled in an unruly way at the nape of his neck. His pale blue eyes, sharp and discerning, were half-hidden behind a pair of wire-rimmed glasses that were perpetually slipping down his nose. Edgar had lived on the island all his life and established himself as the go-to solicitor for nearly all of the island's residents. He knew every family's history and every bit of gossip, the fact that he kept himself very much to himself making him the ideal keeper of secrets.

'Amelia,' he said, standing as she entered, his voice kind but subdued. 'I'm terribly sorry for the circumstances. Please, have a seat.'

Amelia managed a thin smile and sat down. Feeling anxious, she looked at him. 'Thank you, Edgar. I just ... I don't understand any of this. The accident, this will reading, everything feels wrong.'

He nodded, his face solemn. 'I understand. Your father's passing was a shock to all of us.'

Before Amelia could respond, the door to the office creaked open again, and in swept Vivienne Langford, looking every bit the villain Amelia had come to know her as. She was dressed all in black, her raven hair cascading down her back in glossy waves, her lips painted the colour of fresh blood. The sharp clicking of her heels on the wooden floorboards echoed in the small room like a death knell as she walked to her seat with an air of self-assurance, her dark eyes glimmering as she cast a brief, dismissive glance at Amelia.

'Ah, Edgar, darling,' she purred, her voice thick with faux warmth. 'I trust this won't take too long?'

Amelia stiffened in her seat, her gaze locked on the woman who had come between her and her father. Vivienne had waltzed into Ethan Brown's life like a storm, sweeping him away with her charm and ambition. As a successful literary agent, she knew how to get what she wanted, and she'd set her sights on Amelia's father – and now, apparently, on everything he owned.

Edgar cleared his throat and gestured for Vivienne to take a seat. 'We'll begin shortly.'

Vivienne sat with the grace of a cat, her legs crossed and her hands resting elegantly on her knee, a slight smirk playing on her lips. Amelia's blood boiled as she watched Vivienne's smug composure, knowing full well that this woman had been the catalyst for everything that had gone wrong in her relationship with her father just before he passed away. The fights, the distance, the final estrangement; all of it led back to Vivienne.

Edgar fumbled with a stack of papers on his desk, clearly uncomfortable with the tension filling the room.

After a long pause, he looked up, adjusting his glasses as he prepared to read the will.

'As you both know,' Edgar began, his voice steady but heavy with the weight of what he was about to reveal, 'this is the last will and testament of Ethan Brown. It was drawn up and signed six months ago.'

Amelia's heart hammered in her chest. She had no idea what to expect, but surely her father had not forgotten her. He had always promised that the family home – *their* home – would one day be hers. It was their sanctuary, the place where they had shared countless memories. It was inconceivable that he would leave it to anyone else, especially Vivienne.

Edgar continued reading, his voice monotone as he listed the various assets and minor bequests. Amelia barely registered the details, her mind already racing ahead to what truly mattered – the house. Her childhood home perched on the cliffs, overlooking the endless ocean. It was a part of her soul.

Finally, Edgar reached the critical part of the document.

'To my beloved daughter, Amelia Brown, I leave my personal savings, investments and all possessions contained within my private study.'

Amelia exhaled, a small relief easing the tightness in her chest. She would have some of her father's things, at least. But then Edgar's voice wavered slightly as he continued, and her heart sank once more.

'And to Vivienne Langford,' Edgar read slowly, as if questioning the words himself, 'I bequeath the family home, Dune House, in its entirety, along with the surrounding estate.'

There was a deafening silence in the room as Amelia's world seemed to tilt on its axis. For a moment, she thought she hadn't heard correctly, that her mind had somehow twisted Edgar's words. But the sickening reality settled in quickly. Her father, her own father, had left the house ... to *Vivienne*?

She stared at Edgar, disbelief etched across her face. 'No,' she whispered, shaking her head. 'That can't be right.'

Edgar set the papers down, his hands trembling slightly. Even he seemed shaken by the contents of the will. 'I ... I'm sorry, Amelia. This is what your father signed. But this will wasn't made with me.'

'Ethan decided to use my solicitor.' Vivienne's smirk widened, her red lips curling into a grotesque smile of triumph. She leaned back in her chair, crossing her legs with the grace of a queen, and gave a small, satisfied click of her tongue. 'Well, it seems Ethan knew what was best after all,' she said, her voice dripping with condescension.

Amelia's fury erupted like a volcano. She shot out of her chair, her hands clenched into fists. 'You! You manipulated him! You've been in his life a matter of minutes. This isn't what he wanted ... I know it!'

Vivienne's dark eyes gleamed with a flash of something sinister, but she remained outwardly unfazed by Amelia's outburst. 'Really, Amelia, such dramatics. I understand you're upset, but the will is clear. Dune House is mine now.'

'I'll contest this,' Amelia shouted, her voice shaking with emotion. 'I don't care what it takes. I will not let you steal my family home!'

Vivienne stood, her long coat swishing as she moved. She straightened, towering over Amelia and looking down at her with cold amusement. 'You can try, darling. But the law is on my side. And, as you know, I'm very good at winning.'

She flashed a final, venomous smile before turning on her heels and sauntering towards the door.

Amelia watched her go, rage and despair crashing through her like waves in a storm. The sound of Vivienne's heels echoed long after she'd left the room, each click a reminder of the power she now held.

Edgar sat in stunned silence, staring at the will in front of him, his brow furrowed in disbelief. 'Amelia,' he said softly. 'I … I don't understand it either. This isn't what I expected from your father. I've known him for years, and this … this doesn't make sense.'

Amelia sank back into her chair, her body trembling. 'He wouldn't do this to me,' she whispered. 'There's something wrong. I have to fight this, Edgar. I can't let her win.'

Edgar nodded slowly, his expression troubled but determined. 'We'll look into every option,' he said. 'I promise you that. We won't let this go without a fight.'

As Amelia sat in the quiet office, the weight of what had just happened pressed down on her like a suffocating fog. She'd lost her father, and now, it seemed, she was losing everything he'd promised her.

Chapter One

JACK HARTWELL

London

It was early September, one of those days where the weather couldn't quite decide what it wanted to do. The day was overcast, a thick blanket of grey clouds hanging low in the sky, threatening rain but not quite delivering. Jack Hartwell watched the world outside his flat through the condensation-covered windows, his eyes unfocused, his thoughts spiralling in a tangled mess. September always felt like a month of transition, and today was no different, a pause between what had been and what might come next.

He turned to the long line of books that he'd written, stacked together on the shelf. He had never imagined his career would come to this. He was an author with a string of well-received travel novels under his belt, each one meticulously researched and written with dedication and care, yet somehow it hadn't been enough. His last few books had barely made a ripple in the market, edging their way into the charts for less than twenty-four hours before vanishing as quickly as they'd appeared. Jack had convinced himself that the downturn was temporary, that his readers would return, but the royalty statements each month didn't lie. Worse still, his accountant had turned out to be a crook, leaving him with a tax bill that could sink a small business.

And now, an unexpected helping hand had been extended. Just when he'd thought things couldn't get worse, his former agent, Vivienne Langford, had reached out unexpectedly. He was very surprised to hear from her given they hadn't spoken in a couple of years, not since his sales had started to stall and they'd parted ways, and even more surprised when Vivienne acknowledged the challenges she assumed he was facing with the general slump of book sales in his genre, and mentioned she had a contact looking for a freelance writer. She reminded him that travel, wrapped up in fiction, had always been his forte, and said the article her contact was looking for would be right up his street. Jack had hesitated initially. When he and Vivienne had parted ways, it hadn't exactly been on the best of terms, but it seemed she still thought enough of him to put him forward for the assignment, and he couldn't deny that the idea of writing quick articles for cash was appealing. It would help him to keep his head above water for the time being, and he had experience of writing these kinds of articles in the past. He dropped the editor an email and received a quick response and an invitation to meet and discuss the commission in person.

Jack glanced at the clock on his wall. His appointment at

the headquarters of *The Morning Ledger* – one of the most-read papers in the city – was in an hour's time.

Five minutes later he threw on his coat, grabbed his briefcase and headed out the door towards the Tube, which was the usual blur of grey metal, blue and yellow worn-out upholstery and the faint smell of old coffee. As Jack boarded the train, he squeezed himself into a corner, clutching the metal pole for balance. His mind raced, as it had done for weeks, never settling on one thought for long before being swept into the next wave of anxiety. Would this job help him dig himself out of his financial hole? It would surely help, and he wondered briefly if he might be able to suggest writing more than one article a week to bring in the cash faster. He had one last book in his contract to deliver in the next six months, but he was sure he could balance doing both, especially if it made it somewhat less painful to check his bank balance.

As the train raced through the underground tunnels he thought about his career. He used to love to travel, and he'd found endless inspiration to write about different places and meeting new people, but now the familiar screech of the train on the tracks grated on his nerves, and even this short trip across London felt exhausting. And it wasn't just because of the decline in his sales or the debt he now owed because he'd trusted the wrong financial planner. There was something else getting to him. A hollow feeling in his gut that told him he wasn't just stuck. He was lost.

The train stopped at his station, jolting him out of his reverie, and he stepped out onto the platform and walked briskly through the maze of tunnels and up the escalator to the exit. The newspaper's headquarters were just a few streets ahead, a modern glass building that stood out amid the older architecture that surrounded it. The building was sleek, corporate and, in Jack's opinion, cold. It rose into the sky like a monolith, its surface polished and reflective, somehow making the overcast day seem even gloomier. He stood for a moment at the base, staring up at the towering structure, feeling as small and insignificant as his current sales. He had been in offices like this before, in the days when his agent used to call him in for meetings with publishers. Back when he still had an agent...

Shaking off the memory, he pushed through the revolving doors, stepping into a spacious lobby. The interior was all marble and steel, the floors gleaming under artificial light. A massive logo for *The Morning Ledger* hung on the far wall, imposing in its boldness.

Jack walked towards the reception desk. 'I have an appointment with the editor-in-chief,' he said to the woman behind the desk who looked up and smiled. She nodded and pointed towards the lift. 'Top floor. As soon as the doors open, there will be another reception desk in front of you.'

'Thank you,' he replied.

As the doors slid shut, his reflection stared back at him from the polished steel. The elevator chimed as it reached the top floor, and Jack stepped out into a hallway lined with glass-walled offices. He was shown to a waiting area, the receptionist telling him that the editor would be with him shortly. He sat down in one of the plush chairs and suddenly felt nervous. The door to his right opened and, to Jack's surprise, Vivienne Langford stood there. The last time he'd seen her was at his publisher's annual summer party, shortly after he'd sent her an email giving notice of his decision to leave her. She hadn't taken it well; in fact, her parting words had been far from amicable: 'You'll be nothing without me.'

For a moment they stared at each other.

Vivienne Langford looked as imperious and sharp as ever. Tall, slender, with perfectly styled black hair and a wardrobe that looked like it cost more than Jack had earned from his last book, she hadn't changed a bit. Her dark red lipstick was as sharp as her smile, which curled at the corners with smug satisfaction as she locked eyes with him.

'Jack,' she said, her voice as smooth as glass, yet still with an edge that hinted she had power over him.

'It's been a while.' He stood up, his heart pounding, unable to mask his surprise. 'What are you doing here?'

'I've just had breakfast with the editor, Miles. Let me introduce you. Miles, this is Jack Hartwell. Jack, Miles Thornton.'

Miles Thornton was now standing in the doorway of his office. He looked to be in his late twenties, with a lanky frame and a slightly hunched posture. He had a pale complexion, as though he rarely ventured outside. His messy mop of dark brown hair looked total chaos, and his rectangular glasses were perched slightly crookedly on his nose. Jack had been expecting a sharp suit, but Miles apparently favoured a wrinkled buttoned shirt with a cable-knit cardigan. The sort Jack's granny used to knit as Christmas gifts.

Miles extended his hand and Jack shook it.

'How are the book sales going?' asked Vivienne, leaning casually against the doorframe.

Jack was sure she knew exactly how his book sales were going, and it wasn't a conversation he wanted to get into at this moment, especially in front of Miles.

'You know how the publishing world is,' he replied evasively.

'Indeed,' she replied. 'Well, I'll leave you in Miles's capable hands. It's good to see you, Jack, we must catch up soon. I'll drop you a line.'

Jack nodded, feeling flustered. Despite their differences in the past, she'd thought of him for this opportunity, and for that, he was quietly grateful.

'Would you like to step into *my* office?' said Miles as Vivienne waved goodbye and headed towards the lift.

It seemed that despite Miles's casual appearance, he was determined to show an assertive demeanour.

Jack walked into the room, which was as sleek and modern as the rest of the building. Floor-to-ceiling windows framed the view of the city skyline, and the desk was immaculate, with no clutter or sign of personal touches, just polished surfaces. Miles gestured towards a chair and Jack sat down opposite him.

'Vivienne speaks very highly of you.'

'That's good to hear,' replied Jack, slightly surprised and unable to shake a lingering sense of unease.

'I understand you're a very successful writer.'

Jack hesitated, a polite smile forming as he quickly masked his discomfort. 'I've been fortunate,' he replied diplomatically, steering clear of the fact that his latest books hadn't reached the heights of his earlier successes. 'Writing's always full of ups and downs, but it's been an incredible journey so far.'

'Let's talk about your first article. I'm sending you to Puffin Island.'

Jack raised an eyebrow. 'Puffin Island?' he repeated. 'The tidal island attached to the town of Sea's End by a causeway?'

Miles looked impressed. 'That's the one,' he replied, his tone casual. 'We're looking for a real inside look at the place. I don't want the usual kind of fluff piece about how beautiful and idyllic it is. No, I want you to dig a little deeper. Focus on the flaws. The residents. What's really going on there. Let's show our readers that it's not all sunshine and puffins.'

Jack blinked, trying to process what he was saying. 'You want me to write something specifically negative? About Puffin Island?'

'Exactly that,' Miles replied, his smile widening. 'I've heard the locals are … less than friendly. Isolated, strange. I want you to show that. Highlight the cracks in the façade. Puffin Island is no paradise, Jack. It's just another backwater full of people hiding from the real world.'

Jack shifted in his seat, feeling uncomfortable. He had written about places all over the world, and he'd always tried to capture their beauty, their uniqueness. He had never been asked to tear a place apart before. 'I don't know if that's my style,' he said carefully.

Miles waved a hand dismissively. 'You're a writer, Jack. You adapt. Write this piece well and there will be plenty of opportunity to earn more money with the newspaper. Unless, of course, you don't want the job?'

There it was … the hook. It was clear that Miles knew exactly what had brought Jack here today. Jack took a breath, his mind racing. He didn't want to do this. He didn't want to destroy a place he hadn't even visited yet. But the tax bill was looming, and he had no other options. He forced himself to nod. 'I'll take the assignment.'

Miles's smile grew. 'Vivienne said I could count on you. I expect a draft in four weeks. Payment is on delivery. Oh, and the purpose of the piece isn't to be shared with the residents. In fact, it would be a good idea to make friends with them, as you never know what they might share.'

Jack stood and Miles extended his hand. He had no option except to shake it. Miles's voice followed him as he walked out the door. 'Welcome to *The Morning Ledger*, Jack. I think you're going to fit in just fine.'

As he stepped back into the lift, Jack was disappointed with himself. Miles reminded him so much of Vivienne, and given that he'd never agreed with Vivienne's cutthroat tactics when she was his agent, it made him uncomfortable to be starting this new relationship with someone who appeared to have the same killer instincts, asking him to destroy a community for the sake of a paycheck. The thought left a bitter taste in his mouth, but as the lift doors closed behind him and he leaned his head against the cool metal wall, he knew he needed to go along with it. He needed the money, and it wasn't as though he was ever going to go back to the island or see these people again. And who knew? Maybe the next article would be one he actually wanted to write.

Chapter Two
AMELIA

Puffin Island

Amelia prided herself on her ability to handle whatever life or the weather might throw at her, but this was one of those mornings that tested her resolve. She'd nipped out for breakfast then battled the wind and the rain as it blew her back towards The Story Shop, the quaint little bookshop nestled in the heart of Lighthouse Lane. It was everything a bookshop was meant to be. The exterior had a charming weathered frontage, the stone walls covered in ivy that seemed to have a life of its own, climbing to the peaked roof. A hand-painted wooden sign swung gently above the door. Slightly faded by the salty sea air, it depicted a puffin perched on an open book. As Amelia fished her keys from her bag, she tried to close her battered umbrella, its spokes now bent at odd angles and looking as if they were bravely hanging on for dear life. The small brass bell that jangled as she stepped inside sounded more cheerful than she felt. She stared at the furious downpour lashing the windowpanes, making the charming bookshop seem to be sitting under a waterfall. She propped up the umbrella in the stand with a touch of sympathy for its valiant efforts. Then she heard a disgruntled meow.

'Good morning, Pawsworth.' The bookshop's now resident cat had taken refuge there just two weeks ago. Amelia had no clue where it had appeared from, but she had immediately named it and made it feel at home. Pawsworth was currently draped over a stack of romance novels with an air of discontent, probably as displeased with the weather as Amelia was. 'We might be each other's only company today if the weather stays like this,' she warned as she filled up Pawsworth's bowl. 'Breakfast for you,' she said cheerfully. Immediately, he jumped down with a thud and with a swish of his tail began to eat. 'I'm going to follow your example,' said Amelia, switching on the lights just as a loud crack of thunder made her jump.

She made her way to the back of the shop, into a space she called a kitchen, though it was little more than a broom cupboard. It boasted a kettle, a small sink and a cupboard filled with puffin-decorated mugs, souvenirs from over a decade of the island's annual summer fetes. She picked her favourite, a mug adorned with a particularly plump puffin, and flicked on the kettle. As she waited for the water to boil, she caught sight of herself in the mirror she'd hung on the wall to make the space feel less cramped. The reflection staring back was less than glamorous. Her rain-drenched pigtails, held up by puffin-themed scrunchies, clung to her face, and there wasn't a trace of makeup left after her battle with the morning's squall.

After brewing a pot of tea in her favourite teapot, decorated with a charming puffinry of puffins, she grabbed a plate and the oversized croissant that she'd just bought from the bakery. Thankful for the now steaming hot mug of tea in her hand, she sat behind the counter as another roll of thunder boomed across the bay.

Amelia had lived on Puffin Island her entire life, and from the moment she could read, she was captivated by two things: books and puffins. Growing up amidst the island's rugged cliffs and windswept shores she found adventure exploring the landscape just as often as she did when diving into a new book. By the time she was a teenager, she was certain that her future would be devoted to pursuing two dreams: becoming a writer and owning her very own bookshop.

Fate, it turned out, was on her side, and when the charming, ivy-covered bookshop in the heart of the village came up for sale along with the flat upstairs, Amelia didn't hesitate. She poured her heart into the shop from the moment she was handed the keys, transforming it into a literary haven. Now, every day, she lived out her dream, spending her mornings scribbling down story ideas and her afternoons thumbing through well-worn classics, all while warmly greeting customers as they stepped into her cosy, book-filled sanctuary.

Tonight was Amelia's monthly book-club night, and though the wind howled and rain pelted against the windows, she remained hopeful that the weather would calm down just enough for her regulars to venture out.

Now, Amelia's book club wasn't your typical gathering where everyone read the same book and discussed it. She always went to great lengths to create something memorable, adding that little extra touch that made book-club nights special. Her plan for that evening was to transform her quaint bookshop into a cosy refuge from the storm. She'd arrange the mismatched chairs and plump cushions around the rustic wooden table, with flickering candles casting a warm glow and small vases of fresh flowers adding a touch of charm. This month, she'd come up with a creative twist and she was feeling pleased with herself. She'd decided to pair beloved romcom books with themed cakes. Amelia would carefully select five books, each accompanied by a cake that embodied the essence of the story, and then pair them with a member of the book club. It was a genius idea, if she said so herself, and she knew already that her friends would just love it. All she needed to do was set everything up, take the cakes out of the packaging and pour the prosecco ahead of everyone's arrival at seven p.m.

Taking a glance outside, she saw that Lighthouse Lane was deserted, but she hoped it wouldn't stay that way for long. With breakfast eaten, Amelia began her usual opening routine. She dusted the counter, set up her laptop, adjusted the display of puffin-themed bookmarks, then tidied the bookshelves. Each one was a work of art, with books rising from the floor to the ceiling. Each shelf represented a category, containing a mix of leather-bound classics with gilded spines, well-thumbed paperbacks and rare first editions. Each nook and cranny held delightful surprises: antique bookends, magnifying glasses, small reading lamps.

Floral bunting hung across the shelves whilst ladders on rails lined the walls, inviting customers to explore the higher shelves.

The shop's ambience was as cosy as ever, but then a loud crack of thunder made her jump and she watched lightning fork across the sky. She glanced at Pawsworth, whose bowl was now empty. He leaped up with effortless elegance, landing softly on the worn wooden counter. With a delicate stretch, he extended his front paws, claws splayed wide as he arched his back. His tail flicked lazily, brushing against Amelia's laptop as he circled once, twice, before settling into a comfortable curl.

'Looks like it will be quiet for a while so we may as well try and write another chapter.' Amelia looked at the screen where her work in progress – a small-town romance, her own personal slice of paradise – was being shaped. It was the kind of romance that had never happened to her, but Amelia, ever the hopeless romantic, clung to the idea that if she wrote it, perhaps it would manifest in real life. Pouring her heart into the story, she envisioned a dashing stranger strolling into her life and sweeping her off her feet. Yet, after years when no one of any real interest had entered her life, her optimism was starting to fray at the edges, and her dream of any type of romance was beginning to feel more like fiction than ever.

Hearing her phone ping, Amelia glanced down to see a text from Clemmie.

CLEMMIE

> How's life in the bookshop? The tearoom is dead thanks to this storm. But I'm looking forward to book club tonight!

Amelia typed back with a grin.

AMELIA

> Today's the day! The storm is going to blow the most handsome man through the bookshop door, and we'll live happily ever after. Looking forward to tonight too!

She added a smiley face for good measure and hit send.

CLEMMIE

> No-one would ever tick all the boxes on your long list of requirements.

AMELIA

> But I live in hope. Ha ha!

As Amelia placed her phone down, she couldn't help but imagine it: windswept, dripping wet and devastatingly handsome, her perfect man would rush through the door before pausing to push the wet hair from his eyes, their gazes meeting and a bolt of electricity shooting through her… She laughed at herself. She expected her only visitor today would be the postman, but hey, a girl could dream!

Her plan was to write for at least an hour while she waited for the latest delivery of bestsellers. There was a particular book she was expecting and she couldn't wait to add it to the display at the front of the shop.

She turned back to her laptop and stared at the screen. She'd crossed the halfway mark in the first draft of her novel and the chapters were flowing, the characters starting to feel like old friends, and she was confident she could knock out at least a thousand words this morning.

As her fingers hovered over the keyboard, the relentless storm outside continued to batter the island, thunder booming so loudly it rattled the windows. Suddenly, the lights flickered, casting eerie shadows over the bookshelves – and then the shop was plunged into darkness. Inside, it was as dark as the stormy sky outside, the only sound the relentless pounding of the rain against the glass. With a resigned sigh, she quickly lit the candles she kept around the counter for just such an occasion. Puffin Island was no stranger to power cuts, but in weather like this, she had no idea when the electricity might return and was thankful her laptop was fully charged. As the storm raged on, Amelia couldn't help but feel like she was living out her own story – trapped in a cosy bookshop, surrounded by candles, with only the howling wind and Pawsworth for company. All she needed now was for that handsome stranger to stumble through the door.

For the next thirty minutes, Amelia didn't see a soul, lost in her fictional world, fingers flying over the keyboard. She decided it was time for a short break and just as she stretched her arms above her head, the shop door swung open with a dramatic creak, and in walked the kind of man who would make anyone do a double-take.

For a moment, Amelia froze, staring at the man in the doorway. She blinked, half-expecting the image to blur and fade, but no, he was very much real. Tall, dark and drenched, he looked like he'd stepped straight out of the story she was writing.

Standing at around six foot two, he had a rugged yet refined charm that seemed to draw attention to him without his trying. His dark hair, tousled and wet from the storm, fell slightly over his forehead, giving him a windswept look that suited him perfectly. There was a bit of scruff on his strong jawline, the kind that suggested he hadn't shaved in a couple of days, but he still managed to look effortlessly handsome.

Amelia wasn't one to believe in love at first sight, but as she stared at the soaked stranger standing in her doorway, she found herself reconsidering. Maybe all those romance novels she loved so much had a point. His eyes were a striking shade of deep blue, intense and captivating, and his broad shoulders filled out his rain-soaked jacket in a way that begged for a closer look. He ran his hand through his wet hair, pushing it back with a casual ease that only added to his appeal.

'Good morning,' trilled Amelia.

The man looked in her direction. His smile revealed a dimple in his left cheek, adding a boyish charm to his otherwise mature and confident appearance. 'A bookshop by candlelight.'

'Welcome to The Story Shop,' Amelia said with a cheerful grin, 'where you'll find books, puffins – though obviously not real ones as they're up on the cliffs – a cat that rents space on my counter, and hopefully no rain…' She glanced warily up at the roof. 'We aren't normally lit by candlelight, but it does happen now and again. Puffin Island is kind of known for its power cuts.' She noticed the large suitcase at his side as he dropped his sodden backpack to the floor. Just at that moment the lights flickered and the power came on.

'You're soaked.'

'I can't argue with you there. The storm seems determined to mark my arrival on the island as memorably as possible.'

Reaching for one of the towels she kept stacked behind the counter for Pawsworth, she held it out to him. 'Here, take this, I'm just about to light the fire. It shouldn't take long to get going.'

The man took the towel as Amelia moved towards the cast-iron log burner that was always prepared for these kinds of moments, and soon after lighting the kindle it began to kick out warmth.

'I'm Amelia,' she said. 'And this is Pawsworth.'

'I'm Jack.' His eyes widened with amusement. 'Pawsworth, that's a very bookish name.'

'He wandered lonely as a cloud right into the bookshop and never left.'

Jack laughed then looked down at the towel in his hands, as though noticing the print on it for the first time. 'Nice puffin towel.'

'I'm a puffin-crazy book lover. How about you?'

'I'll admit to being book-crazy but I'm not so sure about puffins,' he replied, taking off his coat and hanging it on the stand by the door before patting his face and hair dry with the towel. 'I've never actually seen one.'

'Never seen a puffin? Well, you've come to the right place. They don't call us Puffin Island for nothing!' She knew she was babbling but the way he was looking at her was making her nervous (in a good way). She couldn't help staring straight into those gorgeous blue eyes. 'Take a seat.' She gestured to the purple wingback chair. 'Feel free to pick a book and settle in. You probably don't want to venture back out just yet ... unless you have your own canoe?' she joked, looking out at the water that was rushing over the cobbled street outside. 'Would you like a cup of tea? I was just about to put the kettle on.'

'A bookshop, an owner crazy about puffins and a cup of tea... I just got lucky. That would be great, thank you.'

Amelia flashed him a smile before disappearing into the back of the shop. As she filled the kettle, she texted Clemmie.

> AMELIA
> The storm has swept in the most handsome man I've seen.

Her phoned pinged almost immediately with a reply from Clemmie:

> CLEMMIE
> Is that a line from the story you're writing?

> AMELIA
> Funnily enough it is, but my dream just came true.

Jack's arrival had brought an unexpected spark to her quiet morning. There was something about him ... something magnetic ... that made her feel unusually flustered. Perhaps it was the way he'd entered so unexpectedly, or maybe it was just the storm outside making everything feel more dramatic. Returning with a steaming cup of tea, she placed it on the table in front of him.

'Thank you,' he said. 'I wasn't expecting to arrive in this weather.' Jack glanced around the shop, his eyes lingering on the shelf to the side of him. 'A great selection of travel books,' he observed.

Amelia's eyes followed his gaze, and she smiled. 'That's a great shelf. Usually, on quiet days like this, I can lose myself in one of those books and pretend I'm exploring the Amazon rainforest or hiking through the Alps. There's something magical about getting lost in a different place, even if it's just between the pages of a book.'

Jack's eyes sparkled with interest. 'Sounds like you have quite the adventurous spirit. You're right though, it's amazing how a good book can take you to places you've never been.'

'Absolutely,' Amelia agreed, her smile widening. 'It's one of the reasons I love running this shop. Each book is like a ticket to a new adventure. And tonight, with the monthly book-club meeting, we'll get to indulge in a different kind of adventure … one filled with romance and cake.'

'Romcoms and cakes?'

'You're welcome to join us if you're free,' Amelia offered, feeling a flutter of excitement at the thought of his company. 'We start at seven p.m. It's always a friendly group and there's no pressure, just good books, good conversation and, of course, good cake.'

'Now there's an offer that's hard to refuse, Amelia…' He

paused, and she supplied her last name, assuming that was what he was looking for.

'Brown.'

For a moment, Jack looked like he was genuinely considering the offer, his gaze lingering on the poster for the book club. 'I might just take you up on that,' he said at last, taking a sip of his tea. 'Thanks for the invite.'

'You're welcome,' she replied.

'This place has a charm all of its own. Perfect for riding out a storm.'

'So, are you just passing through, or staying on the island for a bit?' Amelia asked, curious about this man who had suddenly appeared in her little world.

'I'm staying at the local B&B for a while,' Jack replied.

'Where are you coming from?'

'London.'

'And what do you do in the big city?'

'I work on a variety of projects. Usually in the realms of lifestyle and culture,' he replied, vaguely.

'Sounds interesting. Are you here for work or rest?'

'Hopefully a little bit of both,' replied Jack.

'Puffin Island is the best place to take a break. With patchy phone signal and Blue Water Bay to walk along each day it does wonders for your soul, and of course the islanders are just the best.'

'And this is you, selling books?' He looked around the shop.

'It is.'

'What genre do you usually prefer?'

'Love a good romcom.'

'And do you write?'

'It's one of my passions.'

'You never know, maybe one day these shelves will be filled with your books.'

'That's the dream. I adore love stories. A gorgeous man walks into the bookshop and...' The blush on her cheeks deepened as she realised what she'd just said.

Jack grinned as he handed back the towel. 'And what would your partner say about that?'

Amelia couldn't work out whether he was genuinely curious or whether he was fishing to see whether she was single.

'No partner.'

'Anyone on the horizon?'

She shook her head. 'And I think that's down to the type of books I love reading.'

'Tell me more.'

'People think romcoms give women unrealistic expectations of a man, filled as they are with over-the-top gestures, perfect partners and instant connections, but the reason I read them is because I love the promise of them, the hope they provide that the perfect man *for me* is out there.'

Amelia wasn't single because she couldn't get a date ... quite the opposite, actually, and she'd turned down more dinner invites than she could count. But she wasn't the type to swoon at the first bouquet of flowers, or fall into the arms of the next eligible bachelor who came along. No, she was old-fashioned, the kind of romantic who believed in waiting for the right man, the one who could tick all her boxes, even the oddly specific ones, like appreciating her love for obscure novels and knowing the difference between 'your' and 'you're'. Her friends thought she was certifiable, convinced she'd end up knitting sweaters for cats and talking to houseplants if she kept holding out for Mr Perfect. But Amelia wasn't about to give up on her quest for true love. After all, she figured it was better to be single and happy than settle for someone who couldn't tell a semicolon from a wink emoji.

He met her eyes, holding her gaze a little longer than usual. 'A woman who knows her worth is incredibly attractive,' he said softly, his voice sincere. The intensity of his stare sent an unexpected flutter through her stomach, catching her off guard.

Amelia tilted her head slightly. 'And you? Married, engaged?'

He chuckled, a hint of ruefulness in his smile. 'My job keeps me so busy I don't stay in the same place for long and there's hardly any time left for anyone. Besides, I'm rather set in my ways.' He shrugged, as if to suggest that his life was just as he liked it.

'You take as much time as you want, warming by the fire,' she said, concerned the conversation was getting a bit too personal and not wanting him to feel uncomfortable.

'Your bookshop seems like the perfect refuge from this downpour. You've certainly made a soggy day a lot more bearable.' Hearing his phone ring, Jack looked at the screen. He seemed hesitant to answer it.

'If you need privacy, I'll just…' Amelia nodded towards the kitchen then picked up his empty mug and edged towards the storeroom, closing the door behind her.

As Amelia turned on the tap and washed up the mugs,

she heard Jack's voice through the crack between the door and the frame.

'I didn't expect to see your name on my phone,' he said, sounding oddly strained. There was a pause before Jack continued. 'Yes, I've arrived, and of course I'll deliver on time. Thank you for thinking of me…'

His voice trailed off and she leaned closer to the door. She knew she shouldn't be eavesdropping but she couldn't help herself. Something about this man intrigued her.

'Yes, I won't let anyone down and I understand the angle,' he continued, before hanging up.

Amelia stepped back into the shop, wiping her hands on a tea towel, and saw Jack slipping on his coat. The rain was still lashing down outside, the wind rattling the windows, and she could feel a draught whistling through the bookshop. She felt a strange sense of disappointment that he was leaving so soon. 'You don't need to rush off,' she said. 'It's pouring down out there.' She noticed as he picked up his rucksack that he seemed a little agitated and she could only guess it had something to do with the phone call. 'You're welcome to stay until it eases a bit.'

Jack smiled warmly. 'I appreciate it, really, but I need to get settled into the B&B. I've got some work I need to plan.'

Amelia was still curious to know more about what Jack did for a living, but before she could probe further, she found herself offering, 'Well, if you find yourself at a loose end tonight, you know you're more than welcome to join our book-club meeting.'

Jack paused. 'Do you usually get a good turnout?'

'Depends on the weather,' she laughed, 'but it's a good way to meet the locals, especially if you're staying for a while. You know how it is with small islands. We're all in each other's pockets around here.'

His eyes flickered with something Amelia couldn't quite place. Maybe it was intrigue, or maybe he just wasn't used to that type of community.

'Thanks for the invite.'

'The B&B is down the lane. Just turn left out of the door and follow the road to Anchor Way. It's Lena who owns and runs it.'

Jack extended his hand. 'Thank you for the tea and the use of the puffin towel.' As he shook her hand, his touch firm yet gentle, she felt a wave of warmth and sensation that left her momentarily mesmerised. Amelia withdrew her hand, her cheeks warming slightly as she tried to compose herself. He smiled at her but before she could say anything else, he opened the door and stepped out into the storm. The doorbell jingled softly as it closed behind him, the sound almost drowned by the wind. Amelia stood for a moment, staring at the rain-soaked street through the fogged-up glass.

Walking back towards the counter, she noticed something on the floor. Just beside the chair where Jack had been sitting was a small piece of folded paper. Bending down, she picked it up and smoothed it out. It was a printout of his booking confirmation for the B&B. She glanced at the details and that's when she saw it: 'Jack Hartwell'.

The name struck her like a bolt of lightning and Amelia blinked, her heart skipping a beat as she looked over to the shelf where she displayed the travel books. Nestled among them were several titles by none other than Jack Hartwell, one of her favourite travel writers. His books were always popular with islanders and tourists alike, offering vivid descriptions of remote places and the quirky, tightly-knit communities that lived there, combining actual places with a fictional story. He had a talent for capturing the essence of places that felt untouched by time, places much like Puffin Island. Amelia's mind raced as she connected the dots. Jack wasn't just some random traveller passing through. He was *the* Jack Hartwell, whose words had taken her to the Scottish Highlands, the vineyards of rural France and the wilds of Alaska. And here he was, in her shop, on her island. The realisation made her knees feel a little weak, and almost instinctively she found herself reaching for her phone. She needed to be sure. With trembling fingers, she opened her browser and typed his name into the search bar. It didn't take long to find him.

A professional author's page popped up first, and there, staring back at her from the screen, was Jack's face. The same strong jawline, the same piercing blue eyes that she'd admired only moments earlier. Amelia stared at the image for a long moment, her breath catching in her throat as her inner fan-girl squealed. It was him. *The* Jack Hartwell had been standing right here in her shop, and she'd been oblivious.

Quickly, she texted Clemmie.

AMELIA

I think I've found the man of my dreams!

Her phoned pinged.

CLEMMIE

> There is no man that would ever tick all of your boxes. But we ALL live in hope!

Amelia chuckled, thinking about the countless times Clemmie had tried and failed to set her up. But Jack Hartwell felt different. There was something about him, a sense that he wasn't just another visitor passing through Puffin Island. She had a hunch he was here for more than just the scenery. He had a purpose, and her guess? He was here to weave Puffin Island into his next story. Just thinking about Jack stirred emotions within her that she'd never felt before, sending a surge of excitement through her that she couldn't ignore. It was unexpected and thrilling all at once. For the first time in ages, she wondered if her life was about to change in ways she could never have seen coming.

Chapter Three

JACK

Jack trudged down Lighthouse Lane with his suitcase, following Amelia's directions to the B&B.

When he arrived five minutes later, he found a quaint two-storey building with ivy-clad walls and a bright, welcoming red door. A small brass sign beside the door read: THE DRIFTWOOD LODGE B&B. Jack stepped inside.

The interior was as charming as the exterior, with wooden beams, floral wallpaper and an assortment of knick-knacks that made the place feel lived-in and cosy. The woman behind the reception desk looked up from the fresh flowers she was arranging in a vase.

'Can I help you?' she asked.

'I need to check in. Jack Hartwell.'

'Welcome to Puffin Island! I'm Lena, owner of the B&B. What a morning for you to arrive.'

Jack guessed that Lena was in her forties. Her kind face was framed by a fashionably short silver bob. She wore a floral apron over her clothes, and her demeanour was as inviting as the B&B itself.

'Thank you, let's hope the weather gets better.'

'It should clear by tomorrow and then you'll see Puffin Island in a whole new light.' She took a set of keys from one of the hooks on the wall at the back of the office. 'I'll show you to your room.'

Jack followed Lena through a narrow hallway lined with old-fashioned photographs and quaint decorations, then up a winding staircase, the wooden steps creaking gently under their weight. At the top of the stairs, she opened a door.

'Here we are. Room seven. It's one of our more special rooms, full of character and a great view.'

Lena was right, the room was a delightful blend of rustic charm and whimsy. A window overlooked the water. It was decorated with mismatched but somehow complementary furniture: a wooden bed with a patchwork quilt, a vintage armchair and a small desk with a lamp, pad and paper.

'That's Cockle Bay Cove,' Lena said, pointing at the view. 'And you have Puffin Island Farm to your left. I'll leave you to settle in and I hope you find everything to your liking. If you need anything, don't hesitate to ask.' She smiled as she shut the door behind her.

After Jack set his suitcase down, he took in the antique radio, a collection of ceramic birds on the windowsill, and a bookshelf crammed with well-worn novels. The rain was still cascading down the window and in the distance the cove's shoreline was a patchwork of glistening wet sand and dark slippery rocks. The waves rolled in, their edges frothing white as they met the shore.

Jack switched on the kettle then began unpacking his suitcase. He took out his laptop, placed it on the desk and opened it up. A blank Word document stared back, taunting him.

He'd spent fifteen years travelling the world, telling stories that mattered to him, but recently he'd hit a wall. Writer's block had taken hold, and no matter how hard he tried, he couldn't seem to break it. That might be due to the stress of the tax bill, and the pressure to stay successful, but the fact was that he had one book still to deliver, and he had no clue what to write.

With a coffee in the mug, he began to jot down his initial impressions of the island and the B&B, but his thoughts kept drifting back to Amelia.

It wasn't just her physical appearance, though her rain-dampened pigtails and quirky puffin scrunchies were endearing. It was the whole package: her smile, her enthusiasm and the ease with which she'd made him feel at home. He thought about the way she'd welcomed him into the shop with such warmth, and couldn't help feeling a twinge of discomfort. He was a good judge of character and there was no doubt that everything about Amelia was authentic and genuine, and yet here he was, assigned to show a side of her beloved island that would paint it – and perhaps even her and the people she cared about – in a bad light. He knew he'd have to tread carefully, keeping his purpose hidden until his work was done and he could leave without anyone knowing who he really was. For now, he needed to stay focused. He couldn't afford to get swept up by the island's allure or Amelia's easy charm ... which he already knew would be difficult.

Jack found himself thinking about her more than he'd intended, wondering if she might be the key to unlocking the story he needed to write. In the past, he'd been quick to boast about his career as an author, revelling in the interest and attention it stirred when he arrived in new places – particularly among women. He'd never been short of female company on his travels, but no one had captured his attention for long, and, in the end, most of his relationships had been little more than situationships. He knew, the next time he even considered a relationship, that he wanted something different: a best friend, a genuine connection, a fairytale of sorts. But he'd already decided to keep who he was and why he was here entirely under wraps, so there definitely wasn't going to be any opportunity for genuine connection, let alone a romance. Still, it didn't stop him wanting to know more about the beautiful bookshop owner.

Closing his laptop, he made his way downstairs to the living room of the B&B. He found a comfortable spot by the fireplace, settled into one of the armchairs and took a book from the shelf – a history of Puffin Island, no doubt written by a local. He flicked through the pages searching for any reference to the bookshop, but frustratingly found nothing. Amelia might be a newcomer to the island, or she might have opened the bookshop only recently, but anyway he wanted to know her story. He already recognised that having a friend here like Amelia would make his stay more enjoyable, and from the way her eyes had twinkled in his direction, he knew there could be some fun to be had, even if their paths were destined to part.

Chapter Four

AMELIA

Amelia was unexpectedly grateful for the storm that rattled the old bookshop's windows. With the rain still hammering down outside and the wind howling through the narrow streets, the usual trickle of book buyers had slowed to a halt, which gave her time and the perfect excuse to take a deep dive into the life of Jack Hartwell.

She muttered under her breath as the web page froze yet again. The Wi-Fi in the shop was usually painfully slow, but somehow even slower in the storm, if that was possible. Every page took for ever to load, making her investigation frustrating. But even the lagging internet couldn't deter her curiosity. Jack Hartwell's career was impressive, spanning over fifteen years and taking him around the globe. He was a celebrated writer who had travelled to nearly every country imaginable, collecting experiences that seeped into the rich, layered plots of his novels. Yet, despite his public persona as a globe-trotting literary star, details of his private life were scarce. His personal relationships were kept under wraps, and the rare interviews he gave only hinted at the man behind the words. His settings on social media were tight and for someone like Amelia, who thrived on reading mysteries as well as romance, only made her want to know more.

Finally, the page reloaded. Amelia's eyes were fixed on the screen as she read how, despite the fame and the success of Jack's earlier works, his latest novels seemed to be floundering. Reviews were tepid at best, with phrases like 'lacks the emotional punch of his earlier work' popping up far too frequently. Even more concerning were rumours swirling in the industry, whispers that his publisher was on the verge of dropping him due to poor sales. Several articles speculated on his downfall, some even questioning if his best writing years were behind him. It was a shocking shift for someone who had once been the literary world's golden travel boy. But what truly grabbed Amelia's attention was an article Jack had penned himself. Published in *Literary* magazine, it was a sharp, topical piece questioning whether authors truly needed agents to help their careers or if they were just unnecessary middlemen siphoning off profits. The tone of the article was unmistakable, the undercurrent of frustration, perhaps even bitterness, plain. To Amelia, it read like the words of a man who had recently experienced some kind of professional betrayal. The more she read, the more she became convinced something had gone wrong in Jack Hartwell's relationship with his agent. Her fingers hovered over the keyboard as she began searching to see who his agent had been, intrigued by what sort of conflict might have led him to air his grievances so publicly. It didn't take long before a name and photo appeared.

Vivienne Langford.

Her stepmother.

Her hands shook slightly as she sat back in her chair. It seemed she and Jack had something in common – a dislike of Vivienne.

Not wanting to stare at Vivienne's face for a moment longer, Amelia shut down her laptop. She wasn't someone prone to hatred, in fact she'd always prided herself on seeing the good in people, no matter their flaws, but Vivienne was different. She didn't like her and every time she thought about the woman her chest tightened and angry tears clouded her vision.

Taking a deep breath, she tried to push the thought of that woman to the back of her mind.

Amelia had already scored a win in a way Vivienne would never see coming – not that anyone else could know about it yet. It was her little secret, mainly because of something that had happened after her father had passed away, and she planned to keep it that way until the will was properly settled. She needed the moment to be just right before she could share it with anyone.

She knew one thing for certain though: under no circumstances could she mention Vivienne to Jack. For one, it would give away the fact that she'd looked him up online, which was the last thing she wanted to admit. It would also complicate things between them. Amelia had always admired Jack's novels, and her shop had an entire shelf dedicated to his work, filled with well-worn copies of his most beloved titles; but Jack had not told her who he was, which Amelia knew must have been intentional. Clearly he wanted to keep his true identity to himself whilst he was on Puffin Island so that the islanders wouldn't act differently towards him.

She decided that if he showed up at the book club tonight, she'd stick to her decision, not sharing a word about who he really was unless he decided to spill the beans himself. Sure, she was curious to know more about him, and specifically to know what had happened between him and Vivienne, but she didn't want to scare him off. Still, it ate away at Amelia. What could Vivienne have done to push Jack into writing such a scathing article about their working relationship? The whole thing had *plot twist* written all over it, and Amelia couldn't help wanting to know every juicy detail, but she reminded herself to tread carefully. She knew how it felt to want to keep something to yourself, and, given that she wasn't ready for her own secret to be unearthed just yet, she recognised that some things needed to be revealed on a person's own terms.

By late afternoon, the storm began to pass, and Pawsworth, without a care in the world, moved himself from the counter to the rug in front of the fire as Amelia began setting up for the book club. The meeting always took place around the fireplace, creating a warm, inviting atmosphere that made the evening feel like a gathering of old friends, which was actually just what it was. She carefully arranged the mismatched chairs into a semicircle, ensuring that each seat offered a good view of both the fire and the small display table where she would lay out tonight's selection of books and cakes. In her head, she rehearsed the clever words she'd prepared for each book and how she would artfully tie them to the cakes and the personalities of the book-club members. It was all part of the fun, Amelia's little way of making the evening light-hearted and special.

Book club was more than just a discussion of the latest reads; it was an excuse for everyone to catch up, enjoy a glass of prosecco and indulge in a bit of local gossip. The books were almost secondary to the camaraderie, though Amelia made sure there was always plenty to talk about with her selections. After plumping the cushions and making sure everything was just right, she disappeared into the kitchen to prepare the delicious treats. She plated the cakes she'd purchased from Beachcomber Bakery, and as she disposed of the boxes she chuckled, remembering her school days.

Amelia had always been hopeless at baking. Once, in a fit of desperation, she'd taken a shop-bought sponge cake to class and passed it off as her own. Clemmie, her now-baker-extraordinaire friend, had gushed over her perfectly risen sponge and flawless piping, unaware of Amelia's culinary deceit. Even the teacher was impressed and had high hopes of Amelia acing her baking exams. Unfortunately, when the real test came, Amelia's sponge turned out flatter than a pancake and her piping looked like it had been done by someone decorating a cake on a rollercoaster. She blamed her failure on the faulty oven but deep down she knew she was just hopeless in the kitchen. Since that exam she'd never cracked an egg again – except when she accidentally knocked a box of eggs off a shelf in the supermarket.

As the storm outside calmed and the fire crackled,

Amelia felt a familiar excitement build. Soon, the bookshop would be filled with laughter, conversation and the comforting sense of community that always came with book-club night, but what she hoped more than anything was that Jack would walk through the door to join them.

Chapter Five

JACK

Jack sat in his bedroom at the B&B. The storm was finally passing and as he stared at his laptop screen, his frustration was building. Aside from the two words at the top of the page – *Chapter One* – the page was empty, still waiting to be filled with creativity that refused to come.

His publisher had made it clear that if his sales didn't improve, there likely wouldn't be a contract renewal. Jack had brushed it off at the time, telling himself he was Jack Hartwell and things would pick up, confident he'd find a way to reignite his readership. But now, staring at the empty document, he wasn't so sure he could pull it off, even with all his experience. His travel novels had always distinguished him from the standard travel writer. Instead of merely chronicling the places he visited, he blended fact and fiction, grounding his characters in real-world settings. His readers loved the immersive experience, the ability to visit the exact pubs, restaurants and attractions his fictional protagonists explored. But not this time. This time, he was stuck. The novel was supposed to unfold on a train running through Switzerland, a journey Jack had recently taken. The trip had been spectacular, the train passing through breathtaking mountainous landscapes and quaint villages, and gliding alongside glistening lakes, but somehow, the magic he'd felt during the journey wasn't translating into words. He replayed the memories in his head, searching for a spark of inspiration. None came. Maybe it was time to change something. His formula had worked for years, but perhaps the well had run dry.

His eyes wandered to the pile of letters next to his laptop. The top one, a thick brown envelope, was from the tax office, a cold reminder of the looming debt that hung over his head. The amount he owed was giving him sleepless nights. He couldn't afford to have writer's block now. He was relying on the money he'd get from this book, and from the article about Puffin Island that he'd agreed to deliver to keep him afloat in the meantime.

With a sigh, Jack leaned forward and typed the date just below *Chapter One*. He drummed his fingers on the desk, thinking. His mind wandered to Amelia again. The thought of her sent a warmth through his chest. He hadn't written about his feelings before, not in a direct, personal way. He closed his eyes and pictured her, the image coming easily as he relived the memory of walking into that cosy little bookshop, Amelia standing behind the counter, illuminated by candlelight, her eyes lighting up when she saw him.

His fingers moved across the keyboard. Slowly at first, but then faster. He began writing about that moment, documenting it almost like a diary entry: the shy smile Amelia had given him when he asked about her favourite travel books, the way her eyes sparkled when she spoke passionately about Puffin Island and its wild, windswept beauty. Jack wrote about his own surprise at how drawn he was to her, how he'd found himself wanting to go back just to talk to her some more.

He smiled to himself as he remembered her sweatshirt, oversized and comfortably worn, with the quotation across the front: *Between the pages of a book is a lovely place to be.* It suited her perfectly. He knew she had a great sense of humour; she had to, to have named her cat Pawsworth. He'd chuckled when he heard it, and Amelia's playful grin had confirmed what he suspected, that she was as fun and quirky as her appearance suggested. He wrote about the puffin scrunchies, her twinkling eyes and how perfect her lips were – yes, he'd noticed them, too. Soon, words became sentences, which became paragraphs, and before he knew it, he'd written two thousand words. Jack read back over the entry, surprised at the depth of emotion he'd captured, the vulnerability he'd exposed. It was clear – all there in black and white – just how much he fancied Amelia. He leaned back in his chair, his heart still racing from the rush of creativity. Maybe he was stuck on the novel, but at least now he knew something for certain: Amelia had gotten under his skin, and maybe … just maybe … she was the key to unlocking his next story.

A couple of hours later the rain had finally stopped and Jack decided to take a stroll down to the bay. He'd barely had any fresh air all day except when he jumped off the bus from the mainland and was blown into the bookshop. Before long he found himself looking at the map of the island that was displayed on the notice board at the bottom of Lighthouse Lane. The island had two main coves and one bay: Cockle Bay Cove, which he could see from the B&B bedroom window, Castaway Cove, where the puffins could be found, and Blue Water Bay. He began walking towards Blue Water Bay, noticing a fancy restaurant bobbing on the water – 'The Sea Glass Restaurant' – and further along he saw a hut on the sand called the 'Cosy Kettle', which he headed towards. There was something about this place that made him feel relaxed, which he hadn't been expecting. He had always assumed he needed the noise and constant buzz of a busy city to feel alive, but here it was as if the natural beauty around him had slowed the constant whirlwind of thoughts in his mind, leaving space for peace he didn't know he needed. The view was idyllic, the open sea stretching out before him, a shimmering expanse of blue that seemed to merge seamlessly with the sky at the horizon. The water was surprisingly calm after the storm and he could see Puffin Island Lighthouse, which rose proudly in the distance from the rugged coastline. Everywhere felt timeless, very different from the fast-paced life of London.

He grabbed a coffee from the Cosy Kettle and sat at one of the tables facing the water. He'd just passed the time of day with Becca, according to her name badge, who served him his coffee, and like Amelia she was friendly and down to earth. His stomach growled and he realised he hadn't eaten since this morning. Ordering a toasted cheese sandwich, he sat back and drank his coffee, noticing a book that had been left on a nearby table.

Its spine was creased from use, and as he picked it up, he immediately recognised the author's name. Maris Wilde had soared from obscurity to fame on TikTok, achieving more sales with a single book than all his previous works combined. He'd never read any of her books, but knew from the reviews that they were full of spice, and he found he was curious to see what the appeal was. He opened it and turned to the dedication page.

To you, from me,
May the secrets we share remain as hidden as the tides.

He looked up as Becca greeted him again with a warm smile and placed the toastie on the table.

'It's a beautiful bay,' said Jack, looking towards the water.

'Isn't it just. It's not a bad job looking at that view every day. Even in the storms it's so beautiful.' Becca returned to serve a customer whilst Jack began to read the first page of the book.

'I didn't have you down as a man who liked to read spice.'

Jack looked up from the book in his hands. His eyes widened and his pulse quickened at the sight of Amelia standing there, her gaze flickering with a mischievous glint. He hadn't expected to run into her before the book club later that night, and certainly not while holding a raunchy novel.

'I wasn't expecting to see you again so soon,' Jack said, trying to sound casual, but failing as he awkwardly attempted to shield the book's cover with his coffee cup.

'It's a small island,' Amelia replied with a smirk, her eyes drifting to the book's cover regardless of his efforts.

'And what do you think of Maris Wilde? Her first book, I believe, that one.'

Jack's face flushed a bright red. 'It's not my book. It was left on the table. I was just ... um ... flipping through.'

Amelia raised an eyebrow, clearly unconvinced. 'Oh really? That's your story and you're sticking to it?'

Jack grinned.

'I'm actually just waiting for her new one to arrive at the shop,' Amelia said, her grin widening. 'I could save you a copy if you're interested. And we do have her second book available, the follow-on from that one, for when you've finished reading it.'

Jack raised an eyebrow then shook his head quickly. 'I think I'll pass, but thanks for the offer. I'll stick to, um, less ... intense reading material.'

'Sure,' Amelia said, barely concealing her laughter. 'But if you ever need tips on navigating the spicy side of literature, or just need someone to explain the finer points of romantic subplots, I'm your go-to. Maybe we could talk about it at book club tonight.'

Jack knew he was blushing.

'I'm joking!' She giggled. 'But honestly, you should give it a go.'

'I'll think about it,' he replied, looking at the cover. 'Have you always lived on the island?' he asked, steering the conversation in a different direction.

'I have.'

'What's it like living here? I mean, from what I've seen, it's beautiful and everyone I've met so far is friendly.'

Amelia gestured towards the sea. 'I wake up every day to that view and wouldn't change it for the world.'

'I can see your point there. It certainly beats the view from where I live. I did some research this afternoon but it looks like not many houses come up for sale here...'

'You're right, they don't. Families tend to stay on this island for generations.'

'But doesn't that get a little stifling, everyone knowing everyone?'

'I suppose it depends on how you look at it. I like the fact that we all know each other and have each other's back, but don't get me wrong, we can get on each other's nerves and every place has its secrets.'

'And do you have a secret, Amelia Brown?' he asked with a smile, but held her gaze, noticing how her eyes flickered.

She hesitated then shook her head, laughing lightly.

'And what secrets does this place have?'

'Well, if I told you, then it wouldn't be a secret, would it?' Amelia gestured towards the bottom of the lane. 'I have to go. I just needed a breath of fresh air now the rain has finally stopped.'

Jack watched her disappear up the lane before turning back to the book and smiling. Maybe it wouldn't hurt to read a little spice whilst he was away. After all, sometimes a little fiction could just be the thing to stir things up.

Chapter Six
AMELIA

Amelia hoped Jack hadn't noticed the way she bristled when he'd asked if she had a secret. His question might have been light-hearted, just a bit of teasing, but she couldn't help feeling a flicker of guilt, given that she was guarding one of the island's biggest secrets. It wasn't that she'd originally intended to keep it hidden for so long; quite the opposite, in fact. But the timing had never felt right to reveal all, especially not in the aftermath of her father's passing.

Even though Amelia found Jack insanely drop-dead gorgeous, she knew exactly why suddenly she felt defensive. She wasn't daft; Jack was a writer and no doubt always looking for a story, and the last thing she needed was her secret getting out, as she knew it would make a great story. Her instinct told her that he might be seeking out the island's more intriguing, perhaps even scandalous, elements to incorporate into his latest novel. It was significant, she thought, that he'd kept his cards close to his chest and hadn't admitted who he was, even when he'd had the perfect opportunity – standing inside a bookshop! – to tell her he was an author. She wasn't against the idea of the island's unique charm being the subject of his writing, but she had her own reasons for keeping some aspects of it under wraps.

As she continued walking up the lane, her thoughts turned to her secret. She hadn't told a soul, not even Clemmie, and that was probably because her grandmother was Betty, co-owner of The Café on the Coast and the keeper of secrets on the island. She had a knack of uncovering or being involved in everything and Amelia didn't want there to be a sniff of anything until she was ready to come clean.

But Amelia also knew that shutting herself off entirely wasn't the only way to navigate this situation. She knew all about Jack's job now and so there was no reason why she couldn't enjoy his company and have a little fun with him whilst he was here. After all, he was undeniably charming and his presence was a refreshing change. But falling for him, or letting him too close, was out of the question because it could complicate things.

As Amelia arrived back at the bookshop she was delighted to discover that her delivery had arrived. Picking up the box, she hurried inside. Pawsworth lifted his head for a second, possibly hoping it was food, but when it was just another cardboard box he fell back asleep in the chair. Amelia's heart raced. She knew exactly what was in the box and couldn't wait to see it. Grabbing some scissors from the drawer of her desk, she carefully sliced through the packing tape on the box. She hesitated for a moment, excitement bubbling in her chest, before flipping open the cardboard flaps. Inside, stacked neatly, were the fresh copies of Maris Wilde's brand-new novel, *The Temptation Bucket List*. Without hesitation, Amelia reached in, her fingers trembling slightly as they brushed over the smooth, glossy surface of the book on top. The cover gleamed, the title embossed in gold. It was perfect. She brought the book up to her face, inhaling deeply. There was nothing quite like the smell of a brand-new book. Opening it, she flipped through the first few crisp pages and stopped at the dedication.

Patience is the sharpest weapon.

The words seemed to pulse on the page, a quiet promise that everyone would face their reckoning … eventually. It wasn't just a dedication. It was a warning, a reminder that justice, or revenge, was sometimes simply a matter of waiting.

Taking the rest of the books out of the box she laid them out on a nearby table, knowing that tonight the book-club members would snap up the copies.

A few hours later Amelia prepared for what promised to be the most entertaining book-club meeting yet. The prosecco was poured, the cakes laid out and the candles lit, making the entire room feel like a secret nook in a whimsical fairytale. Everything was ready, so all she needed now was for the avid readers to arrive. Pawsworth was sitting on the counter, grooming himself, with one eye on his paw and one eye on the cakes.

'I'm watching you,' Amelia threatened, looking the cat in the eye.

'Who are you watching?' Clemmie breezed in and immediately swiped a glass of prosecco off the tray before kissing Amelia on both cheeks. 'I'm in need of this,' she said, swigging it back in one gulp. 'Granny is about five minutes behind me.'

'Clemmie!'

'Sorry! I had the date from hell last night. These dating apps are just horrific.' Clemmie rolled her eyes.

Amelia loved Clemmie's dating stories, which were so far-fetched that never in a million years would you think they were true. But Clemmie had been a prolific dater for ages, believing that *the one* was out there. You just had to kiss a million frogs before you found your prince.

'He has got to be out there, somewhere.'

'Maybe he's not been born yet.' Amelia grinned.

'Amelia! Honestly, I know I've been on a lot of strange dates, but nothing prepared me for this one. Picture the scene … The Sea Glass Restaurant—'

'Isn't that a bit close to home?' Amelia interrupted.

'It's the ideal. I'm not making the effort to travel anywhere and Sam looks out for me. I even have my own table overlooking the stunning ocean views and it's perfect for a romantic evening.'

'Thank God our friend owns the restaurant.' Amelia smiled.

'Sam is worth his weight in gold; in fact he saved me.'

'I'm all ears,' said Amelia as they settled on the chairs.

'The date started off normal enough. His name was Ian, he had great hair, a charming smile and an interest in architecture that seemed refreshingly grown up. Things had started well and Sam gave us time to look over the menu. Ian said he was going to order garlic bread with extra garlic, then, for his main, the garlic shrimp pasta with a side of garlic butter…'

Amelia raised an eyebrow.

Clemmie continued. 'I've come across some fetishes in my time, but this was a new one on me. He shared with excitement that he can't get enough of the stuff, even making garlic-based snacks at home – including smoothies.'

Amelia picked up a glass of prosecco and took a sip.

'And he even brought me homemade garlic fudge. I nearly choked.'

'What did you do?'

'I plastered on my best smile, made my excuses and pretended I needed the bathroom but instead I nipped into the kitchen and enlisted Sam's help. When I returned to the table, Sam came over to take our order and asked if we had any allergies. I piped up straightaway that I'm deathly allergic to garlic! I told Ian I was sorry but it just would never work and then I scarpered. I owe Sam big time.'

Amelia threw back her head and laughed. 'Only you!'

'Could you imagine the garlicky fumes clinging to your clothes for ever? And just think of his breath!'

'I'd rather not. This is why you need higher standards for the men you date.'

'If I had your standards, I'd end up like you, on the shelf,' Clemmie said with a glint in her eye, gesturing to all the books on the shelf.

Amelia swiped her playfully. 'You need to use the old-fashioned methods,' she whispered. 'Someone will walk into the café when you least expect it.' As soon as the words left her mouth, she thought of Jack and felt her heart give a tiny flutter.

'I live in hope,' replied Clemmie, her eyes immediately glancing towards the table of cakes. 'Shop-bought?' Clemmie asked, one eyebrow arched, though a playful grin danced on her lips.

Amelia widened her eyes in mock horror. 'How dare you! I slaved over these cakes for hours, Clemmie. Do you see these flour-dusted hands?' She dramatically showed off her palms, pristine and flour-free.

Clemmie laughed.

The door swung open and Amelia welcomed the troops, handing each a glass of prosecco before they sat down in their usual seats. Her book-club members were creatures of habit and it made Amelia smile. Almost immediately she could hear whispers of admiration for the cakes. 'Gorgeous, aren't they?' Betty said, bending down to inspect the red velvet cake, her hand hovering dangerously close to the creamy frosting.

'I hope you're not only here for the cakes,' teased Amelia, taking her place in the semicircle and peering out of the window hoping to see Jack. Just as she was about to quiet the chatter, the door swung open again and in he came, everyone turning to look in his direction. He wore a simple white T-shirt that hung just right, paired with well-fitted jeans that accentuated his laid-back style. There was a casual elegance about him that made him devilishly gorgeous, even without the athletic build. His tousled hair fell just so, framing his face, and when he flashed Amelia that charming grin, her pulse began to race.

His eyes sparkled with warmth, pulling her in like a magnet. 'Hope I'm not late!' he called out, his voice sending a thrill down her spine. The room fell silent, the energy shifting around them as he unexpectedly walked over to her and kissed her on both cheeks. As he leaned in, Amelia briefly closed her eyes, taking in his intoxicating aftershave, a blend of sandalwood and fresh citrus that made her go weak at the knees. She saw Clemmie's eyes flicker between her and Jack like a hawk tracking its prey.

'You've changed your jumper, it suits you!' he observed.

'I have,' Amelia said, trying to sound breezy but likely coming off as flustered.

Just before seven p.m. Amelia had changed into a cosy fluffy jumper adorned with two adorable puffins cuddled up against each other, perfectly capturing her whimsical spirit. She'd paired it with ankle-length jeans and small kitten heels that added just the right touch of elegance to the outfit.

'Now, where do I sit?'

Immediately, Clemmie patted the arm of the chair next to her. 'Are you going to introduce us?' She looked towards Amelia, clearly itching to know who this handsome stranger was.

'This is Jack, our newest member of the book club for one night only.'

'If I could just have him for one night only,' muttered Clemmie before turning towards Jack. 'What are your thoughts on garlic?'

Jack looked confused. 'Not a huge fan if I'm truly honest.'

'You can definitely sit here next to me then.'

Amelia shook her head in playful exasperation, giving Clemmie a look that silently pleaded, *Please, not the interrogation*!

Before Clemmie could unleash a flurry of questions, Amelia threw her arms wide open with a bright smile. 'Welcome, everyone, to The Story Shop … our little haven by the coast! I'm Amelia Brown, your book-loving host, and this is Pawsworth, our honorary book club mascot!' She stroked the cat, who looked more than a little disgruntled to have his seventeenth nap of the day interrupted.

She gestured towards the table and its array of delectable cakes. 'You know,' she began, 'I've always felt that cakes and romcoms are a lot alike … they both have layers, a sprinkle of sweetness and, sometimes, a little unexpected drama!' Amelia's voice rose in enthusiasm. 'Tonight, we dive into romcoms and cake, but we're adding a touch of your personalities into the mix!' She glanced at the stack of books wrapped in brown paper, their titles still a tantalising mystery.

'Ooh, this is very clever,' Betty remarked, looking round the group with an approving nod. 'It's like a recipe for a perfect evening, just the right blend of flavour and fun!'

'So, grab a glass of prosecco, settle in and let the stories unfold!' Amelia declared, as she beamed at the group. She'd already carefully matched each book with a cake and chosen which resident would receive them, but they didn't know that. With a playful twinkle in her eye, she pretended to shuffle the wrapped books as if at random, adding a sense of mystery. 'Let's see who gets the first surprise!' she said, handing the first book to Robin, the owner of Beachcomber Bakery. 'Let's see what you got.' As all eyes were on Robin, Amelia took the opportunity to glance at Jack, only to find he was watching her. He flashed her a grin, his eyes not leaving hers as he took a sip of prosecco, clearly amused at what was going on around him.

They all waited as Robin carefully peeled back the paper to reveal the first title. She held it up for everyone to see. '*Me Before You* by Jojo Moyes,' she shared, handing the book back to Amelia who pretended to think. She was quite enjoying herself.

'For Robin, I'm going to pair this book with the lemon drizzle cake.' She held up the cake on its plate in one hand and the book in the other. 'Much like Louisa Clark in *Me Before You*, Robin is someone who embodies resilience and hope. Running Beachcomber Bakery requires grit and a sweet touch, which is perfectly symbolised by lemon drizzle cake. The tartness of lemon represents Robin's ability to tackle the sour moments in life, while the drizzle of sweetness is her way of adding light and warmth to those around her. Much like Lou and Will's bittersweet romance, Robin's life isn't without challenges, but she always finds a way to bring joy to others.'

Everyone began to clap as Amelia sliced the cake. After offering everyone a piece, she couldn't help stealing another glance at Jack. He seemed suitably impressed with her little speech, watching her with a look that sent goosebumps skittering across her skin. There was a playful glint in his eye, the kind that made her both nervous and excited all at once. As he reached out to take a piece of cake from the plate, he leaned in slightly and murmured, 'That was impressive.' A flicker of warmth spread through her. She liked that he was impressed. In fact, she liked it a lot.

After a light discussion about the first book as everyone enjoyed their cake, everyone eagerly awaited the next selection. Voices bubbled with excitement, each person hoping it would be their turn. Ever the thoughtful hostess, Amelia moved gracefully around the room, topping up their glasses. The anticipation grew as she approached the table of wrapped books, and pausing for effect, she looked over her guests with a playful smile before picking up the next book. The room fell silent, all eyes on her before she finally handed the book to Cora, the owner of the local pub, who was known for her sharp wit and big heart. 'Cora, you're up!' Amelia said with a grin.

Cora peeled back the wrapping, eager to see which story would accompany her next quiet evening in the pub. '*Crazy Rich Asians,*' she announced, holding up the book.

Amelia moved towards the table of cakes and immediately held up the black forest cake. 'Cora's pub may not scream luxury...'

'Hey!' she protested, and everyone laughed.

Amelia grinned. 'But! Her character has a rich backstory, much like the layers of intrigue and drama in this book. She is complex, confident and knows how to handle secrets and tensions.'

'Very true. The things I hear in that pub...' Cora smiled ruefully.

'The richness of black forest cake, with its indulgent chocolates and cherries, mirrors Cora's own layers. She's tough on the outside but there's plenty of hidden sweetness beneath. Her pub is a gathering place where drama unfolds, much like the world of *Crazy Rich Asians*.'

Everyone clapped.

'I'm going to be bursting at the seams eating all this cake,' Clemmie said with a grin.

'There's a few more cakes to go yet! So maybe we wait until the end and then you can help yourselves. Next up...' Amelia handed the next book to Clemmie.

'Ooh, I was hoping it was me next!' Clemmie tore off the paper and burst out laughing. '*To All The Boys I've Loved Before.*' She waggled the book in the air. 'If only! With my dating history!'

Amelia walked over towards the cakes. 'Let me find a cake that doesn't have a whiff of garlic,' she teased and picked up the Funfetti cake. 'I think this is the perfect cake for Clemmie.' Amelia thought for a second. 'Clemmie's personality shines with a youthful energy, much like Lara Jean's romantic daydreams in *To All The Boys I've Loved Before*. Her tearoom has a light, playful atmosphere and of course she brings joy to all around. The Funfetti cake with its colourful sprinkles and cheery vibe reflects Clemmie's optimism and the sweet charm she brings to her business. She's all about finding beauty in the little things, which makes this cake the perfect match.'

Everyone again erupted into applause. 'And now for the last book of the day. This one I'm going to give to Betty.'

Betty ripped open the paper to reveal *The Hating Game*.

The room fell silent, waiting for Amelia to begin. She held up the red velvet cake. 'Like the intense push and pull between Lucy and Josh in *The Hating Game*, Betty's life is filled with layers of mystery and subtle emotions. As the keeper of secrets on this island, she mirrors the deep red layers of the cake, fiery yet elegant, hiding passions beneath the surface. Her ability to balance the past's intensity with her calming demeanour parallels the contrast of the cake's rich flavour and its smooth, sweet, cream-cheese frosting. Betty is all about depth, much like the book and the cake.'

All the book clubbers were nodding at each other with big grins, and Amelia knew she'd nailed it.

The room was soon filled with the soft hum of conversation and Amelia was chuffed with herself. Once again, she'd pulled off a successful night. She made her rounds, chatting with her friends, topping up drinks and soaking in the sense of community that always flourished at her beloved Story Shop. Jack, still sitting in the middle of the room, had been watching her the entire evening. Every time Amelia looked in his direction, he caught her eye, his gaze lingering a fraction longer than was usual. It wasn't just the kind of casual, friendly look she'd become used to receiving from men over the years. It was the kind of look she'd always hoped someone, particularly someone like Jack, would give her. He found her attractive, she could tell. The way his eyes followed her every move, the slight, playful smile that tugged at his lips whenever she caught him watching, and that glint in his eye that hinted at something more. She felt a flutter of nerves, but it wasn't the uneasy, anxious kind. It was the exciting, electric kind that comes when you sense the first spark of something new.

As she chatted with Dilly about the new art gallery she'd recently opened, and the whirlwind of motherhood that had come with the birth of her twins, Amelia kept one ear on the conversation that was now going on between Jack and Clemmie. Clemmie, ever the nosy investigator, had wasted no time trying to interrogate Jack. Amelia heard snippets of her rapid-fire questions, cleverly disguised as casual conversation, digging for any morsel of information she could unearth. 'So, Jack, what exactly brings you to Puffin Island? Any interesting projects? A girlfriend, perhaps?' Clemmie's eyes sparkled with mischief as she probed, but Jack, with a smile that was equal parts charm and deflection, gave very little away. He skilfully dodged each question with grace, offering just enough to keep Clemmie intrigued but never enough to satisfy her curiosity. Even though Amelia knew exactly who Jack was, she kept his secret to herself.

As the evening began to wind down, people started to gather their things and say their goodbyes, the laughter and lively discussions carrying on down Lighthouse Lane as they filtered out. Amelia, still basking in the warmth of the evening's success, stood by the door, waving everyone off with her signature bright smile. Clemmie was the last to leave and she leaned in and whispered, 'Anyone can tell he's got the hots for you.'

Amelia playfully pushed her friend out of the door before shutting it behind her. Everyone had left except for Jack.

'I think Pawsworth has found his new favourite person,' she said.

In the course of the evening Pawsworth had made himself comfortable on Jack's lap and Jack didn't seem to mind in the slightest.

And there was that smile again, the one that made her pulse quicken.

'You were impressive tonight,' Jack said. 'Funny, engaging, and you clearly know your book clubbers inside and out. It's no wonder they love it here.' He paused, his eyes searching hers for a moment before adding, 'And today you mentioned you liked writing. I'd love to take a look at what you've written sometime.'

Amelia felt both flattered and slightly overwhelmed. 'Oh, it's not as good as my words tonight or even the cake.'

'Don't put yourself down … and you were amazing tonight.'

'Thank you,' she replied. Not wanting him to leave just yet, she took her chance. 'Would you like anything else to drink? I have beer in the fridge.'

'Now you're talking.'

Amelia returned from the kitchen with two beers and handed one to Jack.

'Where did you come up with the idea for your cakes, romcoms and islanders pairings?'

She shrugged. 'Just something I thought of in the spur of the moment.'

'Well, it was a very clever idea. You have me wondering though … which book would you pair me with?'

She studied his face and took a swig of her beer, her eyes locked with his. 'How about you go first.'

Jack slowly moved Pawsworth from his knee and gently placed him on another chair. He got up and slowly browsed the romcom shelves.

'You never know, I might be a dark, bury-strangers-who-frequent-my-bookshop-under-the-patio type of girl,' she mused.

'I'll take my chance,' he said, grinning, pulling a book off the shelf. He turned it towards her. '*Bridget Jones's Diary.*'

'Interesting. You do know you have to pair me with a cake as well.'

He sat back down. 'I'm going to pair you with my favourite cake … carrot cake.'

'That's my favourite too!'

'Your warm, welcoming vibe here at The Story Shop aligns perfectly with Bridget Jones's blend of self-deprecation, charm and sincerity. She's attractive, humorous and lovable. Like a wholesome carrot cake, your character is filled with a down-to-earth appeal. And I suspect that your bookshop is much like Bridget's life, full of mishaps, adventures and love – but hopefully not crime – and at the heart of it all, an all-round gorgeous individual.'

'Can you just repeat that bit in the middle about being attractive, humorous…' She was teasing, but she really did want to hear it again. 'And the part at the end.' His words wrapped around her like a cosy blanket, resonating deeply within her. Hearing him liken her to Bridget Jones, with all her charming quirks and relatable mishaps, made Amelia's heart swell with a mix of pride and vulnerability. The comparison to a wholesome carrot cake also struck a chord. She'd always hoped to be seen as approachable and genuine, and his description affirmed that perception. What set Jack apart from other men she knew was his maturity and depth. The connection between them felt rare. She truly felt seen, and for the first time in a long time, as undeniably attractive.

'Now you're milking it.' He grinned. 'Your turn,' he said, swigging his beer.

Amelia stood and walked over to the new display table. Her fingers brushed the cover of the brand-new Maris Wilde novel. She picked it up. 'This one is for you,' she said, her voice warm and teasing as she gave him a mischievous smile. 'Paired with devil's food cake, which is dark, rich and a little bit wicked.'

'Interesting,' mused Jack.

'This book is called *The Temptation Bucket List*, and it's all about a sexy bucket list ... adventurous to say the least.'

Jack's eyebrows quirked, a smile playing on the edge of his lips. Amelia had got his full attention.

She felt her pulse quicken as his gaze lingered on her, sparking a flutter deep inside. 'The main character, Asher Knight, is charismatic, an irresistible, sexy, adventurous hero, and the devil's food cake is just like him – layered, decadent and a little dangerous if you have too much.'

Jack smirked, shaking his head with a chuckle. 'Dangerous, huh? I'll take that as a compliment,' he said, sending a flutter of nervous excitement through Amelia.

'You should read it and let me know what you think. Who knows, you might get some ideas from the list.'

He took the book from her, his fingers brushing hers. She felt a rush of heat bloom through her as Jack's eyes locked onto hers yet again. He leaned in a little closer. 'A sexy bucket list, you say.' His voice was low and teasing. 'Sounds like a list that's worth pursuing.'

'You tell me after you've read it.' Her words danced between teasing and daring. 'And if you find you wish to try anything on that list...'

Amelia's heart raced at the playful exchange. She smiled, trying to keep her cool, but the way he looked at her left her feeling flustered and intrigued. It was clear they were both thinking the same thing. It was a private game of sorts, a silent understanding between them that was strangely thrilling.

'Well, I'm game if you are.'

Jack leaned in. 'Me, too.'

Chapter Seven

JACK

Jack arrived back at the B&B with only one thing on his mind: Amelia Brown. They'd had a moment. He knew it and so did she. After a quick shower, he climbed into bed, the book by Maris Wilde resting on his lap, its colourful cover inviting him to dive into a world of passion and adventure. He leaned back against the plush headboard, his mind racing as he replayed the evening's events. Amelia had captivated him immediately. There was something undeniably magnetic about her, a chemistry that sparked between them from the very first moment.

The feeling lingered long after they had stood by the door, both teetering on the edge of something more. The way Amelia had looked at him ... her soft, inviting eyes told him everything. She'd wanted him to kiss her, and he'd wanted to, too. The air between them had practically hummed with unspoken desire. His pulse quickened just thinking about it. But something had made him hold back.

He knew that if he hadn't stepped away in that moment, the evening could have taken a very different turn, one they both seemed to want. In a strange, undeniable way, Jack liked the idea of letting the tension simmer between them. He smiled to himself, knowing that if the time came, it would be worth the wait.

He picked up the book Amelia had given him. He was fully aware who Maris Wilde was. In her short career, she'd sold hundreds of thousands of books on pre-orders alone, which always took her to the number one spot, but he'd never read one. This was her third book and after his innuendo-filled back-and-forth with Amelia at the bookshop, he had to admit he was intrigued. What was in this sexy bucket list? But before losing himself in the fictional world of Maris Wilde, Jack grabbed a pen and a notebook. He was here on Puffin Island for a purpose, to gather stories about the islanders and their lives.

He began jotting down notes, inspired by Amelia's lively descriptions of the people who made Puffin Island unique. He paused as he recalled Amelia's description of Betty as the keeper of secrets and wondered what hidden knowledge about the island Betty held. As he continued to make notes about the other book clubbers, he could feel the pull of the novel sitting next to him. He glanced at the cover again, the playful title hinting at themes of romance and adventure. With a deep breath, he opened the book, his eyes landing on the dedication page.

Patience is the sharpest weapon.

The second he read those words he immediately thought of Vivienne.

Vivienne Langford was the kind of agent who did the bare minimum. Instead of actively seeking out new deals or opportunities for her authors, she sat back and waited for them to do the legwork. As soon as they caught a lead, she'd swoop in and take over, claiming credit if it all panned out. The truth was, Jack's success had come from his own passion for writing, not because of any effort on her part. He had made a name for himself through his talent, perseverance and sheer love of storytelling, not because of her so-called guidance. Looking back, he wished he'd been more cautious, that he'd read the small print or sought legal advice before signing that first contract. But when you're just starting out, the excitement of landing an agent and the promise of breaking into the industry clouds your judgement. You're too eager, too naive, to notice the trap you're walking into. And now, years later, he was paying the price for that mistake. She owned a stake in his books indefinitely. For as long as he lived, she would continue making money off his work, no matter what. She would probably continue to do so even when he was ten feet under. Every royalty payment that landed in her hands felt like another blow to his autonomy as a writer.

But he had a plan. After he fired her, he'd set his sights on writing a book that would surpass all his previous works. A novel so compelling it would be snapped up by Netflix, turned into a global phenomenon and outsell all his existing books combined. And best of all? She would have no rights to it. But now that plan was starting to unravel. Writer's block had gripped him tightly, and the pressure to outdo himself only made the creative process harder. That was why he needed the money from this article for *The Morning Ledger*. But given that there was no love lost between them, why had Vivienne put his name forward in the first place? The more he thought about it, the more it didn't make any sense to him.

From the very first page of *The Temptation Bucket List*, he was drawn into the story, captivated by the sizzling chemistry between the two main characters, Zara Quinn and Asher Knight. Jack was instantly transported into a world filled with passion and excitement as Zara, a free-spirited woman, embarked on a quest to complete a sexy bucket list. The pages turned quickly as Jack became engrossed in the protagonists' escapades, each chapter introducing a new thrill. The story captured the essence of living boldly. And when Zara and Asher met for the first time in a bookshop, it reminded him that he and Amelia had met in exactly the same way.

He leaned against the headboard, finding it difficult to tear himself away. The hours were slipping into the early morning and still he continued reading. The book was more than just a story. It was an exploration of desire, a tale of two people discovering their connection through their sexy bucket list. Jack was enthralled, already imagining himself in the characters' shoes alongside Amelia. It made him think about his own desires. He was stuck in his career and stuck in his love life. He carried on turning page after page, and when he finally set the book down, he was surprised to find that it was four a.m. He couldn't believe how quickly time had passed. As he turned the light out he wondered how he was going to get any sleep, his mind still turning over the plot of the book and all those sexy bucket list items…

It only felt like moments later when there was a knock on his door.

'Last call for breakfast!' Lena's cheerful voice rang out from the other side.

Jack rubbed his eyes, momentarily disoriented as he sat up in bed. The Maris Wilde novel was still resting beside him, its pages slightly rumpled from his late-night reading.

'I'll be down in five, thank you,' he shouted, bringing himself around quickly.

After dressing, he made his way downstairs, the aroma of freshly brewed coffee wafting through the air and guiding him towards the dining area.

Sitting in the quaint dining room of the bed and breakfast with a full English untouched on the plate in front of him, Jack couldn't focus on anything but Amelia. His thoughts were consumed by her … her smile, the way she'd laughed nervously last night, the sparkle in her eyes when she talked about books. He could see she shared a great bond with the islanders, and the camaraderie among them was unmistakable. He wasn't sure if it was the lack of sleep, or the fact that he might have dreamed about her, but the effect was the same. He couldn't get her off his mind.

As he sipped his coffee and began to eat, his gaze drifted out of the window. The island was peaceful in the morning light, unlike his thoughts, which were far from calm. *The Temptation Bucket List* had been playing on his mind, especially the two main characters. Neither of them had been looking for a relationship, and that resonated with him more than he cared to admit. Zara knew her worth; she wouldn't date just anyone, but was always searching for the real deal, the person that had everything, with no compromise. Asher, on the other hand, was a bit of a player, a famous actor who used his charm and status to lure women into bed. Jack couldn't help but see shades of himself in Asher. He wasn't famous in the Hollywood sense, but when he mentioned his name, people knew his books.

This time, things felt different. He liked Amelia and he wanted her to like him for who he was, not because of his books or his name. But Jack knew that's where the problem lay. He couldn't tell her who he really was as he was here under false pretences. When she discovered the truth about the article he was here to write, she would never speak to him again, and he didn't like that thought. His appetite dwindled and he pushed his plate aside.

He returned to his room and opened up his laptop. The diary entry he'd written yesterday was staring back at him. He read back his words and the first thing that struck him was his own enthusiasm for the island. He'd written warmly about the place, the islanders who had participated in book club and of course Amelia.

His inbox pinged and there, at the top, was an email from Vivienne. He clicked on it reluctantly.

Subject: How's it going?

Hope you're settling in well and finding your feet! I thought I'd check in to see if you've arrived safely. Because we know each other, I offered to step in while Miles is away on business. Do keep me updated from your end and let me know how the assignment is coming along? And of course any interesting stories or juicy gossip from the island. Oh, and just a thought – Amelia Brown, the owner of The Story Shop, might be worth connecting with. It sounds like her place is the heart of the community, so she could have some valuable insights. Don't hold back – treat her to a coffee or lunch, wine and dine her, or whatever it takes to get her talking (feel free to expense it!).

Looking forward to hearing how it's going and reading the article!

Best wishes, Vivienne.

Jack stared at the email. The suggestion of using Amelia as some sort of pawn to get the story, to exploit her kindness, made him feel uneasy. Something about this whole assignment wasn't sitting right with him, and the more he thought about it, the worse it got. Closing the laptop, Jack leaned back in his chair and exhaled. The payment for this article was more than generous; it was over the odds, actually. That should've been a red flag from the start, but he hadn't thought much of it then, too grateful for the relief it would provide. Now, though, the weight of what he was doing hit him full force. If this article went into print, was it something he wanted his name associated with?

He stood up and paced the room, feeling a tug of conflict. The tax bill was lying on the desk and he knew that despite his differences with Vivienne she'd recommended him knowing he was dependable and would deliver. Her email message lingered in his mind.

Don't hold back – treat her to a coffee or lunch, wine and dine her, or whatever it takes to get her talking (feel free to expense it!).

She'd made it sound so cold, so transactional. And Amelia? She wasn't just some means to an end. The night before, over prosecco and laughter, she'd shown him a side of herself that was open, kind and refreshingly real.

And then there was *The Temptation Bucket List* and their playful conversation about it last night. Reading the book after, he'd been taken aback by how much he had in common with Asher Knight. But he wasn't that man anymore, or at least he didn't want to be.

The Story Shop would be opening soon, and Amelia would be there, setting out books, chatting to the customers. Jack grabbed his jacket and his laptop and headed for the door.

As he walked through the cobbled streets towards Blue Water Bay, the soft hum of conversation drifted through the air, children's laughter on the beach mingling with the sound of the seagulls in the distance. He stepped up to the small window counter at the Cosy Kettle, where Becca, the café's owner, stood pouring frothy milk into a mug.

'Good morning,' she greeted him brightly. 'Good to see you again. What can I get you today?'

'A hot chocolate, please,' Jack replied.

Becca prepared his drink, the sound of the milk steamer hissing softly in the background. 'So,' she asked, 'how was your first night on Puffin Island? Wasn't book club so much fun?'

'It was. I have to say I've loved every moment so far and waking up to all this feels surreal,' he replied.

'It's the best place in the world.'

'I think I agree.' He smiled and held up the polystyrene cup in a toast then began walking towards the bookshop. He decided there and then that he wasn't going to wine and dine Amelia to extract information from her. He was going to spend time with Amelia because he wanted to.

Chapter Eight

AMELIA

Amelia was up with the lark, as she was most mornings. She cherished her early walks before the bookshop opened when the world was still quiet, the only sounds the soft lapping of waves against the shore and the occasional moo of a puffin. The air was crisp, carrying a faint tang of salt, as she strolled along the bay. The weather was completely different from the stormy clouds of yesterday, the bright, chilly sunshine a welcome change. The walk had taken her past her old family home, reinforcing an ache she could never quite lose. The whitewashed cottage, perched on the edge of the island amongst the sand dunes, looked just as it always had, the weathered stone walls standing strong against the harsh elements that had battered them for generations.

Her heart clenched as she gazed at it from a distance, memories flooding back like a wave crashing onto the shore. The front garden, once teeming with wildflowers, was now overgrown, neglected for the past six months. The pale blue window shutters that she and her father had repainted every summer were peeling, the colour faded and tired. She could almost hear his voice in the back of her mind, laughing as they worked side by side, their hands covered in paint.

It had been seven months since her father's tragic death, and the grief still consumed her on a daily basis, often when she was least expecting it. Ethan Brown had always been a sensible, measured man, the kind who planned his steps carefully and rarely took risks. He'd lived in the same house all his life, like his parents before him, and he loved to write, hoping that one day his dream of becoming a published author would come true. It had been such a shock when he shared with Amelia he'd bought a boat. And not just any old boat, but the kind that looked like it belonged to a rockstar or a millionaire, which was far from the humble life her father had led. It wasn't his style at all. He was a man of simple pleasures, more likely to enjoy a quiet afternoon tending to his garden than anything extravagant like sailing … until his new wife changed everything. Amelia wished with all her heart their paths had never crossed.

'What on earth possessed you, Dad?' she'd asked, dumbfounded by his purchase.

'Why not? It's an adventure!' he'd replied.

That adventure had ended in disaster. Not long afterwards, he took the boat out one day for its maiden voyage around the island. According to Vivienne, they'd been enjoying a lavish lunch on the boat and, while she sunbathed, Ethan had decided to go for a swim. But when he dived into the water he hit his head on a rock, the head wound killing him almost immediately.

But none of it made any sense to Amelia. Her dad had liked watching the ocean from the comfort of their cosy family home, but he had never been a fan of actually getting into the water, so why had he that day? Amelia couldn't make peace with the fact that something so out of character had stolen him away from her.

Dune House had been filled with good memories, memories made before her stepmother had come into their lives and changed everything. She'd swept in just over a year ago, marrying Ethan after a whirlwind romance. Vivienne had been all charm and sophistication at first, but Amelia had quickly realised her true nature: cold, manipulative, and always looking for a way to gain control. The legal battle contesting the will was wearing Amelia down but she wasn't going to give up and hand everything to Vivienne on a plate.

Thankfully, there was one thing that Vivienne could never take away from her. The memories Amelia shared with her father, those belonged to them alone.

There were the laughter-filled mornings in the kitchen every Sunday, and the hours spent in the little study where he would sit and read her favourite books to her as a child. The living room, where they'd spend cold winter nights huddled by the fire, sharing stories. The little annexe that led onto the cobbled street was her favourite part of the house, and as a child she'd always imagined turning it into her own writing studio or even a bookshop. And there was the garden he'd carefully tended, full of vibrant flowers and shrubs he'd planted with his own hands.

Her father had loved Puffin Island, its raw beauty, its wild nature and of course the close-knit community that were like family to him. He'd championed everyone on the island, supported whatever venture they engaged in and was an all-round decent guy, which was why it was so hard to understand what the hell he could possibly have found attractive in a woman like Vivienne Langford, whose heart was black if it existed at all.

Amelia's phone buzzed in her pocket and she glanced at the screen. It was a message from Clemmie, thanking her for last night and seeking gossip, wondering what, if anything, had happened between Amelia and Jack after everyone else had left.

AMELIA
Jack left straight after you.

She texted the little white lie, fully aware that if he'd suggested staying for another beer she wouldn't have hesitated to say yes.

CLEMMIE
Boring!

As Amelia arrived at The Story Shop, she unlocked the door and flipped the sign to 'OPEN', propping the door ajar to welcome the day's first visitors. Pawsworth leaped gracefully down from the counter and rubbed against her leg just as she picked up *The Sunday Times* from where it was lying on the mat. On a good Sunday, she could double her weekly takings, so she usually took Tuesdays off instead.

As she placed the newspaper on the counter, Amelia

nearly jumped out of her skin as a voice trilled, 'Morning.' As she spun round she was hit by the scent of freshly baked scones.

'What are you doing? You nearly gave me a heart attack, and you literally just texted me!' Amelia exclaimed, clutching her chest as Clemmie stood there grinning from ear to ear.

Clemmie held up a white paper bag, placing it on the counter. 'Two things, my gorgeous friend,' she began. 'First, I know how much you love a freshly baked scone in the morning, and even though the café is only open for a couple of hours on a Sunday, I thought you might like one. Because, well, I'm that kind of friend.'

Amelia peered into the bag, her mouth already watering at the thought of buttery, crumbly goodness. 'That's very kind of you, thank you,' she said, grateful but eyeing up Clemmie. There was something else.

'And secondly'—Clemmie's tone shifted, and she took a seat on the nearest chair, folding her arms with all the seriousness of a detective about to crack a case—'you're busted. We need to talk.'

Amelia's heart skipped a beat. 'Busted?' she repeated, her pulse quickening. Her first thought was that Clemmie had somehow uncovered her secret.

Clemmie narrowed her eyes, her gaze laser-focused on Amelia. 'I know…' she said, drawing out the moment like she was savouring it.

Amelia remained silent, swallowing hard, her mouth suddenly dry. She could feel the heat rising to her cheeks. She hadn't meant to keep it from Clemmie, she'd intended to tell her all along, but struggled to find the right moment due to her dad's passing. And then, as time went on, it became harder to bring it up without it seeming strange.

Clemmie's expression softened for a second. 'Would you say I'm your best friend?'

Amelia nodded, hoping that it wasn't going where she thought it was going.

'And yet,' Clemmie continued, her voice tinged with disappointment, 'you didn't think you could be honest with me. You lied to me.'

She knew.

Amelia sank onto the chair beside her and let out a long breath. 'I couldn't tell anyone until I was ready. I'm so sorry, Clemmie. It just ... happened ... then...' She fidgeted, looking for the right words. 'How did you even find out? And please, please tell me no one else knows.'

Clemmie raised her hands in surrender then reached for the glove she'd evidently left on the arm of the chair. 'I left one of my gloves here and only realised when I got home. I decided to come back and there you were ... both of you! Engulfed in candlelight. Enjoying a beer! Jack didn't leave straight after me ... I want details!' Clemmie leaned forward.

Amelia stared at her in stunned silence for a moment, then burst into a relieved laugh. 'You saw me and Jack enjoying a beer? That's what you're on about?'

Clemmie looked scandalised. 'Don't laugh, Amelia! You lied! And my guess is you lied to cover up the truth.'

'Which is?'

'You kissed.' Clemmie tilted her head to the side, waiting for answers.

Amelia exhaled in relief. Thank God the actual secret

she'd been harbouring was safe ... for now. 'We didn't!' she said, still giggling, holding her hands up.

Clemmie narrowed her eyes playfully. 'Don't think you're off the hook. I don't believe you! Tell me! It's just not fair ... I get garlic guy and you get Jack, the deliciously hot man that suddenly appeared at book club ... how? Who is he?'

Amelia grinned. 'I told you! He got blown in with the storm and I invited him to book club because he'd only just arrived and it was a good way of meeting the islanders.'

'But then you invited him for a drink after hours?'

'One beer and then he went home ... well, home to the B&B.'

'I want to believe you...'

'You had me going there for a minute. I thought—' Amelia cut herself off, realising she was about to spill more than she intended.

Intrigued, Clemmie asked, 'Thought what? What else are you hiding?'

Amelia stood up quickly grabbing the white paper bag and waving it in front of Clemmie. 'Nothing! Now, I think you should go back to work whilst I enjoy my scone.'

'Mmm. Okay, but I know that look.'

Amelia held up her hands. 'I'm hiding nothing.' Another white lie.

'I'm disappointed in you, Brown,' said Clemmie, standing up. 'I would have had him stay for a second beer then kept him hostage all night!' She laughed.

'You only call me Brown when I'm in trouble.'

'You are! But I think you can make it up to me. In fact I'll stay silent about what I saw if'—she pointed to the display of Maris Wilde's novel—'you let me have one of those. I've been waiting for this one. Apparently it's very steamy.'

'As you're my friend, you can have a copy for free. It might highlight for you what a real man is all about, and convince you to stop wasting time with all those garlic-loving deadheads you keep finding on dating sites.'

'If only fictional men were real, the world would be a better place.' Clemmie picked up a copy and walked towards the door. 'I'll catch up with you later.'

As soon as Clemmie had left the shop, Amelia could feel her heart calming down. She let out a huge sigh, both relieved and amused by her friend's dramatic interrogation. She loved Clemmie, truly, but she was thankful she hadn't accidentally confessed her secret because it wouldn't stay secret for long.

Pawsworth meowed loudly, his reminder that it was time for breakfast. Amelia smiled as she walked to the kitchen and scooped food into his bowl.

'Here you go, troublemaker,' she said, giving him a gentle scratch behind his ears as he tucked into his meal. She grabbed herself a steaming mug of tea and settled into her favourite armchair, the one next to the large window with a view of Lighthouse Lane and Blue Water Bay in the distance. The Story Shop was still quiet, it was too early for the usual trickle of tourists, and as she waited for the customers, she unfolded the crisp pages of the newspaper. Amelia loved the Sunday supplements, especially the art and book sections. She let her eyes wander over the headlines and as she turned to the book reviews section, her eyes widened in surprise. There, staring back at her, was a headline about none other than Vivienne. That bloody woman was everywhere!

Vivienne Langford: The Agent Behind the Bestsellers, the headline read.

Amelia skimmed through the piece, which highlighted just how successful a publisher Vivienne was and explained that she was setting up a new writers' scheme within her company whereby they could pay to receive feedback and help with polishing their manuscripts, thus bringing fresh voices to the literary world. Typical Vivienne ... fingers in so many pies, always trying to be the puppet-mistress. Vivienne's strategy was as shrewd as it was brilliant. Aspiring authors would leap at the chance to have their manuscripts refined under the guidance of a renowned literary agent, knowing it would vastly improve their chances of landing a coveted spot on the roster of one of the most prestigious agencies in the industry. Meanwhile, Vivienne would be paid to handpick the manuscripts that showed true promise, stories with raw potential that she could nurture, polish and eventually represent. It was a win-win for both parties, and Amelia couldn't help but admire how seamlessly Vivienne wrapped her pursuit of business advantage in fake generosity.

But one line in the article made Amelia sit up straighter. When asked if she'd had any regrets during her illustrious career, Vivienne had answered: 'Rejecting Maris Wilde's manuscript.'

Amelia's eyes widened in surprise. So, even the invincible Vivienne had her regrets. And it was no wonder. Wilde's debut had gone on to sell millions. Amelia allowed herself a small, satisfied smile. The fact that Maris Wilde sat at the top of *The Sunday Times* Bestseller list with her new novel, which had only been released this week, would undoubtedly eat Vivienne alive. Good. Let her stew in it.

Amelia reached for her phone, her fingers tapping rapidly as she Googled Maris Wilde. It wasn't the first time she had done this. The internet was unusually silent about this elusive author. Maris Wilde had managed to keep her personal life thoroughly hidden from the world. There were no photos, no interviews, no social media presence, and not a scrap of personal information had leaked out. Just like Cillian Murphy, an actor who had shunned social media, preferring to be known because of his body of work, Maris's success was entirely due to her talent and the quality of her books.

Amelia's thoughts drifted back to Vivienne's regret. If only the woman could regret other things in her life, like stealing Amelia's inheritance after her father's death. She tried to push those thoughts aside; she wasn't going to let Vivienne ruin another Sunday.

As The Story Shop was starting to stir with life she shut the newspaper and concentrated on greeting her customers. The warmer weather had brought out a flood of tourists eager to explore the island. Amelia loved these moments, the way the shop buzzed with visitors, each one with their own story, their own reason for visiting Puffin Island. Some came for the rugged beauty, others for the solitude, and some had memories that tied them to the place. She chatted with customers as they wandered in, helping them find books or sharing her recommendations. As each new visitor crossed the threshold, Amelia found herself glancing towards the door, hoping Jack would appear. When she'd climbed into bed last night all she could think about was the charged energy as they stood in the doorway, the air between them practically crackling with tension. She'd felt it keenly, and she knew he had, too.

She smiled as she handed a book to a customer and watched them walk out, her gaze – finally – colliding with Jack's as he confidently walked in and placed a hot chocolate down on the counter.

'For you.'

Amelia's heart flipped in her chest, the sight of him sending a thrill through her. She grinned, knowing the exact reason he'd brought her a hot chocolate. 'Thank you.' She couldn't stop smiling at him. 'You've started the book then?'

He leaned against the counter, his captivating eyes locked on hers. There was a hint of mischief in his gaze. 'Asher Knight stumbles upon a bookshop and is intrigued by the beautiful Zara Quinn. The next day he brings her a hot chocolate and, well … the truth is I finished the book in the early hours of this morning.'

'You finished it? That's very good going, I'm impressed.'

'It was a different book to what I'm used to reading, I have to admit.'

Amelia's pulse quickened. There it was again, that charged energy between them. The unspoken attraction that seemed to simmer beneath every word they exchanged. She swallowed, trying to keep her composure. 'Well,' she said, her voice softer, 'I'm glad you stopped by.'

His eyes lingered on hers for a moment longer, and she could feel the weight of everything that wasn't being said. Jack reading that book had changed things, upped the stakes between them, and she could tell by the way he looked at her that he knew it, too.

'What's that you're reading?' he asked, gesturing towards the newspaper still spread out on the counter. Amelia glanced down, momentarily distracted from the tension between them.

'Just *The Sunday Times*. Maris Wilde's new book is at the top of the charts. She's quite the mystery,' Amelia replied. 'She's practically a ghost. No photos, no social media, just a trio of bestsellers. Maybe that's the key to success. Stay hidden, let the work speak for itself.' Amelia smiled.

Jack's eyes flickered to hers again, and she felt her heart beat just a little faster. 'So, Amelia,' he said, his voice lowering slightly, 'about last night…'

Her breath caught in her throat.

Jack leaned in just a fraction more, his smile slow and deliberate. 'What was it you said about this temptation bucket list?' He walked over to the display table, picked up a copy of the book and set it down in front of her. 'Three weeks I'm here, maybe four. If you want to be Zara Quinn, well … I don't mind being your Asher Knight.'

Amelia let out a nervous laugh, the memory of last night's prosecco-fuelled bravado rushing back. Now, standing in the daylight with Jack teasing her, she realised he might actually be daring her for real. She wasn't sure what to say, her thoughts bouncing back and forth like a tennis match in her head. Should she flirt back or retreat to safety? Her heart raced as Jack's playful smile lingered, waiting for her response. This was no longer the buzz of a tipsy evening. This was real, and the excitement of it made her feel alive, like she was standing on the edge of something thrilling.

Jack leaned in just a little more, watching her with quiet intensity, giving her the space to decide but letting her know that he was very much invested in whatever came next. The moment stretched, filled with anticipation and excitement. Amelia could feel her pulse in her throat, her skin buzzing with the electricity of being so close to him.

Finally, she met his gaze, her eyes filled with a mix of excitement and uncertainty. 'Last night, I might've been a little ... bold, thanks to the prosecco,' she admitted, her cheeks flushing slightly.

They both looked at the customer approaching the counter. 'Damn,' whispered Jack. 'Would you mind if I work at that table for an hour or so?'

'Be my guest,' she replied, as he stepped out of the way to let her serve the customer.

As soon as she'd finished ringing up the purchase she dared a glance towards Jack, who'd settled himself and opened up his laptop. He caught her eye and Amelia shook her head, laughing softly. There was no denying that they were on the verge of something extraordinary.

Five minutes later the bookshop was empty. 'All right, Asher Knight,' Amelia said, her voice teasing but full of warmth, 'let's see where this takes us.'

'Yes, let's,' he replied.

Chapter Nine
AMELIA

The four friends were huddled around their favourite table in The Sea Glass Restaurant, anchored to the wooden jetty of Blue Water Bay. The restaurant's glass-bottomed floor allowed them to watch sea life glide beneath them as they caught up on the latest gossip. They made a ritual of these monthly get-togethers, a non-negotiable girls' night complete with seafood platters, laughter and, of course, scandalous revelations. Tonight, though, Amelia was about to drop a bombshell. Her eyes sparkled mischievously as she leaned in, her voice lowered for dramatic effect. 'I have something to tell you…'

Her three friends froze in mid-bite, their forks hovering in the air. Verity, Dilly and Clemmie exchanged glances before turning their full attention to Amelia.

'I'm about to sleep with a stranger.'

Clemmie laughed loudly. 'For a moment there I thought you said you were about to sleep with a stranger!'

Verity picked up her glass and took a sip of wine. 'Is this some sort of new TV show like *Married at First Sight*? Because as your friends we don't want you to involve yourself in any car-crash TV. Just think, when you do become a famous author this will come back to haunt you. I'd definitely advise against it.'

All heads turned towards Dilly to see what she had to say about the situation.

'Is this our friend Amelia Brown? The same Amelia who once made a pros and cons list before agreeing to hold a guy's hand?'

Amelia rolled her eyes but couldn't suppress the grin tugging at her lips. 'I was eleven years old.'

Dilly, who was currently wearing a lobster bib but still managed to look chic, leaned forward, her eyes wide with curiosity. 'I am *loving* this. After the birth of the twins, Max and I are so knackered we haven't had a moment of excitement. I need *every* detail.' She picked up a shrimp from the platter and dipped it into some sauce before eagerly leaning in, waiting for Amelia to explain.

'And who is this mystery man?' asked Clemmie. 'Oh my, it's him, isn't it? The guy from—'

'The guy from book club,' Amelia interrupted casually.

Clemmie raised an eyebrow looking clearly impressed. 'So, this Jack guy rocks up on the island and you don't know who he is, he comes to book club, and then the next thing we know you're sleeping with him? It sounds like something out of a movie.'

'I may have exaggerated a little when I said I'm going to sleep with him,' Amelia admitted, and saw the looks of disappointment that flashed across their faces. 'But you all know how fussy I am. I just ... well, there's this ... chemistry, and we've been, um, flirting a lot. He's here for a few weeks, and there's just ... something about him. He's funny, and charming, and, well, last night we were talking about this book, and now he's teasing me about us being like the characters. I may have ... sort of ... agreed to a flirtation.'

'Which book?'

'*The Temptation Bucket List*, and we may have dared each other to take part in some activities from that list.'

Clemmie gasped dramatically, placing a hand over her heart. 'Amelia Brown! I love this for you!'

'But isn't that book a little—'

'Steamy!' Verity interrupted Dilly. 'I've heard things about this book.'

'What I'm more interested in is how this conversation even came about.' Clemmie grinned at her friend. 'Get talking.'

'Just like in the book, he walked into the bookshop and we hit it off straightaway.'

'Why didn't he walk into the café first?' Clemmie rolled her eyes. 'Do you know how many dates I've had to put myself through from those dating apps? It's torture. There's never a normal man.'

Verity, ever the practical one, leaned in. 'Okay, but is Jack a *normal* stranger or one of those "might-have-bodies-buried-in-his-back-garden" strangers?'

Amelia laughed, shaking her head. 'Normal, I think. Mostly.'

Dilly waved a crab claw in the air like a gavel. 'I declare this is the best gossip we've had in *months*.'

'Definitely the best gossip, but this guy can't be normal. There's no denying he's hot but there has to be something wrong with him, like … he has three nipples … or doesn't like mugs…'

Amelia raised her eyebrows, chuckling. 'Doesn't like mugs? What's that supposed to mean?'

Clemmie rolled her eyes dramatically. 'I once dated this guy who, by the third date, brought his own china mug to my place because he didn't like the thick-rimmed mugs I use. Then, he had the nerve to ask if he should bring me one next time! I was like, "No, thanks. It's *my* house." Honestly, that was just the tip of the iceberg. For Christmas, he bought me two gifts … wait for it … a diet cookbook and shampoo for frizzy hair. Do I look like I need to go on a diet or have frizzy hair? The cheek!'

The entire table erupted in laughter, with Verity shaking her head in disbelief. 'He sounds like a real barrel of laughs!'

'I know, right?' Clemmie grinned. 'Safe to say, he didn't last long after that. Can you imagine, though? A diet cookbook? Who does that?'

Dilly, still wiping away tears of laughter, chimed in, 'Honestly, that's a gift from someone who doesn't want to make it to New Year! You definitely dodged a bullet. And for what it's worth, there's nothing like drinking a cup of tea from a proper mug.'

'I'll check out Jack's mug game,' said Amelia with a chuckle. 'But I think he's normal.'

'How did the temptation bucket list come about?' pressed Clemmie.

'After book club, we chose a book and paired each other with a cake. I chose Maris Wilde's new novel for him.'

'That's very clever,' admitted Verity. 'And you said he was here for a few weeks? What else do you know about him?'

'He's from London, works in social affairs.' Amelia kept to herself that Jack was *the* Jack Hartwell, famous author, and that she'd done a fair bit of internet stalking for information about him since his arrival. 'I know that I'm usually dead boring Amelia who won't even consider a date unless they tick every box but ... there's something about him.'

'Basically, what you're saying is you've agreed to have a holiday fling.' Dilly took a sip of her drink.

'You're going to fall in love,' stated Clemmie.

'I'm *not* going to fall in love,' Amelia protested, though the warmth in her cheeks betrayed her.

Clemmie leaned back, laughing.

'You girls are always telling me to push myself out of my comfort zone, and that's exactly what I'm doing!'

Clemmie shook her head, still grinning. 'We never said to recreate the plot of *The Temptation Bucket List* with a stranger.'

'I'm going straight home to read this book,' declared Dilly. 'I need to know exactly what you're going to be getting up to.'

Verity raised her glass. 'To Amelia and her sexy stranger!'

This catch-up had been far juicier than any of them had

expected, and though Amelia was careful not to reveal Jack's true identity, she couldn't help feeling another flutter of anticipation at what was to come. She was about to discover not just the man behind the public persona, but also the personal and intimate side of Jack Hartwell, and she was more than ready for the adventure.

Chapter Ten

JACK

Jack sat at the small wooden desk in his cosy B&B bedroom, the distant sound of waves gently lapping against the shore drifting through the open window. His laptop glowed faintly, casting a warm hue over the room as he leaned back, letting out a thoughtful sigh. The day had been eventful, and as he began typing his diary entry, the words flowed easily.

He wrote about the way Amelia looked at him, how her laughter was sexy and how the playful teasing between them felt electric. Within half an hour he'd written nearly 2000 words. If only writing his novels would come that easily. As Jack read back through the entry, it almost felt like he was reading the beginning of a love story. His feelings for Amelia were clear and it surprised him that he'd written so openly and honestly. He'd never been one for talking about his feelings, and kept his private life very much private, but maybe that was because he'd never actually been in love. He thought back to his previous relationships, realising that none of those women had ever inspired him to plan a proper, meaningful date. With Amelia, he wanted to know what made her smile and what made her heart race. He wanted to peel back the layers and get to the heart of who she was.

Even though he wrote about love in his novels he'd often questioned what love was, wondering if everyone had the same feeling when they fell in love, and, if not, what it meant to different people. Now he was beginning to get an idea for himself. Because there was no use denying it; in a short space of time he had started falling for Amelia Brown.

After he finished reading his diary entry, he opened his emails. Vivienne's still sat unanswered and he knew he couldn't avoid replying for much longer. He rubbed the back of his neck, deciding to put it off just for a while. Vivienne could wait. What mattered to him right now was arranging something special for Amelia.

Even though the temptation bucket list from Maris Wilde's book had started as a playful dare between them, Jack knew he couldn't simply tick off items from a fictional list. And besides, the list in the book was a little too steamy for what he had in mind. He really wanted to make Amelia feel special, to create moments that would mean something to both of them. He smiled to himself as an idea began to form. Grabbing his jacket from the back of the chair, he headed out into the afternoon air. He had something to plan, and the first step was finding the perfect spot for their first real date … cliffside stargazing but with a twist.

Jack made his way along the rugged cliff path that curved around the far side of Blue Water Bay, the salty breeze ruffling his hair and the distant cry of seagulls echoing overhead. He passed the old boat house, weathered by years of coastal winds, and the whitewashed lighthouse. Now, he was on the coastal path that wound its way over the dunes, finally bringing him to the top of the cliff. The panoramic view stopped him in his tracks. Below him, the ocean stretched endlessly, a canvas of deep blues and greens. Waves crashed rhythmically against the jagged rocks below, sending sprays of white foam into the air. And there, bobbing on the surface of the water, were the puffins. His breath caught slightly as he saw them for the first time. Their black-and-white plumage and colourful beaks made them look almost comical, like little clowns floating on the waves. Some flapped their wings, trying to take off, while others simply drifted, enjoying the current as if they didn't have a care in the world. As Jack watched the puffins continue their amusing routines, he felt peaceful and relaxed for the first time in a long time.

Before he'd arrived on Puffin Island, Jack had researched the island and knew that Cliff Top Cottage was indeed nestled at the top of the cliff and was occupied by Pete Fenwick, whose story intrigued him, not just because the man had been in the news lately for his involvement in setting up automatic barriers to protect tourists from crossing the dangerous causeway at high tide, but because of Pete's more colourful past. Once on the verge of stardom as a member of a band that had been adored by swooning fans, Pete had retreated into a quiet life on the island, all but disappearing from the public eye after tragedy struck and one of the band's members died in an accident. He eventually became the island's vet, occasionally making headlines for his community efforts, like the causeway project he'd organised alongside Sam, the owner of The Sea Glass Restaurant.

Ahead, Jack spotted the stone cottage, its weathered walls blending seamlessly with the landscape. Just beyond it, perched near the cliff's edge, was a bench. Jack walked over and sat down, gazing out over the vast expanse of the ocean.

Hearing footsteps behind him, he spun around to see a man approaching him whom he recognised immediately: Puffin Pete.

'Can't fault that view,' Pete said, nodding towards the horizon.

Jack smiled, turning back to face the sea. 'I agree. I don't think I've seen anything quite like it.'

Pete stepped closer, his hands resting casually in his pockets as he gazed out over the water. 'Not seen you around these parts before,' he said. 'Passing through?'

'Staying for a few weeks at the B&B,' Jack replied. 'Trying to escape work for a bit, maybe figure out what comes next in life.'

Pete nodded slowly, as if he understood all too well. 'It's a good place to sit and contemplate life. It has a way of making you think about what really matters.'

Jack smiled, appreciating the man's insight. 'That's exactly why I came up here. I'm planning something, a ... date, I guess you could call it. But I'm not sure if this spot is too exposed for stargazing. I want it to be special, something that makes her feel like she's the only person in the world.'

Pete raised an eyebrow. 'A special girl, then?'

'I think so, but we've only just met so I need to impress

her,' Jack admitted, a warmth spreading in his chest at the thought of Amelia. 'All I know is she's different; there's something about her.'

Pete smiled, his weathered face softening. 'I know that feeling. It's rare, but when you find it, you hold on to it. As for this spot, well...' He looked around thoughtfully. 'You'll see the stars here, that's for sure, but it's not exactly cosy, and believe me, the winds up here at night can get a bit gusty. There's a spot on the other side of the island in Cockle Bay Cove. If you walk along until the farm clock tower is in view there's an empty house on the right called "Dune House", which backs onto the cove there but is high up. Cut through the garden and I suspect you'll find it's the perfect spot to stargaze.'

'Am I able just to walk through the garden?'

'The property is empty and if anyone does question you, you send them in my direction. It's all in the name of love and something tells me she's worth it.' He smiled, his eyes twinkling with the kind of understanding that only comes from experience.

'Thank you.'

'No problem. In case you haven't picked the day yet, it's rumoured we may see the Northern Lights on Wednesday night.' As Pete walked away, Jack sat for a few more moments, watching the waves roll in. The idea of witnessing the Northern Lights, the elusive, magical aurora that had always been on his bucket list, was exciting – particularly if he could see them with Amelia beside him. There was something deeply romantic about the idea of sitting side by side, wrapped up against the cool night air, watching the sky put on its magical display. It was intimate and meaningful. All he had to do now was figure out the details, send the invitation, find a tent and plan the night so everything would fall into place. Jack stood up, brushing off his jeans, and headed back down the coastal path with a newfound sense of purpose. Wednesday night couldn't come soon enough.

He shouted after Pete, 'You wouldn't by any chance have a tent I could borrow?'

'There's plenty of camping stuff in the shed. Help yourself to whatever you need.'

Chapter Eleven
AMELIA

The next morning, Amelia breezed downstairs and noticed a letter resting on the mat by the bookshop's front door. Pawsworth sauntered over, rubbing against her legs. 'What have we here?' she asked, scooping him up in her arms. She cradled him close as she examined the envelope ... handwritten, no stamp, and addressed to her. Intrigued, she set Pawsworth on the counter and ripped open the envelope. Inside was a beautiful handwritten invitation, its elegant script making her heart skip a beat. She read it aloud to Pawsworth.

Our first Temptation Bucket List adventure begins at Cockle Bay Cove, 7:30 p.m. Wednesday. Meet me there.

Jack x

A smile tugged at her lips as she brought the letter to her nose, inhaling deeply. A familiar woody scent clung to the paper, and instantly she recognised his aftershave, the fragrance that had filled the air when he'd leaned close to her, teasing her at the bookshop just a day ago. Her heart gave a small, delighted leap. What could he possibly be planning?

Still holding the invitation in her hands, Amelia felt a wave of excitement rush through her. She'd been thinking about him endlessly since their flirtatious exchanges, and now this. A first date. A bucket list of temptations. Whatever Jack had in store for her, it sounded thrilling, mysterious and, if she was being honest, just a little bit nerve-wracking. Without hesitation, she grabbed her phone and opened up her WhatsApp group, quickly typing out a message to the girls,

AMELIA

> Wednesday is the first date! He's invited me to Cockle Bay Cove. What do you think he has planned?

It didn't take long for the replies to roll in. Clemmie, always the cheeky one, was first.

CLEMMIE

> Whatever it is, make sure you're wearing matching underwear!

Amelia laughed out loud, shaking her head. Clemmie could always be counted on for advice that bordered on scandalous. She stared at the phone, her smile lingering as she felt another flutter of anticipation. Truthfully, she was nervous. It wasn't like her to jump into something so daring and spontaneous. She'd always been the sensible one, the one who planned everything to perfection, the one who made sure all the boxes were ticked before she took a risk. But with her thirtieth birthday looming on the horizon, she couldn't help but wonder where all that cautiousness had gotten her. Sure, she had her beloved bookshop, her close-knit circle of friends and Pawsworth, but something was missing. Adventure. Passion. A little bit of recklessness. And maybe, just maybe, Jack was exactly what she needed to throw caution to the wind. Amelia glanced back at the invitation, running her fingers over the elegant writing. Her phone buzzed again as Dilly chimed in.

DILLY
I agree with Clemmie!

Amelia grinned, picturing her friends, each of them eager to hear every detail of this mysterious date as soon as it was over.

She glanced at the clock, already counting down the hours until Wednesday night. Whatever happened at Cockle Bay Cove, Amelia knew one thing for certain: this was the start of something exciting and she couldn't wait to see where it led, but in the meantime, she had a bookshop to run.

There was a steady stream of customers all morning and just after eleven a.m. the door opened and in walked her solicitor, Edgar Carmichael.

'Edgar, how lovely to see you,' said Amelia with a smile. 'Have you not retired yet?' she teased, something she always said to him, knowing Edgar showed no signs of slowing down.

'Retirement? What would I do with my time?' He

smiled. 'How are you? I thought I'd look in on you ... especially because...'

'It's nearly my dad's birthday,' Amelia filled in the gaps. 'I can't believe we're no further on in getting the will sorted.' She sighed, looking across the counter at him with an expression of disbelief and frustration.

'I know,' Edgar replied with a sympathetic nod.

Amelia shook her head in exasperation. 'I just don't understand it, Edgar. How could my father have left the house to her? He always told me I didn't have to worry and everything was left to me. And here we are, over six months later, and she's still sitting on it all, as if I don't exist.'

'I see this a lot in my job,' Edgar said, his voice a bit unsteady. 'But even to this day, it still completely baffles me that your father handed over the family home to her. The will didn't make any sense, and it didn't sound like the Ethan I knew,' he said meaningfully.

Amelia leaned in. 'He married her within a few months of meeting her and now this. What did you think of Vivienne when she first appeared, Edgar? You've known my father for such a long time. When you saw them together ... what was your impression of her?'

Edgar hesitated, his fingers drumming on the wooden counter, as though considering how best to answer without reopening old wounds. 'When your father first introduced Vivienne to me, I thought. "Well, it's not very often you get a second chance at love." Your father had been alone for so long after your mother passed and I think everyone was hoping he'd find happiness again, and at first, Vivienne seemed to bring him that.'

'But…' Amelia prompted, sensing the unspoken truth behind Edgar's words.

'As the months went on, it became clear that they were like chalk and cheese. Your father was warm, traditional, he valued family, heritage, that sort of thing. Vivienne, well, she was … sharp. Ambitious. She'd this way of taking control of a room, but not in a way that made people feel at ease. I never really understood what kept them together or why he actually married her … and so soon. He was always so grounded, and she … well, she always had her eye on something else. Some bigger game.'

'That's what worries me. I can't help feeling that she was with him for the wrong reasons. The house, the estate … it was never meant for her. He'd promised me that much. And yet here I am, with nothing but memories and legal battles.'

His tone soft but firm. 'I know it's difficult, Amelia. I've seen many people fight over estates, and ultimately, it's never about the money, really. It's about legacy, about what we think we deserve, what we think we're owed. But your case is different.'

'And in Vivienne's case, she's just out for everything she can get. I saw that article in *The Sunday Times*, painting her in such a good light. She has everyone fooled; all she craves is fame and status.'

'I saw it too,' Edgar replied, his expression thoughtful. 'But hang on in there.'

Amelia bit her lip, feeling a knot of resentment forming in her chest. 'That woman ruined my relationship with my father. We were so close until…' Her voice faltered. 'And now my family home stands empty and she's changed the locks so I can't even get inside. It's like she's moved on from my father's death as if it were nothing more than a minor detour in her grand plan. Sometimes I just want to give up fighting and move on too. But I don't see how that would ever happen.'

'I know it seems like everything is dragging, but we can't let her win,' Edgar said quietly but with conviction. 'She might think she's in control now, but time has a way of balancing things out. Your father's estate, his legacy, will come to you. It might not be immediately, and it might not be easy to get to that point, but the truth always has a way of surfacing, and I'm confident you'll triumph in the end.'

Edgar's words planted a seed of hope in her heart.

'I suppose you're right. My father always believed in fairness. Maybe I just need to trust that things will work out, even if it's taking longer than I expected.'

Edgar smiled, a rare glint of optimism in his eyes. 'Exactly. You have every right to what's yours, and you've got the strength to see this through. Vivienne's power ... whatever it is ... is temporary. And you've got something she doesn't – integrity. In the end, that's what endures.'

Amelia returned his smile, feeling a small but significant shift in her perspective. The bitterness, though still present, was beginning to soften, a sense of resolution and an energy to fight she hadn't felt in months slowly returning.

'Thank you, Edgar,' she said, her voice lighter now. 'You've always known how to put things into perspective.'

'Anytime, Amelia,' he replied warmly. 'You're not alone in this.'

'As you're here, can I interest you in any of my books

today? We have one last copy of the Maris Wilde novel and more arriving this afternoon.'

Edgar chuckled as he picked up a copy and flicked through the pages. 'I think this may be a little too raunchy for me, but I hear she's doing very well.'

'Sometimes you have to step out of your comfort zone and read something a little different,' she teased. 'You never know, you may find you enjoy it.'

He smiled, shaking his head. 'I think a temptation bucket list would finish me off at my time of life. A cup of tea, a chocolate digestive and a glass of whisky before bed are all I need to be happy.' He chuckled before touching her arm affectionately and leaving the shop.

Cuddling Pawsworth, Amelia watched Edgar walk down Lighthouse Lane, then she took a duster and began dusting off the shelves. Her thoughts drifted back to the first time she'd been introduced to Vivienne. It was one of those memories she wished she could forget, but it lingered, stubbornly vivid, as if it had happened just yesterday.

The day had been idyllic, with the sun blazing in a cloudless sky, and she and Clemmie had spent it lazily at Blue Water Bay. They'd taken a bottle of prosecco and their favourite paperbacks, and enjoyed a peaceful day on the beach.

But that peaceful feeling had evaporated the moment Amelia returned home. As she stepped into the garden of Dune House she was surprised to see her father with company – especially as it was a woman. She could hear them talking as she approached, her father's laughter ringing out and filling the late afternoon air as he explained the origin of the cottage's name. 'It's called Dune House because it's nestled right into the sand dunes!' he'd said between chuckles, clearly charmed by his own storytelling. The woman sitting opposite him, her leg brushing against his, was taking in her surroundings. 'The view from here,' she'd said, 'is simply divine. Overlooking the water like that. This place must be worth an absolute fortune.'

Her father noticed Amelia and gestured her over with a huge beaming smile on his face. He introduced her to Vivienne, who wore a wide-brimmed hat, designer sunglasses and a flowing summer dress over a bikini. She was the picture of effortless elegance and they were sipping wine together, lounging in the garden like they had been doing it for years. Amelia's dad poured her a glass of wine and began telling the story of how he and Vivienne had met. He'd gone to London to a book fair, hoping to network, share his work and maybe, just maybe, find someone interested in his new project. Her father had always dreamed of becoming a published author, and even though he'd always been secretive about his projects, he was convinced that this latest venture would be his big break, if only he could secure the right representation.

And Vivienne was exactly that right representation, or at least that's what Ethan had thought. They'd met by chance in a bar after one of the book fair events, and he'd been stunned to learn that she was not only a literary agent but a *well-known* one at that. His hopes had soared. But Vivienne, ever pragmatic, had quickly dashed those hopes. 'I'm afraid it's just not marketable,' she'd told him, coolly, after a brief glance at the manuscript. 'There's nothing terribly unique about it and in this genre it's a tough sell unless it's extraordinary.'

And yet, despite her rejection of his book, their relationship had blossomed almost overnight. Vivienne, with her endless charm, had swept him off his feet, and soon she became a permanent fixture in his life. Amelia could hardly believe how fast it had happened. One day, it had just been her and her father at Dune House, their familiar routines, their shared space. The next, Vivienne was lounging by their pool, claiming the best sunbed for herself, and sipping her way through the vintage wines Amelia's father had painstakingly collected over the years.

It hadn't taken long for Amelia to see Vivienne for who she truly was. From the moment they met, Vivienne had looked at her with thinly veiled disdain. Amelia was just an inconvenient detail, an obstacle in the way of her new, comfortable life.

It had been shortly after Vivienne's arrival in their life that Amelia, hoping to make a good impression on her dad's new girlfriend, had dared to show her a manuscript she'd been working on. She'd been so eager, hoping it might spark a connection between them or at least open up some common ground. But Vivienne had only glanced at it, a barely concealed smirk on her face as she handed it back with a remark that still stung. 'It's cute,' Vivienne had said, 'but it reads like a bad GCSE project. I'd just stick to selling books in your bookshop if I was you.'

Amelia had stood there, dumbfounded, as Vivienne clicked her perfectly manicured nails against her wine glass, clearly pleased with herself. In that moment, Amelia had seen exactly what kind of woman Vivienne was, someone who thrived on power over others, who delighted in asserting her dominance. It was why Amelia knew Vivienne would stop at nothing to make sure she got what she wanted, and that apparently was Dune House.

'Good morning, Amelia!'

Amelia turned towards the door just in time to see Liam, the local delivery driver, struggling to juggle an armful of cardboard boxes. His face was flushed, and a grin tugged at the corner of his mouth as he attempted to maintain balance.

'Here, let me help,' she said, hurrying over to take the top box from him. She placed it carefully on the counter as Liam, now a little more relaxed, handed her the delivery notice to sign.

'Every time I see you, I get excited!' Amelia teased, signing her name.

Liam chuckled, leaning against the doorframe. 'I'm taking that as a win because I'm guessing it's for my good looks and charm, not the fact that I'm bringing you books, your favourite thing in the whole wide world!'

'You've guessed it,' Amelia replied with a grin, watching him roll his eyes dramatically. He tipped an imaginary hat before heading out.

She tore into the top box and revealed a pile of pristine, glossy books. 'Another shipment of Maris Wilde,' she muttered to herself, smiling. *The Temptation Bucket List* had been flying off the shelves faster than Amelia could keep up. Every woman who walked into the store seemed to want a copy, and Amelia couldn't blame them. Wilde's writing was addictive, full of wit, romance and just the right touch of scandal.

Amelia reached for the second box, and as she pried it open, her heart gave a little leap of excitement. Nestled inside was another batch of bestsellers, but with a new arrival. Right there – currently at number two on *The Sunday Times* Bestseller list – was *The Forgotten Portrait* by Ellis Ford. The buzz around his debut novel had been impossible to ignore. The cover was sleek and moody, with bold lettering and a hauntingly beautiful image of a faded portrait that caught the light just so, promising intrigue and mystery.

Sliding a copy behind the counter for herself, Amelia promised herself she'd read it as soon as she finished her current book. Just as she was about to start adding the books to the display shelves, the familiar sound of giggling caught her attention. A group of schoolgirls burst into the shop, their excitement bubbling over as they made a beeline for the counter.

'We're looking for *The Temptation Bucket List* by Maris Wilde!' one of the girls piped up, her eyes wide with anticipation.

'You're in luck! I've just had a delivery,' Amelia replied, pulling copies of the book from the new stack. The girls practically squealed with delight, each grabbing a book as if it were the last one on earth.

Within seconds, the book had sold out again. Amelia barely had time to ring up the purchases before the girls eagerly skipped out of the shop, clutching their copies to their chests. As the door swung shut behind them, she shook her head in disbelief. Maris Wilde's popularity was showing no sign of slowing down and she jotted a note to order more copies.

As she stood behind the counter, surveying the stacks of books still waiting to be shelved, she smiled to herself.

'Looks like you're going to get the chance to dominate the display,' she muttered, gathering up the Ellis Ford hardbacks. She stacked them carefully on the wooden table that served as the centrepiece for new releases, then reached for her phone. She quickly Googled his name, expecting to find the usual array of author photos, interviews and social media profiles, but to her surprise there wasn't much to be found beyond a brief author bio and links to buy his debut novel. Reading the bio, she discovered that his agent was none other than Vivienne Langford. Amelia wasn't surprised to see Vivienne's name attached to another high-profile project. After all, she always seemed to come up smelling of roses.

Chapter Twelve

JACK

Jack closed his laptop, the Word document filled with his observations from the last couple of days on Puffin Island. He'd spent long hours walking through the cobbled streets and chatting to the locals in the shops, café and pub. The brief that Miles had sold – of cliques, secrets and hidden animosities – couldn't be further from the warm welcoming feeling Jack had found everywhere on the island. Deep down, he suspected the article might never be written, unless he stumbled across something truly extraordinary. And even though he needed the money, a part of him secretly hoped nothing would surface.

Attempting to push the article to the back of his mind, he focused on the day ahead. As Pete had mentioned earlier in the week, due to a combination of strong solar winds and unusually clear weather conditions, the auroras might just be visible. The idea of witnessing such a rare spectacle while on a date with Amelia filled Jack with excitement. It would be the perfect backdrop for the romantic evening he'd planned.

This morning, he had been busy getting everything ready. He'd borrowed a tent from Pete, which was ready to be pitched at the spot Pete had recommended, and he had a bundle of soft, cosy blankets lent to him by Lena, who had also thrown in some cushions and pillows. Tucked away in the fridge in the B&B was a picnic for later, full of treats: scones, fresh fruit, cheese, crackers and salami along with a bottle of champagne.

In the late afternoon, Jack made his way to Cockle Bay Cove. It was just as breathtaking as Blue Water Bay on the other side of the island, though perhaps more secluded, the rolling dunes protecting it from the wind, and the empty pale golden sand stretching out before him. He could see why Pete had suggested this place.

As he walked along the shore, Jack's eyes wandered up to Dune House, sitting proudly at the top of the dunes. He stopped for a moment, taking in the sight of the cottage, its name perfectly suited to its surroundings. Pete had said the house was empty, which was a shame, as there was something mesmerising about it.

He found the perfect spot to pitch the tent, a little nook nestled between two dunes that offered just the right amount of privacy while still giving them a view of the stars and, hopefully, the Northern Lights. The sand beneath his feet was soft, and the sound of the waves gently lapping at the shore set the tone for the perfect evening ahead. He set to work, fastening the tent securely and spreading out the blankets, arranging the nightlights in a semicircle to create a cosy, intimate atmosphere. Everything was coming together

The Story Shop

perfectly. Just as Amelia had done on book-club night, he'd paired their first date from the bucket list with a book, which he laid on a cushion inside the tent. In a few hours Amelia would arrive. He couldn't wait to get to know her at a deeper level. With everything ready, he decided to go and explore Dune House, taking the path from the cove that led to the cobbled street in front of the house.

It was a stunning cottage, its weathered stone façade softened by creeping vines and a riot of wildflowers bursting with colour. The pale blue shutters framing the windows needed a fresh coat of paint, but it was a perfect blend of charm and rustic elegance, and, for a moment, Jack felt as if he'd stepped into a romcom.

As he rounded the corner, he discovered a swimming pool, which took him by surprise. Then he wandered further around the beautiful garden, which was a little unruly but still had beautiful blooms clustered in the overgrown borders. That's when he spotted an outbuilding, its weathered wooden door ajar.

Jack knew he was trespassing but curiosity soon had him pushing the door open. The place seemed like it had been used as an outdoor office; there was a desk and chair, and paintings of the cove on the walls. His attention was drawn to the top of a filing cabinet, where a half-empty bottle of whisky stood alongside a single glass. On the desk lay a notepad. It was charred at the edges, almost as though it had been deliberately set alight. He picked it up and flipped through its blackened pages, but the contents were unreadable so he placed it back down and opened the filing cabinet. It was empty apart from a chunky notebook stuck at the back of the drawer, its cover worn but still intact.

Thinking he heard something, he froze, his heart hammering as his ears strained for any further sounds of movement outside. A sudden jolt of panic gripped him and he hastily stuffed the notebook in his rucksack, hurried outside and made his way back past the swimming pool and down into the dunes where he'd set up camp. That's when he saw a man in a suit, standing near to the tent.

The man turned and his eyes widened in recognition.

'Jack, is that you? Jack Hartwell?' asked Edgar.

For a second Jack could only stare, shocked to have run into someone he knew, and then he grinned. 'Edgar Carmichael! Out of all the beaches in all the world…' He walked towards the older man with his hand outstretched and Edgar shook it.

'The last time I saw you, you were an unruly teenager! I've followed your career over the years though, thanks to my brother.'

'The best godfather any unruly teenager could wish for.'

'Yes, I heard he used to buy you beers from the shop when you were most probably underage.'

'I couldn't possibly comment on that!' Jack mimed locking his lips then laughed heartily.

'I've just had some business at the farm and I've got to get back to the office now. Do you want to walk with me?'

Knowing the tent was all zipped up and everything was safe for later, Jack happily agreed.

'So, what brings you here?' asked Edgar as they began to walk along the beach towards the main bay.

'A little holiday, a little work,' Jack replied. 'I've not seen you since…'

'It would have been your dad's sixtieth birthday. I was in London and was my brother's plus one.'

'That's right; would you believe that was over fifteen years ago now?' Both men shook their heads in disbelief.

'And how is your father?'

'All good, and still playing golf with Arthur most days. Wait until I tell him I've bumped into you, they won't believe me.'

'We need to have a proper catch-up before you leave. How's the writing going?' Edgar asked, his tone warm.

'Between you and me, it's the last book in the contract and for the first time ever I'm struggling with writer's block. I used to think it was a myth but…' He trailed off.

'Well, if I know anything about this island it's that it's a great place to relax and get back on track. Something about the sea air clears the mind.' They'd reached the bottom of Lighthouse Lane and Edgar gestured towards the cobbled road. 'My office is above the antiques shop, just up there on Anchor Way. Make sure you pop in and we can arrange dinner.'

'I'll do that,' Jack replied, watching Edgar walk away. He could hardly believe he'd just bumped into his godfather's brother.

Jack glanced up Lighthouse Lane and immediately spotted Clemmie, Dilly and Verity gathered at the door of the bookshop, their animated chatter carried faintly down the lane by the breeze. Each of them held carrier bags, and it didn't take much to guess they were there to help Amelia prepare for tonight. There she was, standing in the doorway, smiling warmly as she spoke to them. She caught his eye, and her expression shifted as she whispered something to the group. Almost instantly, the women turned to look in his direction, their faces lighting up with mischievous grins. Before he could fully process it, they ushered Amelia back into the shop, giggling and shooting him playful glances as they disappeared inside. Jack couldn't help but laugh out loud, a warm, buoyant feeling rising in his chest. If her excitement about tonight matched his, it was going to be an evening to remember.

Chapter Thirteen
AMELIA

Clemmie, Verity and Dilly burst into the bookshop with a flurry of laughter.

'As I was saying, haven't you all got jobs you need to be at?' Amelia teased, folding her arms and raising an eyebrow.

'Luckily for you we're all self-employed and it's officially closing time,' Clemmie declared with a triumphant smile.

Amelia's gaze drifted to the suspicious-looking carrier bags that they were all clutching. 'And what have you got in there?' she asked, narrowing her eyes in mock suspicion. The three friends exchanged conspiratorial looks before Verity reached for the door and flipped the sign to 'CLOSED'.

'You'll see,' she said mysteriously as they took hold of Amelia and steered her towards the back of the shop.

'We,' Clemmie began, her eyes sparkling with mischief, 'are here to prepare you for the date of the century. Mainly because, let's face it, you haven't had a date in ages.'

'That's right,' Verity chimed in as she placed the carrier bags on the table with a satisfying thud. 'Which is precisely why you need our help.'

'We've thought of everything,' Dilly added confidently, her grin wide enough to suggest they'd left no detail unconsidered.

Amelia fought back a laugh. 'And what exactly do you think I need?' she asked, her tone more amused than alarmed, though the glint in her eye hinted she was bracing herself for whatever antics they had in store.

'Oh, just the essentials,' Clemmie said with a cheeky grin, reaching into one of the bags and, with a flourish, pulling out a bottle of prosecco, like a magician revealing a rabbit. 'Such as Dutch courage!'

'We're also talking makeup,' Verity added, rifling through another bag. 'The good stuff. And…' She paused dramatically, holding up a set of lingerie that looked like it belonged in a high-end boutique. 'Sexy underwear.'

Amelia raised her eyebrows. 'Lingerie? Seriously?'

'Deadly serious,' Clemmie exclaimed. 'Haven't you been reading Maris Wilde's *The Temptation Bucket List*? The first item is something along the lines of "Unleash your inner goddess." Well, this'—she waggled the lingerie in front of Amelia's face—'is your first step.'

Amelia laughed, shaking her head. 'I'm fairly certain Jack isn't expecting anything even close to this tonight.'

'Exactly. He'll be expecting you to turn up in a fluffy jumper featuring puffins and mismatched underwear,' Dilly said, popping the cork on the prosecco. 'Which is why you need to surprise him. He's taking you to Cockle Bay Cove, right?'

'Yes,' Amelia said, nodding, 'but I have no idea what he has planned.'

'That's all the more reason to look fabulous,' Clemmie declared, pouring the prosecco into plastic cups and handing them around. 'Whatever he's got in store, you'll be ready.'

Amelia rolled her eyes as she accepted the cup. 'You three are ridiculous.'

'We're amazing,' Verity corrected her, plopping down on a plush chair. 'And you'll thank us when Jack's jaw hits the sand tonight.'

Clemmie turned Amelia towards a mirror that hung at the back of the shop. 'Now, sit down. Let the experts work their magic.'

Amelia sat sipping her prosecco while Verity pulled out a palette of makeup that looked like it belonged backstage at a fashion show.

'Close your eyes,' she ordered, standing over Amelia like a determined makeup artist. 'We need to make you look irresistible but natural. That *I woke up like this* vibe.'

'Pretty sure I actually woke up looking like I fought a hurricane,' Amelia muttered, but she did as she was told, closing her eyes.

'We'll fix that,' Verity promised, dabbing glittering shades onto Amelia's eyelids. 'Just trust us.'

Clemmie leaned against the table, a playful smile on her face. 'What do you think Jack's got planned for tonight? A romantic dinner on the beach? A sunset boat ride?'

Amelia shrugged, feeling her stomach flip at the possibilities. 'You know as much as I do.'

'Well, if he's mirrored Maris Wilde's book, you'll be having the best sex of your life on a yacht by midnight!'

'Clemmie!' Amelia laughed, though the image her friend's words conjured in her mind was hard to shake. 'I highly doubt it. He's probably just planned a nice walk along the beach.'

Verity gave a mock gasp, still focused on her makeup masterpiece. 'Girl, don't sell yourself short. He's clearly smitten. After all, he's only known you five minutes and he's gone to the effort of handwriting an invitation.'

'And if he hasn't got something magical planned,' Dilly said, wagging her finger, 'we'll have words.'

Amelia rolled her eyes again, though her heart did skip a beat. She had no idea what Jack was planning, and the mystery of it all was driving her nuts.

It was nearly two hours later, after lots of girly chat and an empty bottle of prosecco, when Verity stood back, admiring her handiwork with a proud nod. 'You look stunning. Like a woman who could get away with anything.'

Amelia opened her eyes, blinking at her reflection. Her normally simple, fresh-faced look had been elevated. Her eyes sparkled, her lips were glossed with just enough colour to catch the light, and her skin seemed to glow. 'Wow,' she breathed, barely recognising herself.

Holding up the scarlet lingerie set with a grin, Dilly said encouragingly, 'Now all you need is to slip into this and you'll be a knockout.'

Amelia snatched the bra and knickers from her and laughed. 'Okay, okay, I'll wear it. But I'm telling you, if Jack so much as raises an eyebrow at this, I'm blaming you all.'

'You won't regret it,' Clemmie said, clinking her cup against Amelia's. 'To a night full of surprises.'

With her makeup done and her stomach constantly flipping with excitable nerves, Amelia changed into the outfit they'd picked for her. It was a simple but elegant dress, with just a hint of mystery in the flowing fabric, a silk scarf, and a cropped cardigan. The lingerie, however, made her feel like she had a secret, even if it was buried under layers of modesty.

She took one last look in the mirror. 'I don't know if I'm ready for this.'

'You are,' Verity said firmly. 'More importantly, Jack better be ready for you!'

Amelia took a deep breath, her heart racing with a mix of excitement and anxiety. 'Okay. Let's do this.'

They walked her to the door. 'Go knock him dead! ... But not literally,' said Clemmie.

Dilly giggled. 'It feels like we're fifteen again, getting ready to go to the island hall for the Friday night disco. Remember, we want all the details tomorrow!'

As Amelia stepped into the cool evening air, she felt a surge of adrenalin. Whatever Jack had planned for Cockle Bay Cove, she knew one thing. She was ready. Ready for surprises, ready for adventure, and maybe, just maybe, ready for whatever temptation lay ahead.

Chapter Fourteen

JACK

Jack stood in front of the small wardrobe in his room, staring at the limited selection of clothes he'd brought with him to Puffin Island. He ran an unsteady hand through his hair. Why did picking an outfit for tonight's date with Amelia feel like such a monumental decision? He hadn't felt this nervous about a date in years. He didn't know quite what she was expecting, but he hoped she wasn't disappointed. He wasn't aiming for anything wild or extravagant like *The Temptation Bucket List*, it was more about creating a simple, old-fashioned romantic evening with her. Just the two of them, under the stars, with no pressure, no distractions, and hopefully a glimpse of the Northern Lights.

After much internal debate, he settled on a long-sleeved navy polo shirt and jeans. After a quick spray of deodorant, he grabbed the chilled bottle of champagne from the mini-fridge in his room, and collected his coat. He was just about to head down to the main fridge in the B&B's kitchen to collect the hamper when his laptop pinged. Jack paused and stared at the screen, his eyes landing on a name he'd often dreaded seeing ... Vivienne Langford. He clicked the email open. She was following up on her previous message, enquiring if he'd received it and, as expected, pressing for an update.

Quickly typing back, he kept it short.

Hi Vivienne,

Thank you for checking in on me and, once again, for considering me for this article. Puffin Island is absolutely charming, and I'm enjoying my time here. I'm actually meeting with Amelia tonight, and I'll be sure to send Miles an update soon.

Best,
Jack

Annoyed that she'd chased him instead of waiting for a response, Jack told himself he shouldn't feel the need to provide Vivienne with regular updates. Miles was his boss, and he preferred communicating directly with him rather than going through a third party.

He hit send and closed the laptop, thinking about his assignment. As far as Jack was concerned, there wasn't a single bad thing he could write about Puffin Island. The place had charm and a peaceful quality that made it hard to imagine anything untoward happening here. Beside his laptop sat the notebook he'd taken from Dune House, its worn cover slightly creased. Guilt at having taken something that wasn't his had prevented him from opening it yet, though curiosity about what was inside nagged at him constantly. He couldn't shake the feeling that eventually the temptation would win out.

Taking the picnic from the fridge, he set off to Cockle Bay Cove. The weather was ideal and he was keeping everything crossed that they would witness the Northern Lights. As he arrived at the cove, he breathed in the salty air and took a moment to enjoy the view. Pete had been right, this was the perfect spot. The gentle curve of the bay, the rolling dunes and the soft, powdery sand made it feel like their own private beach. To add a little more romance, he pulled out from his bag the battery-operated fairy lights that he'd bought on a whim earlier that day and began hanging them on stakes in a semicircle around the tent, adding a touch of magic. He unzipped the tent and fluffed up the cosy blankets and cushions he'd borrowed from Lena, making sure it all looked inviting. With the hamper safely tucked inside and the champagne chilling in a bucket of ice, everything was set. All that was missing now was Amelia.

Jack sat on the picnic bench outside the tent, glancing at the sea as he waited. The gentle sound of the waves lapping against the shore was soothing, but the real excitement hit when he saw her in the distance. Amelia was walking up the cove, her sandals swinging casually in her hand. Her light dress fluttered gently in the breeze, and with her hair tied up in a messy bun she looked utterly gorgeous.

Jack stood up, feeling warmth rush through him as their eyes met. She beamed at him, making his heart skip a beat.

'You look absolutely stunning,' Jack complimented her as she approached, then noticed her sideward glance towards Dune House. 'Don't worry, I have it on good authority that it's empty. No one's watching us,' he said, gesturing towards the house with a playful grin.

'All this looks amazing,' Amelia replied, her eyes scanning the set-up around them. 'It's such a perfect spot.'

'We have a picnic, champagne, and ... true to your style, Amelia ... I've paired our first date with a book,' Jack added, his tone teasing but warm.

'Ooh, I'm intrigued!' she said with an excited laugh, her eyes widening with curiosity.

Jack smiled. 'And not only that,' he continued, 'we're also in with a good chance of seeing the Northern Lights tonight.'

Amelia's eyes lit up. 'No way! That's on my bucket list.'

'And mine,' Jack admitted, smiling as he gestured for her to take a seat on the blanket. 'Now, sit down, and I'll get you a drink.' As Amelia settled in, Jack placed a couple of champagne flutes carefully on the picnic blanket and grabbed the bottle of champagne. With a twist and a soft pop, he released the cork, sending a faint spray of bubbles into the air.

'I feel like I'm being spoiled rotten,' Amelia said, watching him pour the champagne. 'I wasn't sure what you had planned, and I'll admit there was a teeny part of me that was a little bit worried.' She paused, her voice playful. 'I've finished reading *The Temptation Bucket List*, and it's a lot steamier than this romantic set-up.'

Jack grinned. 'Well, I'm most interested in getting to know you, talking and spending some quality time together,' he admitted. As he handed her a glass, he pressed a light kiss to her cheek. She blushed. He could feel the electricity sparking between them. 'But just to be clear,' he added. 'I do find you very attractive.'

'You do?'

'I think it may be down to your obsession with puffins.'

She swiped him playfully.

'Only joking. If I'm honest, I think you're beautiful, you intrigue me, and your love for literature is a real attraction. And I think there's a lot more to Amelia Brown that I'm still to discover.'

'Oh, there is,' she replied softly.

For a moment there was a comfortable silence between them as they looked out over the water and sipped their champagne. Then Jack reached inside the tent and handed her a book neatly wrapped in brown paper. 'For our first date.'

Eager to know what was inside, Amelia tore open the paper and saw the familiar cover of *Pride and Prejudice*. 'Of course!' She grinned, holding up the book. 'How did I know you'd pick this one?'

Jack leaned back on his hands, smiling at her reaction. 'What can I say? I thought it suited the occasion. You, me, a bit of stargazing... It has that Elizabeth and Darcy vibe, don't you think?' His eyes glinted with affection.

'So, are you comparing yourself to Mr Darcy?' she teased.

'Maybe, but I'd like to think I'm a little more charming than he was in the beginning.'

Amelia laughed, tucking a loose strand of hair behind her ear. 'Well, you haven't insulted my family yet, so you're off to a better start than Darcy.'

'True, but I don't know anything about your family yet.'

Amelia was quiet. 'It's actually just me left in the world. My family is the wonderful community of Puffin Island. If it wasn't for them...' Her voice faltered.

'Hey, I didn't mean to upset you,' he said softly.

'You didn't. It's just ... my dad passed away recently and it's his birthday coming up, the first without him being here, and I get emotional thinking about it. It's a good job I have the best friends that I do on this island. They've helped me so much... But let's not talk about that now, let's get back to the book.'

Jack's eyes locked on hers. 'I have to admit, there's something about the tension between Elizabeth and Darcy that's ... fun. The banter, the misunderstandings, the way they circle each other before finally seeing what's been there all along.'

Amelia tilted her head, enjoying the flirtatious tone in his voice. 'And do you think we have the same dynamic going on?'

'Possibly,' he replied.

'Good.' She leaned a little closer, her heart racing at the way he was looking at her. 'So, if you're Mr Darcy, the brooding but secretly sweet gentleman who just needs someone to show him the way, I suppose that makes me Elizabeth?'

'Absolutely,' Jack replied without missing a beat. 'Strong, humorous, beautiful ... and, at a guess, I would say you don't put up with any nonsense.'

'I definitely don't – and, to add to your list of qualities, I would usually class myself as a fair person and honest.'

'I think honesty is a wonderful trait to have. By the way, I'm not that brooding.'

Amelia raised an eyebrow. 'Not even a little?'

'Maybe just a touch,' he admitted, holding up two fingers to show a small gap between them.

They both laughed.

'I love *Pride and Prejudice* because they both grow,' said Amelia. 'Elizabeth and Darcy … neither of them are perfect by the end, but they make each other better.'

Jack nodded. 'Yeah, I've always thought that's what makes it so timeless. They see each other for who they really are, flaws and all.'

Amelia glanced down at the book in her hands. 'I guess we all hope to find that … someone who sees us, even the not-so-perfect parts, and still wants to stick around.'

Jack's voice was lower now, more sincere. 'I think it's more than just sticking around. It's about wanting to grow together, to challenge each other, like they did.'

Amelia looked up at him, her heart skipping a beat at the intensity of his gaze. 'You really have thought this through, haven't you?'

Jack smiled, his voice warm and teasing again. 'What can I say? I wanted tonight to be perfect. I'm a romantic at heart.'

Amelia laughed softly, feeling a little blush rise to her cheeks. 'I wouldn't have guessed.'

'Let's eat.' Jack opened the lid of the picnic basket.

As the sun began to set, he took a sideward glance at Amelia, acknowledging to himself that this was the first time in ages that he was right where he wanted to be. All his troubles lifted from his mind when he was with Amelia, the world around them fading away.

They spent the next hour enjoying the food, sipping

champagne and looking out to sea. The warmth of the sun was beginning to ebb away and Jack draped a blanket around Amelia's shoulders. 'Here, have this.'

He looked at her, grateful for how easily their conversation flowed, and for a moment he nearly lost himself completely and started talking about his job and his career. He managed to stop himself just in time, but found himself questioning why he wasn't revealing his identity to her. Probably because it was nice to connect to someone that actually liked him for him, and wasn't only interested in his career. It was refreshing.

With the temperature dropping, Jack suggested they build a fire to keep warm. Despite having written about starting fires countless times, he'd never actually done it himself, but he figured it couldn't be that difficult.

They set to work, gathering large pebbles to form a makeshift circle around their DIY firepit, then headed up the sand dunes to collect sticks and kindling before attempting to light the fire. After a few tries Jack managed to get the flames to catch, and though crackling warmth took some time to achieve, the wait was worth it. With blankets wrapped snugly around them, they cuddled at the entrance of the tent, watching the flames dance. He pulled her in closer. 'And I have something else.' He reached towards the rucksack at the back of the tent and pulled out a telescope.

'You really have thought of everything.'

'Pete gave me this.'

'You've met Pete?'

'I have, he was the one who told me about this spot.'

'Did you say who you were preparing all this for?'

Jack shook his head. 'No, I just told him it was for someone special.'

'Say that again,' she teased.

It wasn't long before the sky began to twinkle with the first stars, and the gentle sound of the waves rolling onto the shore filled the air, a peaceful backdrop to the night's quiet magic. Jack adjusted the telescope and aimed it towards the brightest star in the sky. 'As a kid I was always fascinated by stars. Now that I'm older I still think there's something humbling about looking up and realising how small we are in the grand scheme of things.'

'The stars just keep on going, always there, always twinkling.'

'There's an app that allows you to point your phone at the sky and it'll tell you what the planets are.'

'No way! Really?'

Jack nodded and took out his phone, pointing it skyward. 'That one there is Jupiter.'

Amelia leaned forward and peered through the telescope. 'Wow!' she whispered, her breath catching. 'I can see Jupiter! It's so clear.' She moved aside, offering Jack a turn. 'Take a look.'

Jack peered through the lens. The planet was small but unmistakable, its distant light somehow bringing them closer to the cosmos. 'Amazing,' he murmured, straightening and looking at Amelia. 'It's funny how we spend so much time using technology when we have all this for free. I think we should look up more often.'

'Looking up makes everything feel possible, doesn't it? Like, if we can dream big enough, maybe we'll touch the stars one day.'

Jack smiled at her words, watching as she wrapped the blanket a little tighter around herself and stared at the constellations above. 'You know,' he said after a pause, 'my dad used to point out the constellations when I was a kid. He always made up his own stories about them ... said it made the stars feel more like old friends than something out of reach.' He chuckled. 'He'd tell me Orion wasn't just a hunter, but someone who'd gotten lost and was trying to find his way back home. I think that's why I always liked him best ... because he planted the idea that even the stars can get lost sometimes.'

'I love that,' she said softly. 'I love that your dad gave you that kind of imagination. And I love the idea that even when we feel lost, we're still always part of something bigger.'

For a moment, neither of them spoke. The stars were growing brighter as the sky darkened. Jack glanced at Amelia, her face lit up by the glow of the fire.

'I think sometimes we just need to let ourselves be a little lost. You know, let go of trying to figure everything out and just ... enjoy where we are.'

Amelia turned to look at him, her eyes locking with his. There was something unspoken in the air between them, an understanding, a connection that felt as old as the stars themselves. 'Maybe being lost isn't so bad.'

'Not if you're with the right person.' Jack's heart raced.

The fire had now started to dim, but still Jack could feel a palpable heat between them. Slowly they leaned into each other. 'You know,' he whispered, 'I think this is the best view I've ever had.'

Amelia smiled, her gaze flickering towards his lips. 'I

think I have to agree.' She closed the last few inches between them, placing her lips on his.

'I've been wanting to do that since the moment we met,' Jack admitted when they finally pulled apart, his voice low and warm.

Amelia's smile widened. 'Me too.'

The warmth of their first kiss lingered and they just sat there, Amelia snuggled into his chest.

Jack lightly kissed the top of her head before his eyes flicked upwards. He leaned back slightly, his breath catching in his throat. 'Amelia … look!' he exclaimed as an ethereal dance of light began to ripple across the sky. 'It's the Northern Lights!'

'But … it's shades of grey and white. I thought they were going to be colourful,' she said, her voice tinged with disappointment.

'You can't always see the colours with the naked eye, but you can usually see them through the camera lens.' Jack opened up the camera on his phone and snapped a few shots.

There they were, the Northern Lights, shimmering and dancing in glorious colour.

'Wow!' Amelia breathed, completely mesmerised. Her hand instinctively reached for Jack's, and he squeezed it gently, their fingers interlocking as they watched the spectacle above. The sky seemed alive, filled with colour and movement as the aurora borealis painted the horizon with streaks of luminous green, violet and hints of pink and blue.

'I can't believe it, it's even more beautiful than I could have imagined.'

Jack smiled, his eyes never leaving the sky. 'I know,' he replied. 'I wasn't sure if we'd get lucky enough to see it tonight ... but this? This is incredible.'

For a while, neither of them said anything else. They simply watched, entranced by the beauty of the lights above. The air felt electric, charged with both the energy of the Northern Lights and the connection between them.

'The perfect end to a perfect evening,' murmured Jack, his voice soft as he gazed at the sky.

Amelia smiled, her eyes reflecting the light of the fading fire. 'I'm not sure I want it to end.'

'Me neither,' Jack replied, his eyes locked on hers once more, the quiet intensity of the moment pulling them closer until their lips met once more in another gentle kiss.

As the kiss deepened, they backed into the tent and, with a quiet zip, closed the flap behind them, cocooning them in their own little world.

Chapter Fifteen
AMELIA

Early next morning, Amelia hurried up Lighthouse Lane, hoping to remain unseen. The night had been nothing short of magical; she'd fallen asleep under the stars, wrapped in Jack's arms. It was the kind of first date she would remember for ever, dreamlike from start to finish. Barely having slept, Amelia knew she was going to have to fight to stay awake through the day, but every second had been worth it.

The reality of sneaking back to her shop at the crack of dawn hit her then and she couldn't stop grinning, feeling like a teenager.

Just as she was about to reach the shop, she heard a voice she recognised immediately.

'Well, well, well ... if it isn't Amelia Brown doing the walk of shame!'

Amelia spun round to see Clemmie and Dilly standing by the entrance to the café, both grinning from ear to ear, clearly enjoying her moment of awkwardness.

'It's not what it looks like,' Amelia protested.

'Sure it isn't! Do you know how unconvincing you sound? Even a stranger would know you were lying, and as your best friends we can read you like a book,' Clemmie teased.

'Walking back to the shop at sunrise, hair a little messy, looks like you've not slept a wink ... all so totally innocent.' Dilly giggled. 'Please tell us you spent the night with Jack.'

Her friends stared at her intently, as though willing her to confess.

'Okay... I spent the night with Jack!'

Clemmie and Dilly squealed and grabbed hold of her.

'I can't get away with anything around here, can I?'

'Nope! Get the kettle on, we want to hear every detail,' said Dilly, linking her arm through Amelia's.

The three of them stepped inside the bookshop and Amelia flicked on the lights. Clemmie and Dilly plonked themselves in the armchairs in the shop whilst Amelia scooped up Pawsworth from the counter and took him into the kitchen with her.

As soon as the tea was made, Amelia joined them and placed the tray of mugs on the table.

Clemmie's eyes were wide with anticipation. 'So,' she began, 'let's get this straight ... you spent the night with Jack under the stars? Amelia Brown doesn't do stuff like that!'

'I know! That's what makes it so perfect,' Amelia replied with a dreamy smile as she handed out the drinks. 'It was spontaneous, and well, a bit unlike me, I guess. But it was perfect.'

Dilly leaned closer. 'What happened? Don't leave out a single detail!'

'Well, we had this amazing picnic on the beach – he'd set up a tent filled with cosy cushions and blankets – and we talked about everything: books, life, you name it. And the stars, oh my goodness, the stars were incredible. Then, the Northern Lights appeared, and … well, one thing led to another, and we kissed.'

'Under the Northern Lights?' Clemmie gasped. 'That's like something out of a novel! You can't make this stuff up!'

Dilly shook her head, grinning. 'It's almost too perfect.'

'Honestly, it was the best date – the best *night* – I've ever had. It felt … easy. Like we've known each other for years.'

Clemmie took a sip of her tea. 'Who exactly is this Jack? I mean, we all know he's charming and good-looking, but where did he come from? What's his story?'

Amelia paused, suddenly unsure of how much she should share. Jack still hadn't mentioned anything to her about being the famous author Jack Hartwell; he seemed to be keeping that side of himself very much under wraps. And as much as she wanted to confide in her friends, something told her it wasn't her place to reveal his identity just yet. She shrugged. 'He's a lifestyle guru or something like that, from London. Here on holiday.'

Clemmie raised an eyebrow. 'He doesn't exactly strike me as the typical London lifestyle guru type.'

'You always said you would never have a holiday fling with a tourist,' said Dilly. 'Are you sure you aren't setting yourself up for disappointment, given he'll have to head home eventually?'

'It's just a bit of fun,' said Amelia, trying to sound

breezy. She didn't actually want to think about Jack going back to where he'd come from just yet. 'And I can't wait to see what happens next. In the book, Zara Quinn gets a large bouquet of flowers at eleven a.m. the day after the first date with a note about the next one!'

Both Clemmie and Dilly looked as excited as Amelia felt. 'We want to know as soon as you know,' declared Clemmie.

'I promise you will.'

'I don't suppose you've looked at social media this morning, have you?' asked Clemmie, suddenly looking concerned.

Amelia shook her head.

'We should warn you then as it's all over TikTok. Apparently, Ellis Ford's new book has been picked up for a movie adaptation, which means Vivienne will be raking it in even more than she already was.' Dilly flicked on her phone and passed it to Amelia.

'Don't even get me started on Vivienne,' Amelia muttered, her mood shifting. 'That woman... I'm still fighting her for my inheritance, and she doesn't even care that she's creating all this emotional stress in my life. The relationship with my father was so strained at the end, and all because of her.' Her voice faltered and tears immediately welled up in her eyes.

'Don't go getting yourself upset over her. That woman will get her comeuppance. I believe in karma,' reassured Clemmie.

Dilly nodded. 'There will come a time when the tide turns for Vivienne, and we'll all be sat watching with popcorn,' she said.

'She was a very controlling woman, a born manipulator.

It was like she'd hypnotised my father in some way. Despite the distance between me and Dad at the end, my gut is still telling me there was no way on this earth he would leave Dune House to her. It's infuriating is what it is.'

They all sat finishing their drinks. 'Try not to think about her. I'm sorry I mentioned it now,' said Clemmie. 'Let's get back to Jack. At least he'll keep you distracted while he's here. He seems like a good guy.'

'I think he is,' confirmed Amelia, her smile returning.

'You're actually glowing, but we need to go. We have businesses to open and you need a shower!' Clemmie leaned forward, theatrically sniffing the air in Amelia's direction. 'You stink of ... well, you know.'

Amelia's face flushed. 'No, I don't!'

'The lady doth protest too much!'

'I'll share with you only that he was the perfect gentleman, and we just lay in each other's arms all night. It felt…' She hesitated, searching for the right words.

'So perfect,' Clemmie finished for her, placing a hand on her heart.

'Just like a fairytale romance,' added Dilly. 'Now, make sure you text us at eleven a.m. when the flowers arrive!'

Amelia smiled as her friends left the bookshop, locking the door behind them. She made her way up to the flat, her mind still replaying the events of the night before. The memory of lying next to Jack under the stars filled her thoughts, a warmth spreading through her chest. But then the smile faded slightly. The mention of Vivienne had made Amelia wonder again about Jack's past. Why had he parted ways with her as his agent? And did he know her on a personal level or just professionally?

She couldn't ask him directly, not yet. If she did, it would mean revealing that she knew far more about him than she'd let on. Amelia felt a pang of frustration. She wanted to know, wanted to understand what had caused that rift, but she knew it was something Jack had to share when he was ready to trust her.

Chapter Sixteen

JACK

Jack returned to the B&B with a wide grin, his mind entirely occupied with thoughts of Amelia. Everything about last night had been perfect. The star-filled sky, the warmth of the fire, the easy conversations and, of course, their kiss under the Northern Lights. It had been like something out of a dream. When Jack had first arrived on Puffin Island, the last thing on his mind was starting a relationship. He was seeking peace, quiet and material for his article, whilst hoping the act of writing – something, anything – would help him to get his mojo back. But now, after being on the island for a few days and getting to know Amelia, everything seemed different.

The thought of leaving the island weighed on his mind. He tossed his bag aside and flopped onto the bed, the exhaustion from the sleepless night catching up with him, but every moment had been worth it. Jack pulled out his phone, scrolling through the photos he'd taken. A smiled tugged at his lips as he looked at the images of them roasting marshmallows over the fire, the Northern Lights shimmering above them, and that spontaneous moment when they'd kicked off their shoes to paddle in the cool ocean under the stars. Each photo captured a perfect memory.

Just before his phone battery died, he plugged it into the charger, thinking he'd take advantage of the few moments he had to relax. But his phone buzzed almost immediately, an email from Miles coming through requesting a call in an hour's time. Jack sighed.

He had time to grab a quick shower so he padded into the tiny bathroom and switched on the water. As it cascaded over his head and he massaged shampoo into his hair, his thoughts drifted. The looming tax bill and his unwritten book nagged at him, yet he was finding the diary so easy to write. Writing about the island came naturally, the words flowing with ease. He couldn't help marvelling at the sense of community here. Pete had immediately offered him the tent and telescope, and Lena had assembled a thoughtful picnic hamper and provided blankets and cushions for the night without hesitation. He was taken aback by how everyone seemed to care for one another.

He thought about his place in London, where he didn't have a huge circle of close friends, his university friends having scattered in different directions. He didn't even know his neighbours in London, and there was no one nearby whom he could pop in on for a chat and a brew ... which led him to ask himself: why was he still living there?

Jack finished his shower, wrapped a towel around his waist, made a cup of tea and headed back to his phone. He opened his laptop and began scrolling through the entertainment news. The first article that popped up was about Ellis Ford. Jack's eyes narrowed as he read the bold headline:

Reclusive New Author Ellis Ford Signs Major Movie Deal for Debut Novel.

There was Vivienne's name, front and centre in the article. Jack scoffed. Vivienne had never been one to shy away from self-promotion and in the interview she gushed about Ellis Ford, emphasising how this brilliant new talent had been her personal discovery. Jack shook his head. No doubt Ford, like him, was locked into a contract where Vivienne would be making a substantial cut, leaving the actual writer with peanuts. It was how she operated, and Jack had seen it happen enough times to know the score.

His phone buzzed again, and he glanced at the time. Miles was early. He quickly finished his tea and got dressed, mentally preparing himself for what was sure to be a frustrating conversation. Miles was likely looking for updates, and so far all Jack had discovered on the island were good things. There was nothing scandalous, no hidden stories, just a close-knit community that were there for each other. Last night had been pure and simple with Amelia, and so easy, and he didn't want to spoil that by getting tangled in the mess of writing an article that he didn't even agree with. Perhaps it was time to tell Miles that he was out?

Sitting on his desk next to his laptop was the receipt for the bouquet of flowers. Just like in the novel, when Asher Knight sends Zara Quinn a bouquet of roses to announce their next date, Jack had arranged for a delivery of two dozen roses to be sent to Amelia at eleven a.m. Their second date would be a hot air balloon ride. It was a bold move, but after last night, Jack felt confident Amelia would say yes.

His phone rang, and he briefly closed his eyes, preparing himself before answering. He already felt disloyal to Amelia by taking the call and discussing the assignment. 'Miles,' he said, his tone as neutral as he could manage.

'Jack, darling!' came Vivienne's overly cheerful voice.

Jack sat up straighter, his brow furrowing as the voice on the other end of the phone greeted him with an almost saccharine cheerfulness.

'Vivienne?' he asked, unable to hide his surprise. 'I was expecting a call from Miles. Don't tell me you've given up being an agent and are now taking over the world of newspapers?'

Vivienne's laughter tinkled through the receiver. 'Don't be daft, Jack. Miles is my nephew, and he's still finding his feet. I'm on annual leave, so I thought I'd help him out with a few things while he settles in.'

Jack barely registered her words as he pulled up his browser and typed in Miles's name. Seconds later, his screen filled with an image of Miles standing beside Vivienne, both of them smiling broadly outside the offices of *The Morning Ledger*. A bold headline beneath the photograph announced, **Another Family Member Joins the World of Words.**

A pang of unease settled in Jack's chest and he shifted uncomfortably, a fresh wave of guilt washing over him. Discussing the assignment already felt like a betrayal of

Amelia, and now he was speaking to Vivienne directly, the person he'd been trying to distance himself from professionally.

'MilesVivienne,' he muttered, jumbling their names together in a moment of flustered irritation.

'I hope I'm not interrupting anything,' Vivienne chirped, seemingly oblivious to his slip.

Jack tightened his grip on the phone. 'Not at all,' he replied, though his thoughts were anything but calm. 'Just wrapping up a few things,' he replied, standing up and pacing the room. 'What can I do for you?'

'I thought I'd check in and see how your little island adventure is going,' Vivienne said, her voice oozing faux warmth. 'Have you found anything of interest? We could really use some juicy content for the feature.'

Jack kept his voice steady. 'Nothing out of the ordinary at all. The island's community is tight-knit, and everyone works together. It's the kind of place where people look out for each other and treat one another like family.'

Vivienne's laugh on the other end was quick and dismissive. 'Come on, Jack. There's got to be something. No one is that perfect. Dig a little deeper. There's always a story.'

Jack bit back his irritation. 'I'm sorry, Vivienne, but it's exactly what it seems … a peaceful, charming island where people live simple lives and take care of each other. In fact, it seems a wonderful place to live.'

There was a pause on Vivienne's end, and Jack could almost picture her sitting at her polished desk, drumming her perfectly manicured nails as she prepared her next verbal jab.

'The bottom line, Jack, is that if you want to get paid, you'll need to produce something worthwhile. Your dwindling book sales aren't exactly going to cover the bills, are they?' Her voice was sharp, laced with that familiar mix of condescension and faux concern. 'Miles will have plenty more articles for you, quick cash opportunities, but they'll only keep coming if you deliver. So, I trust you'll find something newsworthy to report.'

Jack's jaw tightened as he stared at the phone. Her words hung in the air, a stinging reminder of how tangled his professional life had become and how precarious his situation felt.

'Why is Miles pressing for the article to be written from this viewpoint, when the newspaper could instead highlight how wonderful Puffin Island is and help to boost tourism?' He waited for her response, half-expecting her to dismiss him with a condescending laugh or a curt remark. Instead, he heard a sharply indrawn breath, and there was a pause that stretched a little too long. Jack could almost hear her mind working, formulating the next move in their verbal chess match.

When she finally spoke, her tone was smooth, almost rehearsed, as if sidestepping his question entirely. 'Every article always highlights the good, Jack. Sometimes, the truth has to be told, even if it's not what people want to hear.'

He frowned, sensing she was deflecting, and he was about to push back when her voice brightened suddenly, taking a sharp turn into a completely different topic. 'By the way, have you seen the news about Ellis Ford? Isn't it fantastic? His book is going to be made into a movie, and the buzz is incredible. I really struck gold with that one.'

Jack knew that was a direct dig at him, another reminder of how Vivienne operated. Her point was that he was no Ellis Ford. 'Fantastic,' he said flatly, masking his irritation. His mind, however, was already spinning, caught between her evasiveness about the article and the unwelcome reminder of Ellis's skyrocketing success. 'I read the article. Impressive how quickly it all came together.'

'Isn't it? Ellis is a bit of a recluse, doesn't like the spotlight, but that's where I come in. I'll make sure his work gets the recognition it deserves. He has trust in his agent.' Another dig at Jack. He swallowed and remained silent, knowing now for certain that he'd made a mistake accepting this assignment. He didn't want anything to do with this article, with Miles or Vivienne. The entire situation felt like a trap, designed to exploit him while tying his name to a narrative he didn't believe in. All he needed was a way out, a way to pull in extra cash quickly without compromising himself or betraying the island that had started to feel like home. But he wasn't about to tell either Vivienne or Miles that just yet, because he knew if Miles was that hellbent on getting the article written he would just employ a different journalist, someone eager to climb the career ladder who wouldn't hesitate to churn out the kind of piece they wanted. No, he couldn't let that happen. Instead, he was going to play along. He would let them think the article was on track, let the deadline come and go to buy himself some time, time to find another job, a more ethical way to earn a living, and, most importantly, to shield Puffin Island from the newspaper's cutthroat agenda.

'Just remember, Jack,' she continued, her tone sharpening, 'I put your name forward for this because of your talent, your ability to dig deeper than most. Don't make me regret it, or, worse, make me look like a fool for trusting you to deliver.'

Jack hung up and let out a long breath. Talking to Vivienne always left him feeling drained. She was a force to be reckoned with, and he really didn't want to be part of her world anymore.

Needing a distraction, he remembered the notebook he'd taken from Dune House. He knew he had no business taking it and should return it, but curiosity now got the best of him. As he opened the worn cover, he initially assumed it was a diary. But after reading the first page, it became clear, it was a manuscript … a novel. The writing was in ink, neat and deliberate, each word flowing with confidence. Jack settled onto the bed, drawn in straightaway by the captivating narrative. The prose was surprisingly strong, filled with vivid descriptions and authentic dialogue, and possessing an unexpected emotional depth. He turned page after page, finding himself completely absorbed, as the story unfolded with a quiet intensity. It was as though the writer had poured their heart and soul into these pages. *Who did this notebook belong to?*

Chapter Seventeen
AMELIA

Amelia stood behind the counter of The Story Shop, absentmindedly rearranging a stack of books for what felt like the hundredth time that morning. Pawsworth was sprawled lazily on the windowsill, flicking his tail and watching the world go by through half-lidded eyes. Every so often, he'd give her a sleepy blink as if to say, 'All you need is a little patience.'

But Amelia had no time for feline wisdom today. She was watching the clock, counting down the minutes, secretly hoping for a grand romantic gesture just like in Maris Wilde's book. Maybe it was a little unrealistic, expecting Jack to do the same as Asher had, but here she was checking the time and waiting for something … anything.

It was now 11.03 a.m., and not a single petal had floated through the door.

'I'm being ridiculous, aren't I?' Amelia muttered to herself, adjusting her cardigan for the umpteenth time.

Pawsworth gave a slow, indifferent blink, clearly offering no opinion on the matter. He stretched his paws luxuriously before curling back into a ball.

11.04 a.m.

Amelia sighed, trying to focus on anything but the clock. She started to pull a few new titles from a delivery box, humming to herself. *Nothing to get worked up about,* she told herself. *You're a grown woman running a business, not a character in a romantic novel.* But despite her attempts at self-reassurance, her eyes kept darting back to the clock and then the door.

11.05 a.m.

Still nothing.

Amelia's heart sank a little. She shook her head at her own silliness and decided that it was time to let go of these unrealistic expectations. Flowers or not, Jack was different from any man she'd ever dated, and that was enough.

Just as she was about to settle back into her work, the shop door burst open with a wild jangle of the bell, and in rushed Rosa Bloomfield, the local florist. She looked a bit frazzled, her apron askew, her hair sticking out from under a floral-patterned headscarf, and she was clutching ... Amelia's eyes widened ... an enormous bouquet of red roses.

'Amelia!' Rosa practically panted, rushing towards the counter as though she'd just sprinted a marathon. 'I made it! Sorry I'm a few minutes late! Don't ever let anyone tell you I'm not dependable!'

Amelia blinked in surprise, her heart doing a little flip as she stared at the flowers in Rosa's arms.

Rosa thrust the bouquet towards her, all roses and greenery, the scent instantly filling the shop. 'Here! Twenty-four long-stemmed red roses, fresh from the farm this morning. Oh, and you wouldn't *believe* the chaos! You're lucky I got here in one piece. The sheep got out ... again ... and blocked the road! Had to wait for old George to herd them back, the stubborn little things. I was practically pleading with them, "Please, Daisy, move your woolly butt!"'

Amelia stifled a giggle as she inhaled the fragrance of the roses, still slightly dazed by the sight of them.

'Those sheep!' Rosa said, with a dramatic roll of her eyes. 'George thinks he's got them under control, but between you and me, it was a right sheep show. I was under *strict* instructions not to be late with these, though, so I hightailed it here as soon as the road was clear.' She grinned, looking immensely pleased with herself. 'Only a few minutes late,' she said, checking her watch.

Amelia looked at the bouquet in her arms, her heart racing. It was exactly how it had happened in *The Temptation Bucket List* ... but where was the note?

'Oh!' Rosa continued, reaching into her apron pocket and pulling out a small cream-coloured envelope. 'There's this, too. Nearly forgot with all the sheep drama.'

Amelia carefully laid the bouquet on the counter and opened the envelope, her fingers trembling slightly. Inside, on thick cardstock, was a handwritten note:

Amelia,

I hope these brighten your day. Please accept my

invitation for a second date, Sunday 6 a.m. Meet me on the cliff top just outside Cliff Top Cottage.

Jack x

Amelia bit her lip, trying not to grin like an absolute fool.

'Someone appears to be very keen on you. Twenty-four roses, Amelia! He's not messing around.'

Amelia's mind was already swirling with thoughts of what he'd planned. The invitation didn't give anything away, but after their magical first date, she was already excited.

'I'll leave you to it,' Rosa continued. 'Enjoy the flowers and the man!'

Amelia laughed as Rosa hurried out of the shop, the door jingling behind her. She glanced down at the roses, still in awe of the gesture, and took a quick photo of them to send to the WhatsApp group.

AMELIA
The next date is Sunday on the cliff top

Almost instantly everyone replied, gushing over the flowers.

Amelia spent the rest of the day in the shop with an extra spring in her step. Every time she glanced at the roses, a smile crept onto her face. This was turning out to be one of those days where life felt like a story, one she was eager to keep reading.

Chapter Eighteen
JACK

Jack didn't stir from his bed until early afternoon, he was so engrossed in the story he'd found in the notebook. It wasn't just any story, it was a masterpiece, a vivid tale that was unravelling in a mesmerising way. He felt as though he was living through every emotion, every twist and every revelation alongside its characters. He couldn't believe that something so remarkable had been left to gather dust in an old shed. He didn't know if this story had ever been published, or if it was a lost manuscript and if that was the case, he considered what a gem it would be for any publisher.

Placing the notebook back on the desk, he stared at the clock on the wall. The afternoon sunlight spilled through the curtains, reminding him that he hadn't left the room in hours, and he began to think about Dune House. Why was the notebook just abandoned in the old filing cabinet in the shed? Curious to discover more, he grabbed his phone and headed back to Cockle Bay Cove.

Once he reached the house, Jack checked up and down the beach before he slipped into the back garden and stood by the pool. He knew very well that he was trespassing, but he couldn't help himself; he felt there was a story about this place and he wanted to know what it was. He headed back towards the old shed where he'd found the notebook, and the door creaked open just as it had before, revealing the dim space inside. There was nothing else to see there, though, and so he began walking around the outskirts of the house. It was larger than it had first appeared. It was obvious that at one time it had been a family home. The garden showed signs of great care, though it was now overgrown, a few stray flowers pushing through the tangle of weeds, a rusted bench half-hidden beneath an old oak tree with a rope swing attached. As Jack walked around the side of the house, he noticed a window slightly ajar. He paused, drew closer and looked in. There was no sign of anyone. He hesitated and then, with a quick glance around to make sure there was no one watching, climbed through the window.

The interior of the house was as quiet as a graveyard. The only thing moving was the dust that floated in the beams of sunlight slanting through the windows. Yet, despite the stillness, the house didn't feel entirely empty. There was warmth to it, a lived-in feeling. Jack wandered through the large rooms, taking in the details. The furnishings were simple but elegant, with lace curtains hanging by the windows and bookshelves lined with leather-bound volumes. It felt cosy, like a place that had been loved. Yet, strangely, there were no photographs or

The Story Shop

personal touches, nothing that indicated who had lived here.

As Jack moved from room to room, his footsteps barely making a sound on the creaky floorboards, he came across a door that was locked. Unlike the others, this door had a small brass plaque, reading 'STUDY'. Jack tried the doorknob, but it didn't budge. Then, as he stood in the hallway, his fingers still wrapped around the cool brass, he heard someone at the front door. Panicking, with his heart beating fast, he hurried back to the window he'd entered by. Within seconds he was outside and heading down the path towards the cobbled street. He gave a sigh of relief when he caught sight of the familiar red van parked further up the road. It was just the postman. Feeling calmer, he turned back towards the B&B to gather the tent and telescope he'd borrowed from Pete and return them as promised.

Ten minutes later, he arrived at Pete's cottage, finding the man sitting in his garden, nursing a tumbler of whisky in the afternoon sun. Jack handed over the borrowed items with a grin.

'Afternoon, Pete. One tent and telescope returned. Thank you.'

Pete's eyes twinkled. 'Good to know you didn't ruin my tent with any wild escapades.'

Jack laughed, taking a seat beside him. 'Nothing too wild, I promise. Just a bit of old-fashioned romance. This girl is definitely different.'

Pete disappeared into the cottage for a moment and brought out another glass of whisky and placed it on the table. 'You look like you've been up all night.'

'The Northern Lights were something else.' Jack grinned.

'They were indeed. I sat right here and watched them with Betty, my oldest friend. In all the time we've lived on this island we've never seen the Northern Lights.'

'Betty. She's Clemmie's grandmother, right? From the café.'

'That's the one.'

Jack could feel Pete studying him. 'You know,' Pete said finally, breaking the silence, 'I do recognise you.' He let the words settle as he took a deliberate sip of whisky before continuing. 'I've followed your career. Got all of your books on my shelf. But I'll be honest with you, I'm more interested in the travel bits of the book than the fictional love story.'

Jack blinked, momentarily caught off guard. 'You do surprise me. I'd have thought it'd be the other way around,' he said with a glint of humour.

Pete chuckled. 'There was a time I thought I was going to travel.'

'With the band?' asked Jack.

'So you know a little about me, too?'

'I researched Puffin Island a while ago and you're one hell of an interesting character, Pete Fenwick. A member of a famous band, girls falling at your feet, about to go on tour with Bowie, then…'

'My best friend was caught in the riptide and lost his life; it changed everything.' Pete was quiet for a moment. 'But I'll share with you that even though there was a time we were destined for stardom, I didn't actually want to leave this place. I mean, just look at this view. Those puffins make me smile every day. I didn't want to swap this for travelling from city to city.'

'Not even with all those girls chasing after you?' teased Jack.

'Not even then. This place is just ... life, a community, my home.'

They both looked out over the waves, the puffins bobbing on the sea.

'I know exactly what you mean. I've travelled all over but there's something different – something special – about this place.'

Pete leaned back, eyeing him thoughtfully. 'Has anyone else figured out who you are?' he asked, glancing around as if checking the shadows for eavesdroppers.

Immediately, Jack's mind flashed to Amelia. 'No, I don't think so, and I'm hoping that stays the case.'

'Any particular reason why?'

Jack hesitated, searching for the right words. 'I'm enjoying the chance to breathe ... to just be me, not the author with expectations hanging over my head. Here, I'm just Jack.' He paused, running a hand through his hair. He knew Amelia was a bibliophile, but she didn't seem the type to dig into someone's personal life unless they invited her in. Maybe she hadn't connected the dots, or maybe she had and she was purposely giving him space. Either way, it was what he needed right now.

'I hear you. I haven't said a word to anyone about who you are, and I won't. Believe me, if Betty hasn't figured it out yet, then you're most likely safe. That woman doesn't usually miss a trick.'

Jack chuckled, somewhat relieved. 'Good to know,' he said, relaxing a little.

'Let's hope Puffin Island works its magic for you.'

'I … I'll be straight with you, Pete,' Jack said. He felt at ease talking to Pete and found he wanted to open up to the older man. He thought himself a good judge of character, and he certainly needed someone to talk to right now. 'I'm in trouble. The past few years haven't been easy. My book sales have dropped off a cliff as big as the one in front of us, and there's a chance my publisher might drop me. And now…' He hesitated. 'I can't even write. It's like I've lost the spark, the excitement. I've come here to figure things out. To see if writing still means anything to me.'

Pete listened without interrupting, his gaze sympathetic.

'And it doesn't stop there.'

Pete raised an eyebrow.

'I stupidly put my trust in a dodgy accountant who has scarpered, leaving me with a huge tax bill, and I've been forced to take on a freelance job for a newspaper to try and make some money…'

'You don't look very happy about the job.'

'The topic of the first article I've been assigned is one that I don't particularly agree with.'

'You'll do the right thing,' Pete said with a warm, confident smile. 'And you've come to the right place. Puffin Island has a way of … healing people. Helping them rediscover who they are and what they're meant to do, helping them find their way again.'

'Thank you,' Jack said sincerely. Then he asked, 'Can you tell me anything about Dune House? It looks like it's been empty for some time.'

The Story Shop

'Ah, Dune House,' Pete replied, a trace of sadness in his voice. 'Yes, it's been empty for over six months now. Sad story, really. It used to belong to a man named Ethan. A real creative, talented guy. There was a touch of magic in everything he did. Always wanted to be a writer but never got a break. And then things took a bad turn.'

'Why, what happened?'

'Boating accident. His partner survived but she and Ethan's daughter didn't see eye to eye – lots of tension there, even before Ethan died – and he left the family house to the partner, who hadn't been in his life that long. The daughter is contesting the will and it's all got a little messy. None of us quite believe Ethan would have shut his daughter out of the family home. It doesn't make any sense to those of us who knew him.'

Jack raised an eyebrow, intrigued. 'Sounds awful.'

Pete nodded. 'It is.'

'There's a story in there somewhere.'

'Just don't you go writing about it, as you'll be chased off the island.' Pete gave a little chuckle. 'Too close to home for folks around here.'

Jack raised his hands in mock surrender. 'Don't worry,' he promised. 'My life is complicated enough. Anyway, I must get back. Thanks for the chat and the drink.'

'Any time, and thanks for bringing the tent back. By the way, can I ask who the lucky girl is?'

'Amelia, from The Story Shop.' Immediately Jack noticed a flash of something he couldn't quite identify in Pete's eyes. 'Have I said something wrong?'

Pete shook his head. 'Amelia deserves the best. She's …

well, she's been through a lot... Dune House was her family home, you see.'

Jack stared at Pete, the weight of the revelation sinking in.

Dune House had been Amelia's family home.

'Ethan was her father? A writer, did you say?' He remembered the notebook he'd found. Surely it had to have been written by Ethan?

'Yes, wrote many novels in his time, though never got the break he hoped for.'

Jack felt a fresh surge of guilt at taking the notebook and reading the words of a man he'd never known, especially now he'd discovered it was Amelia's father. He'd read so many books over the years to get a feeling for what was current in the market, but what he'd read that morning was one of the best stories he'd ever read. Ethan Brown's raw talent had shone from each page.

'Thanks for telling me,' he said softly.

Pete nodded as he drained his glass and set it down on the table. 'Just remember, Jack'—his tone was firm—'if your intentions aren't pure ... well, steer clear of Amelia. From what I've seen, you seem like a decent man, but she's been through enough already. She doesn't need anymore heartache in her life.'

Jack met Pete's gaze. 'I have no intention of hurting her. I promise.'

Pete studied him for a moment longer before his expression softened. 'Glad to hear it. She's one of a kind, that girl. More strength in her than most people realise.'

Jack stood, extending his hand. 'Thanks for the chat, Pete.'

Turning and walking back down the quiet cliff path towards Blue Water Bay, Jack thought of Amelia and her father's novel. He wanted to talk to her about it but how could he? He couldn't admit he'd been snooping and had been startled and accidentally slipped the notebook into his bag, and then had read it. Maybe he should put it back and encourage her to open up about her life, her father and, of course, the stepmother. He wondered if Amelia knew about the novel Ethan had written or if it had been forgotten in the chaos of her father's death. Either way, one thing was certain: Ethan Brown's literary work should not be hidden away. It had bestseller written all over it.

Chapter Nineteen
AMELIA

A steady stream of customers had kept Amelia busy all afternoon. Sales had been particularly strong that day, with the new title by Ellis Ford selling out, and Amelia was glad she'd put a copy under the counter for herself. Finally, there was a lull when she managed to grab a cup of tea and, with Pawsworth sprawled out on the counter, began to read the book that everyone seemed to be talking about. In what seemed like no time at all, she was three chapters in.

Despite her reluctance to admit it, she had to acknowledge Vivienne's knack for discovering talent. There was something magnetic about the protagonist's journey, and she could feel herself slipping deeper and deeper into the story, forgetting her own troubles as she turned page after page.

Just as she reached a particularly tense passage, the bell above the door jingled. She glanced up to see Edgar Carmichael stepping inside. He had the air of a man bearing unwelcome news, and her heart sank. She forced a smile and set the book aside.

'Edgar,' she greeted him, trying to keep her tone light. 'I'm taking it by the look on your face you aren't here to bring me good news?'

He gave her a sympathetic look, his mouth set in a grim line. 'I'm afraid I have some updates on Vivienne and Dune House.'

Amelia's stomach clenched, just as it always did whenever her family home or Vivienne were mentioned. Edgar glanced down at the paperwork in his hands. 'There's no easy way to say this, but Vivienne is adamant that Ethan left her the house in his will. She's not open to any form of mediation, so it looks like we're heading to court.'

Shaking her head in disbelief, Amelia felt a rush of anger and frustration. She wanted nothing more than to resolve this peacefully, but Vivienne had left her no choice. It was as if the woman was determined to erase Amelia from the picture. 'How has she convinced herself that Dune House belongs to her?' Amelia said, barely able to keep the bitterness out of her voice. 'I can't believe I have to go through this. It was my parents' home long before she entered our lives. Urghh! That woman.'

'I understand, Amelia. Believe me, we'll do everything in our power to present your case. The judge will consider all the evidence, including the fact that Dune House was your childhood home. I truly believe there's a strong argument in your favour. Try not to worry too much. I know it's hard but I'll do my very best to get justice.'

Amelia gave him a small, grateful smile. She appreciated

Edgar's reassurance, but it did little to ease her apprehension. There was so much more at stake than just a building. Dune House was a part of her identity, a link to her father and the life they'd shared. Losing it would feel like losing him all over again.

Edgar's gaze drifted to the book that she was reading. 'I see you've got your hands on a copy of Ellis Ford's novel. I've heard remarkable things about it,' he said with a warm smile. 'Would you recommend it?'

Amelia nodded. 'So far, so good. It's ... honestly, it's brilliant. I didn't want to admit it at first, but Vivienne has really found a gem with this one. The writing is captivating. It would be a welcome distraction, except I know how much money she'll be making from it.'

'Any other copies on hand?'

'All sold out, I'm afraid, but you can have this one when I've finished with it.'

'That's very kind but I'll order a copy from you. I'm fully aware that sharing books leaves authors without an income, and I know from your father the hard work that goes into writing a book. It's just a shame he never got to submit his last piece of work.'

'I can't even get into his study to have a look for his notebook. Because of all of his previous rejections, he got very protective of what he was writing, and it'd been ages since he let me read any of it. I'd like to see what he was writing before he passed.'

'We'll find a way. It's likely to be a long, drawn-out process but I'm convinced we'll win.'

Amelia placed the book order with the supplier using

her computer, 'A new delivery will be here in a couple of days. I'll let you know when it's in.'

Edgar admired the freshly arranged bouquet on the counter. 'And these roses ... they're beautiful. You deserve a little beauty, Amelia. Don't let this dispute steal all your joy.'

Amelia felt a wave of warmth at his kind words. It had been easy to lose herself in the anxiety and stress surrounding Dune House, but here, in her bookshop, with her beloved books and roses from a man she wanted to get to know more, Edgar was right. She couldn't let Vivienne rob her of everything. 'Thank you. I know you're doing your best.'

He gave her a reassuring smile before heading to the door. 'Remember, don't let her ruin your day. Enjoy that book.'

Amelia watched as Edgar left. She wasn't going to let Vivienne control her emotions or steal her happiness. She took in the aroma of the flowers and thought of Jack. She wondered if he would pop in and see her or whether, just like in the book, they would only see each other on their dates. But just as that thought flashed across her mind she looked up and saw him standing in the doorway. He grinned and walked towards her.

'Nice flowers.' He slid a coffee over the counter. 'For you.'

'Flowers and coffee. You're a keeper.' She took the invitation out of the drawer and placed it on the counter. 'Meet you "on the cliff top"? And at such an early hour. Sounds intriguing.' Her eyes didn't leave his. 'How will I know which part? That cliff top is quite extensive.'

'X will mark the spot. You won't be able to miss it. Now, according to the book, I shouldn't be here.'

'So why are you here?' She smiled.

'To bring you coffee and...' Jack walked round the counter and slipped his arm around her, pulling her close and kissing her tenderly on the lips. He drew back slowly. 'It's a long time until Sunday ... and I couldn't wait to kiss you.' He edged backwards, his eyes not leaving hers until he disappeared through the door, leaving her engulfed in goosebumps and with a huge smile on her face. Sipping the coffee, she thought to herself that Sunday couldn't come soon enough.

Chapter Twenty

AMELIA

Amelia hadn't slept a wink. It was very early Sunday morning, and she'd spent half the night tossing and turning, wondering what Jack had arranged for their date. She had no clue what she was supposed to wear but after hours of speculating she'd decided on a comfortable pair of jeans, a light blouse and her favourite jacket. The weather was forecast to be perfect from mid-morning.

Just after 5.30 a.m. she walked down Lighthouse Lane and called in at the tearoom, knowing Clemmie would be up baking. Her friend was standing at the tearoom gate.

'You look amazing. Are you all ready for the next big date?'

Amelia smiled. 'I'm feeling so nervous. I've no clue what Jack's got planned. What can we be doing this early in the morning?'

'It won't be long before you find out! I want a full update when you get back, whether that's this evening or tomorrow morning!'

Amelia grinned. 'I'll let you know what we're up to as soon as I can.'

'Have fun!'

Amelia walked along Blue Water Bay, where the sea stretched out in shades of sparkling blue, then made her away across the sand dunes and up the path, thankful for the gentle breeze. She felt a sense of anticipation building inside her as she climbed. What was waiting for her at the top?

As she reached the summit, her breath caught in her chest. Before her, majestic against the sky, swaying gently in the wind, was a massive hot air balloon. Overcome by surprise, she paused to take in its beauty. She'd only ever seen these balloons as dots on the horizon, drifting like lazy clouds in the distance, and yet here was one looming in front of her, huge and vibrant, a magnificent tapestry of colour, with alternating broad panels of rich, velvety red and deep royal blue, interwoven with bands of shimmering, sunlit gold. The fabric seemed to ripple slightly in the heat of the burner, making the colours dance. Her mouth fell open. She was speechless. Nothing like this had ever happened to her before.

'Oh my!' She brought her hands up to her face and stared. Jack was standing by the balloon's wicker basket. He wore a grin as wide as the horizon, and in his hand he held a chilled bottle of prosecco.

'You have got to be kidding me?'

Jack chuckled, his eyes twinkling as he gestured for her to come closer. She walked towards him, still looking up at the balloon. 'Is this actually for me ... for us?'

'It is.'

Amelia's eyes were wide. 'But who is going to fly it and how did it get here?'

'It got here on the back of the truck and I'm going to fly it, of course, if you trust me to.'

She pointed. 'You're going to fly it?'

'Don't look so alarmed. I promise I'm qualified. I became obsessed with hot air balloons many years ago and have always kept my hours up.'

'What else do I not know about you?' Amelia asked curiously. For a second, she thought she caught a flicker of something – maybe guilt? – in his eyes, but it disappeared as quickly as it came.

Jack laughed. 'I'm sure that by the end of our temptation bucket list, you'll know everything about me,' he replied, his tone light-hearted. He looked at her with an openness that felt almost vulnerable, and Amelia wondered he if was feeling guilty that he hadn't yet told her who he really was. She absolutely understood, though, that he would want her to like him for himself.

'I'm sure we will,' she agreed. 'I was not expecting this. Possibly puffin watching or rock climbing … not floating hundreds of feet in the air beneath a big colourful balloon.'

'Trust me, you're going to love this.'

She took a deep breath and placed her hand in his, feeling the warmth of his fingers wrap around hers. 'If I die today, it's all on you.'

'I'll take full responsibility,' he said with a laugh, helping her step over the edge of the basket. She climbed in, careful not to trip on the ropes, her pulse quickening as she felt

Jack's hand at the small of her back, steadying her. She glanced around, marvelling. Overhead, a balloon bursting with colours, deep reds and blues against the clear sky … and below, the basket – sturdy, with cushioned walls to lean against, and much more comfortable than she'd anticipated.

Jack glanced over at her, sensing her hesitation, and gave her a reassuring smile. 'We'll go up quite high, but don't worry, I've been flying for years. Plus, I've got a team keeping an eye on us who know where we're heading. You'll be fine.'

'I trust you,' she replied, looking up at the balloon again, the initial uncertainty abating a little. The idea of soaring over the sea felt a little daunting, but Jack's calm confidence had a way of putting her at ease.

Jack joined her inside the basket, then popped the cork on the bottle of prosecco, making bubbles spill over. 'To adventure,' he said, pouring her a glass. 'You can ride in style, but I'll stay off the alcohol until we've landed safely. Are you ready?'

'I think so!' Amelia took a sip then leaned back against the side of the basket.

Pete and Betty, standing outside Cliff Top Cottage, waved at her and she waved back. She took out her phone and angled it towards Jack. 'We need a photo!'

'We do!' he replied, slipping an arm around her waist and pulling her close so she could take the snap. 'Now I need to concentrate.' He kissed the top of her head then got to work, and Amelia began to record as the balloon slowly began to rise. Suddenly feeling a little nervous, she put her phone away and closed her eyes, enjoying the breeze on her face. When she opened them, Jack smiled at her and pointed towards Pete and Betty, now shrinking into the distance but still waving.

Amelia sipped prosecco as the ground drifted away, and the balloon floated higher, rising steadily over the rugged cliffs and dense greenery of Puffin Island. The view was breathtaking, and for a moment Amelia forgot her nerves. She leaned over the edge of the basket, looking down at the cliffs and beaches below, the ocean stretching out in shimmering waves.

'We're higher than the lighthouse.'

'And about to go higher. See? Not so scary after all, is it?' Jack's voice was soft, and as she turned back to him, she found him watching her, a gentle smile playing on his lips.

'Not scary at all,' she said. 'Just ... beautiful.'

They were silent for a moment, their eyes locked, and then Amelia leaned forward and kissed him softly on the lips. 'There'll be no more of that until we land somewhere safe. I don't want you to get distracted.'

Jack smirked. 'Just one more?'

Amelia laughed and gave him one more quick kiss.

They drifted over the island, the soft roar of the burner filling the quiet afternoon sky. Amelia pointed out landmarks below, describing hidden beaches and trails Jack said he hadn't yet explored, each with a story or some local legend attached. She knew he was hanging upon every word, admiring her knowledge and love for the land.

'If you could go anywhere, see anything in the world ... where would it be?' he asked.

Amelia thought for a moment, watching as a flock of

seagulls dipped and glided below them. 'Italy,' she said, surprising even herself. 'I'd love to visit Tuscany, spend my days wandering through vineyards and tiny old towns, eating my way through the local restaurants. I've never been but I've read lots of books set there.'

Jack's eyes lit up. 'Italy? Great choice. I could see you there, actually ... with a wide-brimmed hat and a glass of wine, wandering the cobblestoned streets, charming every local in sight.'

She grinned, feeling her cheeks warm under his gaze. 'What about you? What's on your list?'

'Hmm... I think I'd go back to New Zealand,' he said, leaning against the side of the basket. 'There's this sense of ... well, it's hard to explain. A kind of wild, untouched beauty that just makes you feel alive.'

Amelia studied him as he spoke, noticing the passion in his eyes, the way he seemed to come alive when he talked about the world.

'Tell me about you and Puffin Island. I want to know everything about Amelia Brown.'

'I'm just Amelia, who owns a bookshop and loves the place where she lives.' She gazed thoughtfully out towards the horizon.

'Do you ever feel ... I don't know, suffocated? I mean, I can't help but wonder ... living on a small island with everyone knowing each other's business all the time... doesn't it feel a little, well, like people around here are sort of stuck, lacking ambition?'

Amelia turned her gaze back to him. 'Absolutely not! You think we're all small-town gossipers with no dreams or drive?' She laughed, shaking her head. 'It's so much more than that. I don't feel suffocated at all. Actually, I feel more supported here than I would living anywhere else.'

'So you actually enjoy everyone knowing everything about you?'

'It's not that they know everything about me, it's that they care about me. There's a difference. You'd be amazed by the kind of support that comes from a place like Puffin Island.' She paused. 'Take Clemmie and Dilly, for example. We've been friends since the day we were born, practically. Our mothers went to school together, and their mothers before them. We're more than just friends, we're family. When my dad passed, their families became mine. That's what Puffin Island is all about. You might lose something, but you're never truly alone.' She knew Jack was watching her carefully.

'You're saying it's more like one big family?'

'Exactly.' She nodded. 'We look out for each other. I mean, if you're having a bad day, everyone knows it before you've even opened your front door. Sure, it can be annoying sometimes, but it's also a relief. When I'm struggling, I don't have to go through it alone. They're just there, without asking. No one here feels like a stranger. I don't think you could find that same warmth or closeness in a city. And if I'm going on a date, everyone knows about it and is cheering me on … though I'm not sure if that's down to the gigantic hot air balloon hovering on top of the cliff or the fact I told everyone.'

Jack smiled. 'But don't you ever want more than this? Something bigger?'

Amelia laughed softly. 'What's bigger than happiness, Jack? Everyone here is chasing after their own dreams, even if they might not look like what you'd expect. Take Dilly, for example: she lives in the lighthouse, runs two galleries and sells her paintings all over the world. Clemmie part-owns the family business and has visions of passing The Café on the Coast down to her own children one day. She pours her heart into every pastry and she has customers who've been coming to the bakery since before she was born. She knows exactly how they like their tea and what they'll order before they even step inside. You could call it small, but she's building something beautiful, something that genuinely brings people joy every day. That's a kind of ambition, isn't it?'

Jack looked thoughtful, nodding slowly as he processed her words. 'Okay, I see what you're saying. But don't you ever get frustrated? Like, if you wanted to do something completely different, do you feel like people would support you, or would they just want you to stay the same?'

'Oh, they'd definitely support me,' Amelia replied confidently. 'I knew from an early age I wanted to open a bookshop and when I first bought the shop, everyone chipped in. Betty donated her old shelves from the café, and Sam gave me lots of bunting that had been used for a wedding, along with the armchairs and old lamps from the restaurant. Dilly painted the pictures of the famous books on the walls to give the shop some character. When you're part of a community like this, your dreams aren't just your own. They belong to everyone, in a way, because they're rooting for you just as much as you're rooting for them. We all want to see each other succeed. Isn't that something special?'

The Story Shop

'So you're telling me you could do anything, and they'd cheer you on?'

Amelia nodded. 'Yes! And it's not just about careers or big life decisions. Even the small stuff counts. Like, when we were kids, Clemmie and I spent an entire summer saving up to buy rollerblades, taking on odd jobs for people around the island, many of which we're pretty sure they made up as a way to contribute to our rollerblades fund without it looking like outright charity. We then rolled around the island like we owned the place, and people would wave or cheer as we passed by. When Dilly decided she wanted to learn how to surf, half the town came down to the beach with their old boards to help teach her. We celebrate each other's little victories, and that's something you don't get when you're surrounded by strangers.'

Jack looked up at the sky. 'You make it sound like a fairytale.'

'It feels like one sometimes,' Amelia admitted. 'Of course, there are flaws, and people disagree, and there's the occasional gossip that gets a little out of hand. But for the most part, it's just ... good. People genuinely want each other to be happy here, and I think that's rare.'

'What about you, Amelia?' he asked, his voice softer. 'What's your dream?'

She paused, momentarily caught off guard. 'My dream?' she repeated, watching Puffin Island become smaller as they floated further away.

'Yeah,' he said, his gaze never leaving her face. 'What makes you happy?'

'My bookshop, the people I love, this island... I don't think I need much more than that.'

Jack studied her quietly. 'You're really content on the island, aren't you?'

She nodded. 'I am. There's something comforting about knowing that I could grow old there and never feel like I missed out on something bigger. Because this is big, Jack. These people, this life, it's big in the ways that matter.'

'You know, I always thought I needed to keep moving, to be on the lookout for the next big thing. But maybe … maybe I've been missing something.'

'Sometimes we overlook the small things because they seem too ordinary. But ordinary things can hold a lot of beauty. Maybe you're just seeing that now. Maybe taking a break on this island is going to be the making of you.' As they drifted over the sea, the gentle sway of the balloon making Amelia feel both exhilarated and calm, Jack pointed towards an island they were approaching. 'That's where we're heading. My friend owns it.'

Amelia raised an eyebrow. 'Your friend owns an island?'

Jack chuckled. 'He does. No one lives there full-time, though. It's more of a private retreat.'

She tilted her head with a sceptical smile. 'What kind of person owns their own island?'

'The kind who's a celebrity chef and lives in a castle,' Jack said with a grin, 'and also owns a hot air balloon. Hence…' He gestured upwards.

'What's your friend's name?' asked Amelia, suspecting she already knew.

'Andrew Glossop. We've flown together many times over the years and I'm also godfather to his boys. He's more like a brother to me than a friend.'

Amelia blinked in surprise. 'And you say he has a castle *and* an island? That's ... something else.'

Jack laughed, enjoying her reaction. 'Wait until you see it, it's even more impressive up close. We're going down. Are you ready?'

Amelia looked over the side of the basket as it began to descend.

'Absolutely ready,' she replied.

Chapter Twenty-One
AMELIA

As they drifted lower, the island unfolded beneath them like the hidden gem it was, nestled within the sparkling expanse of the North Sea, just over a thirty-minute journey from Puffin Island. Amelia could see its dense canopy of emerald-green trees swaying in the gentle breeze. Pristine white sand encircled the island like a ribbon, meeting the sparkling turquoise waters that lapped gently at the shore. A majestic waterfall cascaded down a rugged rock face on the far side of the island, its crystal-clear waters pouring into a sparkling blue pool that looked as if it belonged on a postcard. The scale was breathtaking. Winding paths cut through the foliage, hinting at the untamed wilderness within. The entire scene had a tranquil, untouched beauty. Jack expertly adjusted the balloon's burners, angling their descent towards a stretch of sand that glistened like powdered gold in the sunlight.

With a gentle thud, the balloon landed smoothly. The fabric above them rustled and billowed as it began to deflate. Jack extended his arm to help Amelia out of the basket, and as her feet touched the ground, she instinctively kicked off her shoes.

'Can you grab this for me?' he asked, passing his large rucksack over the side of the basket. 'Breakfast!' Stepping out of the basket, he kicked his shoes off too and quickly finished deflating the balloon and rolling it up, ready for transport.

He turned back to Amelia and took the rucksack. They began to walk, their bare feet sinking into the warm, golden sand that stretched endlessly beneath the azure sky.

'I feel like I've just arrived on a beautiful Caribbean island. This is definitely a place that Asher Knight would own,' she mused, then gave a little squeal and ran towards the water's edge. She briefly closed her eyes and tilted her face towards the sky. It was still very early in the morning but already the sun had begun to break through. She breathed in the fresh salty air. 'It's like we've landed in another world!'

Jack slung the rucksack over his shoulder and took her hand, and as they headed along the shoreline, he pointed to clusters of seashells and a small tide pool teeming with life. He nodded towards a hammock underneath the shelter of trees up ahead.

'Let's have breakfast there.'

'This is just so amazing. You really are something else, aren't you?'

Jack pulled out a picnic blanket and laid it on the ground, and Amelia knelt down, took off her jacket and stretched her legs out in front of her. She watched as Jack unpacked a gorgeous-looking feast of fresh fruit, delicate pastries and a variety of cheeses, along with two small bottles of orange juice.

'I feel like I'm in paradise, on a honeymoon!' She laughed.

'I know Asher and Zara get married eventually but I think you may be being a little hasty,' said Jack with a smile.

'Spoilsport!' replied Amelia, opening one of the bottles of juice. 'The girls are never going to believe me! And what's this?' She took out a brown parcel. 'Another book! Which one this time? And where are you getting all these books from? I know it's not my shop,' she teased.

'The charity shop,' he replied. 'And you'll have to open it and find out.' He sat beside her.

'You really went all out, didn't you?'

He shrugged, his smile a little bashful. 'Well, I figured if we were going to do this, we might as well do it right.'

'This is incredible,' she murmured, taking in the scene around her before unwrapping the book.

'*Jane Eyre* by Charlotte Brontë.'

'I thought you might appreciate this one. As you probably already know, it's about a woman who's both strong and kind, navigating her way through challenges to find happiness.'

She turned the pages and inside found a handwritten note.

> *For Amelia, who deserves the kind of happiness found in the best love stories.*

'You're going to make me cry. I don't think anyone has ever been this lovely to me.'

He leaned across and kissed her on her cheek then paused.

'You look like you want to say something…'

'I don't want you to think I've been prying, but I chose this book because something about her resilience reminded me of you. It's a timeless story, full of depth, self-discovery and love. She's an inspiring character, strong and independent. You have that same kind of spirit.'

'You think so, do you? And what do you mean, you don't want me to think that you've been prying?' she asked.

'After I borrowed the tent and telescope from Pete, and was setting up on the beach, I noticed Dune House and wondered why such a beautiful place was sitting empty. Thought maybe it was going on the market, or it was just a holiday home. Then Pete mentioned your dad.' He looked at her earnestly. 'But he wasn't gossiping, I swear.'

Amelia's expression softened. 'It's okay. Pete was one of my father's oldest friends and I know he's not one for gossip.' She paused. 'Dune House was my family home from the day I was born. I lived there with my mum and dad. They were … incredible parents. I had a fantastic childhood because they made even mundane happenings magical, sometimes in the simplest ways.'

She knew Jack could see her struggling with words, could hear how her voice faltered. 'Then, five years ago, my mum went in for a routine operation. Nothing serious, they said. But then she caught an infection, and she didn't make it.' Her voice cracked, and she looked down, her hands twisting together in her lap.

'Amelia.' His hand reached out to hold hers, giving a gentle squeeze. 'I'm so, so sorry.'

For a second her fingers tightened around his. 'After that, things changed. My dad ... he was so strong, always trying to shield me from his own grief, but I could see it in his eyes. He was hurting too.' She paused.

'Tell me about your dad.'

'He was a creative soul. We'd spend hours sitting together, just writing, me in my journals, him drafting stories. He'd come by my bookshop, rearrange the shelves, dust off the old books; he loved being there. Literature was his escape, his way back to life.'

A smile touched her lips, but Jack could still see the sadness in her eyes. 'He didn't care much about money or the latest trends. If something didn't matter in the grand scheme of things, he'd ignore it. He wasn't tight-fisted, he just ... valued what was real. Time, kindness, unconditional love. He taught me to love books, to cherish words. Those were the gifts he shared with me and that will always stay with me.'

Jack listened and watched as her face clouded.

'Then something changed.' she continued. 'One day, this woman walked into his life. I can't even bring myself to say her name. She appeared charming, beautiful, full of energy, everything he thought he was missing. To be honest, I still don't know what the attraction was for her. Yes, my dad was a nice person, but not someone you would expect her to go for. He was down to earth, loved his comfy shoes and favourite jumper. She was all power suits, high heels and not one bit of warmth to her personality.'

'Sounds exactly like someone I know,' said Jack, a strange look on his face.

'I suspect he had something she wanted – possibly just

my inheritance, though I always got the feeling there was more to her scheme – and I still have this niggling feeling that there's more to discover. Soon Dune House felt different. I wanted him to be happy, of course. But it was like she made him forget who he was. She pulled him away, little by little, from the things that had once meant the world to him. It was like Dune House became less ours, less the place filled with his love and memories, and more of a stranger's possession. He spent more time away, with her, chasing things he used to call distractions. Sometimes I wonder if it was his way of coping, of trying to find something new to hold on to. But it felt like he was letting go of everything we'd built together.'

Amelia stopped and took a huge sip of juice.

'It sounds like it's been a difficult time.'

'It has, it still is. No one on this island can believe that my dad left the house to her. I just wish it was all over already.'

'I can imagine. Pete mentioned a boating accident,' he said gently.

'I was absolutely gobsmacked when he told me he'd bought a yacht. It was just something he would never do. I mean, it wasn't just a boat, it was something a millionaire would purchase, and this from a man who was never interested in materialistic things.' Amelia took a deep breath, her fingers nervously tracing the edge of the wine glass.

Jack listened intently. 'Did he give you any reason for the purchase?'

'That's just it,' Amelia said. 'He didn't. He'd never even shown an interest in boating before. Sure, he loved the beach. He loved watching the waves, feeling the sand beneath his feet. But the ocean itself? He wasn't a huge fan. He'd always said that he liked the water best when it was at a safe, scenic distance. And yet, here he was, dropping an unbelievable amount of money on a yacht that would put him right where he'd never wanted to be.' She paused, glancing up at Jack as if to gauge his reaction. 'I tried to ask him about it, but he just brushed it off, said it was something he felt like he should do, something for a "fresh start", whatever that meant.'

'And the new woman he'd met ... did she have anything to do with it, do you think?'

'That's what I keep coming back to,' she said. 'She was this whirlwind of excitement, so different from him, constantly talking about adventure and luxury and ... well, everything my dad never cared about. They were married within six months of meeting; it was ridiculous. He barely knew her!' She stared out at the water for a moment before looking back at Jack. 'One day he told me he was taking her out on the yacht for the day. They were going to cruise along the coastline, have a picnic on board, just the two of them. I had no idea it would be the last time I'd see him.' Amelia briefly shut her eyes. 'Supposedly, while she was sunbathing on the deck, he decided to go for a swim. She said he just dived in, like he was completely comfortable in the water. But ... that wasn't him. Dad was never a confident swimmer. He wouldn't just dive into open water, especially from that height. But apparently, he did ... and he never came back up.' Her voice cracked. 'The coroner said he hit his head on a rock. But that doesn't make sense either because they were anchored near a stretch of coast where there were no rocks.'

She took a shaky breath, her hands trembling slightly. 'The police ruled it an accident. Just an unfortunate, tragic accident. But I can't shake the feeling that there's more to it. None of it makes sense to me.'

Jack raised his eyebrows. 'And the woman he was with, did she ever reach out to you afterward? Offer any explanation?'

Amelia's expression hardened, a flash of anger in her eyes. 'No. She came to the funeral, all dramatic tears and shallow condolences, but it felt insincere. I tried to talk to her, to get a better understanding of what happened that day, but she kept repeating the same story. Almost like she'd rehearsed it. "He just dived in", she said, brushing away the tears with the back of her hand. But I don't believe it. I don't believe her.'

Jack reached out, placing a reassuring hand on hers. 'Have you thought about looking into it? Talking to someone, maybe?'

She nodded. 'I thought about it, but … what if I'm wrong? What if it really was just a horrible accident, and I'm clinging to some conspiracy theory because I can't accept he's gone, or that he actually did love her so much that he left her our family home?'

A long silence settled between them before Jack spoke again. 'Did he leave you anything?'

'The contents of his study, which I don't even have a key to. I've just got to wait until the court decides.'

Jack stretched out an arm and Amelia shuffled over and

snuggled into him. 'Thank you for sharing all that, it couldn't have been easy.'

'It's actually good to get it off my chest to someone who isn't directly involved. Even though it feels like I've known you for years.'

'That feeling is mutual.' He tilted her face towards his and pressed a soft kiss to her lips.

'What I want to know is how we're going to get home,' asked Amelia, suddenly changing the subject. 'In the balloon?'

Jack's face broke into a mischievous grin. Without a word, he reached down, tugged her to her feet and pulled her along in a spontaneous sprint along the shoreline. The cool, foamy water lapped at their ankles and Amelia's laughter rang out as they rounded a bend in the sand and spotted a secluded crescent. That's when Amelia saw them: two sleek jet skis, their paintwork glistening in the sun, beached. Jack pointed at them. 'Fancy some fun?'

Chapter Twenty-Two
AMELIA

'I don't have a swimsuit,' Amelia said, glancing down at her clothes.

Jack flashed her a mischievous grin. 'Who needs a swimsuit?' With a swift movement, he pulled off his T-shirt, revealing his toned physique, and then stripped down to his boxer shorts. He grabbed a life jacket hanging over the handlebars of the closest jet ski and tossed it in her direction. 'Come on, the water's perfect,' he added, his eyes flashing with excitement.

Amelia hesitated for a moment, glancing first at the jet skis and then at Jack, before she finally shrugged and followed suit. She was secretly relieved to be wearing a matching set of lingerie, even if it was about to be drenched by the seawater. She pulled on the life jacket, her cheeks slightly flushed at the unexpected turn of events.

'A jet ski each or…'

'I think I'll climb on the back of yours,' she said.

'Any excuse to hold on tight to me,' he said with a playful grin.

'Exactly that,' she replied, wading through the water. It felt good to have the sun beating on her skin. As she slid her arms around Jack's waist her heart fluttered with a mix of exhilaration and nervousness. She'd watched jet skis bounce over the waves at Blue Water Bay but had never had the nerve to climb on one herself … until now.

'Ready?' he asked, looking over his shoulder.

'Ready,' she exclaimed as he started the engine.

'Hold on tight!'

Amelia clung to Jack with a grin that matched his, her laughter bubbling up uncontrollably as the jet ski zipped across the waves. The wind whipped through her hair and the cool spray of water hit her skin, every twist and turn making her heart race with exhilaration. The sound of their laughter mixed with the roar of the engine and the rhythmic splash of the waves beneath them.

Jack kept looking over his shoulder, flashing her a carefree smile. She could see the joy in his expression, and it made the moment feel even more magical. The jet ski carved through the clear turquoise water, weaving in and out of the gentle swells. As they circled the island, Amelia's eyes widened with awe. She marvelled at the beauty of the secluded place he'd brought her to, and her thoughts raced. How lucky could someone be to own a place like this? The island, with its untouched beaches and crystal-clear waters, felt like something out of a dream. It was a fleeting moment of freedom and fun, but she wished she could hold on to it for ever.

On the other side of the island, Jack began to slow the jet

ski as they approached a secluded cove. The shore was untouched, with powdery white sand meeting lush greenery that stretched upward towards the towering cliffs beyond. The sound of the waves added to the sense of serenity. Once Jack had steered the jet ski towards the sand and cut the engine, he reached out a hand to help her steady herself as she climbed off. She took it, her fingers brushing against his, sending a jolt of warmth through her. They lingered for a moment, their hands still joined, and then walked together onto the soft sand.

'How was the ride?'

'Amazing! I've never felt my heart beat so fast,' Amelia replied.

Jack cocked an eyebrow. 'Never?' he teased. 'We need to change that!'

'And look at this place.' Amelia was in awe.

'It's beautiful,' he said, lifting her off her feet, spinning her around and making her giggle. 'Come on, this way. I'd say we've officially found paradise.'

Amelia looked around at the untouched beauty surrounding them. 'I think this is the most romantic place I've ever visited.'

'You deserve only the best.'

Amelia's heart fluttered at his words. Here, on this island, with the sound of the waves, and the sun warming their skin, she felt at ease, and for the first time in ages all thoughts of Vivienne vanished from her mind.

'Up in the balloon, we could see the waterfall…' He grabbed her hand, leading her towards a narrow path that wound through the trees. They laughed as they ducked under low-hanging branches, their footsteps muffled by a soft layer of sand. Amelia's heart raced with excitement. After a few minutes they emerged into a clearing, and she gasped at the beauty of the waterfall up close. Sunlight filtered through the trees, casting dappled light onto the surface of the water so that it sparkled like diamonds. It was breathtaking, a scene that belonged in fairytales.

'Jack...' Amelia breathed, awestruck. 'This is unbelievable. Is it real? Are we actually here? I honestly feel like I'm dreaming.'

'It's definitely real. I figured if we were going on an island adventure, we might as well go all in.' He looked at her, his expression playful. 'Fancy a swim?'

The intensity of his gaze sent a thrill through her, and her heart raced in response. Jack climbed over a small cluster of rocks, and Amelia felt a shift inside her, a slight drop in her mood, a momentary flicker of doubt. Nobody had ever made her feel this way before. It all seemed too perfect, too unreal, and a small, quiet fear settled in her chest. Soon he would disappear, returning to wherever he came from, and the thought of it made her wish for something that felt impossible: that this moment could last for ever. She gave herself a little shake. 'Live for the moment,' she muttered to herself.

'What are you thinking about?' Jack asked as he stood on top of the rock.

'That I never want this day to end,' she shouted back, standing at the water's edge.

'It doesn't have to,' he replied, before gliding through the air into the cobalt water.

Splash.

Jack surfaced right under the waterfall and took

Amelia's breath away. He swam towards her, his tousled hair slicked back. 'The water's refreshing!' he shouted.

'That means cold!' she replied.

He laughed, scooping up water in his hands and attempting to splash her. She squealed and jumped backwards. Jack waded out of the deeper water, his shoulders broad, his skin glistening. She couldn't take her eyes off him as she reached for his hand and walked into the water. Side by side, they swam towards the waterfall, letting the spray mist engulf them, then laughing as the water cascaded over their heads. At one point, he reached out and brushed a strand of wet hair from her face, his hand lingering on her cheek. She felt a spark, an undeniable chemistry crackling between them as their eyes met, and for a moment it seemed as if time stood still.

'What do you think Asher Knight and Zara Quinn would do if they found themselves in this position?'

For a second, nothing happened, then neither of them could help themselves. Grabbing each other, they kissed, slowly at first, then with more urgency. Jack slipped his hand around her waist and Amelia pressed herself against him, their lips locked.

'Are you sure we're on our own?' she murmured.

'Absolutely.'

Within seconds she had pushed down his shorts and begun to explore every part of his body. With one swift movement her bra was floating on the water, her chest pressed against his. His hands followed the curve of her back and as he pushed down her pants, he hitched her up, her breasts exposed above the water. Then he kissed her like no one she'd ever been with, dragging his lips down her throat. She moaned and their hips began moving together. Never in her wildest dreams did she think her bucket list would have 'raw, passionate sex with the most gorgeous man she's ever set eyes on under a waterfall on a private island' ticked off.

Two hours later, they'd made their way back to their original landing spot and were reunited with the rucksack and picnic blanket. The jet ski ride back was just as thrilling as the first time. Now they lay on the blanket, Amelia wrapped in Jack's arms. She hadn't had this much fun in ages. She glanced up at him, saw his eyes were closed and couldn't resist leaning in softly to kiss him. 'Fancy going again?'

'Of course.' He smiled, opening his eyes as she began to kiss every inch of his body.

Thirty minutes later, feeling pleasantly hungry, they gathered dry twigs and kindling and built a small fire. They spent the next ten minutes chasing fish that darted just out of reach in the shallows, their splashes and laughter echoing across the quiet beach. Jack finally managed to spear some fish on sticks and expertly propped them over the crackling fire. The scent of roasting fish mingled with the fresh sea breeze, making Amelia's stomach growl with anticipation. As they waited for the fish to cook, Jack leaned back on his elbows, looking up at the sky.

'So,' he said, glancing at her with a soft smile, 'what's on your bucket list, Amelia?'

She thought for a moment. 'Honestly ... I'm not sure. I've never really thought about making one. I always thought it was something you did when you hit a midlife crisis, but maybe I should start to think more, explore more.

It's exciting when you have someone to do these things with.' A familiar sadness washed over Amelia again, and this time she couldn't shake it. Her voice quieter than before, she admitted, 'I wouldn't normally do something like this.'

Jack looked up with a grin and shrugged. 'This is a first for me, too – cooking fish on a private island.' With that, he checked the fish, decided they were done, and handed her her share.

Amelia's gaze dropped to the sand for a moment, her fingers absentmindedly tracing the edge of the picnic blanket. 'You know what I mean...' She trailed off. 'Tell me about Jack's normal love life. Why aren't you all "loved up" with someone else already?'

There was a long pause before Jack answered, his voice steady but laced with something deeper. 'Who says I'm not?' His eyes didn't leave hers, his gaze intense, and her stomach did a flip. He took a bite of his fish and chewed slowly. 'The truth is, no one spectacular has crossed my path ... until now.' The words hung in the air between them, charged with meaning.

Amelia smiled softly, warmth spreading through her chest. She was feeling exactly the same, a sense of connection, something deeper than the simple fun they'd been having. They had shared a moment, and she couldn't deny it. It felt like a rare kind of intimacy. She tried the fish, savoured the smoky flavour and looked over at Jack, her smile lingering. 'This fish is delicious,' she said. She couldn't believe how perfect everything was. It wasn't just the food, it was the company, the place, the way they fitted together so easily.

They ate with their fingers, laughing as they swapped pieces of fish. Amelia took a bite of Jack's fish and raised a mock-serious eyebrow. 'I think I might have caught the better one, actually,' she teased, leaning over to snatch another piece from his plate.

Jack grinned, shaking his head. 'You're trying to steal my catch now, are you?' He playfully nudged her with his elbow, and she returned the nudge, their easy banter making it feel like they'd known each other for a lot longer than they really had.

They ate the last of the fish, crispy from the fire. Amelia leaned back, gazing up at the sky, sad that the day was coming to an end.

'What exactly are you doing with the hot air balloon?' she asked.

Jack smiled, wiping his hands on his shorts before picking up a few small rocks to toss into the fire. 'It's staying here. Andrew's coming tomorrow with his boys for a camping trip and they'll be arriving by boat. It has a carrier on the back for the balloon and the basket. When you're ready, we're all good to go.'

'I've had the best day,' said Amelia as they packed the rucksack and picked up their shoes. Reluctantly, they headed towards the water.

'Me too.'

Climbing onto the back of the jet ski, Amelia looked back towards the island as she slipped her arms around Jack's waist. He gave her one last glance over his shoulder, revved the engine and sped off across the water, back towards Puffin Island.

Arriving at Blue Water Bay not long after, Jack pulled

the jet ski onto the sand and then walked Amelia back to the bookshop. Lighthouse Lane was quiet now, cloaked in twilight.

'I don't think I'll ever forget today.'

He reached out and pulled her close, hugging her. 'I can't remember the last time I had this much fun.'

They stood there for a moment, neither one wanting to end the day. Finally Amelia took a step back, giving him a smile. 'Well … I guess I'll see you soon?'

'Oh, you can count on it,' Jack replied, his grin returning. 'I'll be working on that bucket list.' He kissed her, and with one last lingering glance she slipped inside the bookshop. As the door closed softly behind her, she leaned against it, happiness flooding through her. Her lips still tingled from his kiss, and with a smile she took a moment to breathe, savouring the feeling that blossomed in her chest. She couldn't wait to see what was next on the temptation bucket list. Pawsworth jumped down from the counter and began brushing against her leg. 'Don't tell anyone,' she whispered, 'but I really want to see him again.'

Amelia was in the first flush of love, and she knew that when Jack left the island, it was very likely that she was going to get her heart broken.

Chapter Twenty-Three

JACK

All the way back to the B&B, Jack could feel the smile stretching across his face. All he was thinking about was Amelia: the laughter, the easy conversation, the thrill of the island, and the electric connection that had sparked between them from the moment he met her. There was something so effortless about being with her, something he hadn't felt in years. As he climbed the stone steps of the B&B he shook his head in disbelief at how well the day had gone.

He found Lena behind the reception desk, her attention on the papers in front of her. When she looked up, a warm smile spread across her face.

'I've been waiting for you,' she said, sliding an envelope across the desk towards him. 'There's a note for you. Have you had a good day?'

'Just the best day,' he replied, his voice full of contentment as he took the envelope from her. 'I'll see you in the morning for breakfast. Thanks for this.' He waved the envelope before heading up the stairs.

Once inside his room, he kicked off his shoes and sat on the edge of the bed, looking at the envelope. The handwriting was neat and familiar; he'd seen it on many Christmas cards over the years. It was from Edgar Carmichael.

He opened the envelope.

Jack,

Let's catch up. I'd love for you to join me for dinner tomorrow night at The Sea Glass Restaurant. 7 p.m.

Yours, Edgar.

It would be good to have a proper catch-up with Edgar and he was looking forward to hearing all of his stories about living on Puffin Island.

Placing the note on his bedside table, Jack collapsed onto his bed, staring up at the ceiling with a smile that refused to fade. His mind was still very much on Amelia, her laughter, her quick wit, her warmth. She was ... one hell of a girl. Whilst everything was fresh in his memory, he sat up, grabbed his laptop and began typing out his thoughts and feelings about how wonderful she was, and recapping the adventures they'd shared so far. He quickly filled several pages, and, reading them, he knew that this was it, *this* was the novel he needed to be writing. The last book in his contract. He would write their story with Puffin Island thrown into the mix.

He ended the chapter with: *It was impossible to believe*

they'd only just met. Everything had felt so natural, so right. He knew he'd be seeing her again soon, and he was already anticipating what else they might add to their bucket list.

He saved the document and then his thoughts turned back to everything Amelia had told him that day.

On impulse, Jack opened up Google, typed in 'Ethan Brown boating accident' and began scrolling through the results. A few local newspaper links popped up, some small online news outlets, but nothing major, certainly nothing from the national papers.

He clicked on the first article, a piece from a local news site, which only provided sparse details. It seemed clear that Ethan's death was the result of the sort of terrible accident that could happen to anyone.

Jack thought about what Amelia had said about her dad: how he wasn't the type to dive off a boat, how he was cautious, grounded and wasn't a huge fan of water.

Jack scrolled further down and then stopped in shock as he read a name he'd never expected to see connected to Amelia in any way.

Vivienne Langford, Mr Brown's wife, was reportedly devastated by the incident and declined to comment when approached.

Jack stared and blew out a breath. Surely this wasn't the *same* Vivienne Langford. But it appeared it was.

'Amelia's stepmum, no way,' he muttered. He reread the sentence, his mind whirring, then he Googled some more.

According to the next article he found, Vivienne Langford had married Ethan Brown twelve months ago. The wedding had been a quiet, private affair with only the residents of Puffin Island attending. That wasn't like the

Vivienne he knew. She loved lavish affairs and wanted everyone to know her business, so why had this been kept so quiet? Why didn't she have her big day splashed across every literary magazine or try to bag a lucrative deal with *OK* magazine?

Maybe it had been Ethan who had wanted to keep the marriage quiet? Somehow, that explanation felt too convenient. Jack sat back, staring at his screen. His instincts told him exactly the same as Amelia's had told her: there was more to this story because something – potentially a lot of things – didn't quite fit.

Jack closed his laptop, wondering if he was overthinking it.

The dinner with Edgar couldn't come soon enough. Having lived on the island for so long, there was a good chance he would know more about the couple. Perhaps he'd attended the wedding. If anyone could help Jack quietly dig into the local gossip and facts that surrounded Vivienne, it was Edgar. If there were pieces to this puzzle to find, Jack would find them. Anything to bring Amelia some peace.

Just before seven the next evening, Jack made his way towards The Sea Glass Restaurant, an elegant dining spot moored off the jetty at Blue Water Bay. Owned by a local named Sam Wilson, it was known for its stunning glass-bottomed dining area where guests could enjoy their meals while watching vibrant sea life glide below them. Jack had known about the popular restaurant before arriving on

Puffin Island, and having read the fabulous five-star reviews he was looking forward to the meal almost as much as the chance to ask Edgar some important questions.

As he walked up the jetty, he could see that the restaurant was even more impressive up close. It was a beautifully restored boat, its sides lined with warm, twinkling lights that were reflected in the water. As Jack stepped on board, he took in the details: polished wood, brass fittings and gentle lighting that added an air of sophistication to the entire experience. The restaurant had a unique open-air design, with large windows and retractable panels that allowed an uninterrupted view of the bay. The decor was tasteful, with subtle nautical touches, a hint of old-world seafaring charm mixed with contemporary luxury. The tables were set with crisp white linen, elegant glassware and sea-green candles that flickered softly, casting delicate shadows over the room. The showpiece was the walls, a striking mosaic of colourful sea glass, each piece telling a story. The glass, in shades of soft aqua, cobalt-blue and seafoam-green, had been carefully collected over the years, some pieces washed ashore by the waves, others smoothed by the relentless tide.

The restaurant had a small wooden box of glass pieces and guests were encouraged to select a shard that spoke to them, place it on the wall and stick it there with a special glue. Over time, the collection had grown into a living, breathing canvas, the glass fragments glistening like tiny jewels against the weathered wood of the wall, which had been framed with driftwood collected from the island's beaches. The effect was mesmerising, a beautiful mix of nature and memory, each piece capturing the essence of

Puffin Island and its coastal charm, and recording the many visitors who had come to experience its magic.

A waiter, impeccably dressed in a navy suit with a crisp white shirt and a neat bow tie, greeted Jack with a polite nod as he approached the host stand. His smile was warm yet formal. 'Good evening, sir. Do you have a reservation?'

'I do, booked under the name of Edgar Carmichael,' Jack replied.

The waiter's expression remained courteous, and he checked the reservation book briefly before looking back at Jack. 'Ah, yes. This way, sir. Your table is ready.'

He led Jack through the softly lit dining room, weaving between the tables to a spot near the centre of the restaurant. The table was perfectly positioned, offering a stunning view, through the glass panels embedded in the floor, of the water below. Lights had been installed under the boat, casting a gentle glow that illuminated the depths. Schools of fish darted gracefully, their shimmering silver bodies catching the fading light, while the occasional jellyfish floated lazily by, its translucent form adding a serene touch to the underwater spectacle. The sight was mesmerising, an enchanting blend of nature and design that brought the sea right into the heart of the restaurant.

'This place is incredible,' he murmured as he settled into his seat. The waiter smiled and handed him a menu before taking himself off to the bar to fetch the whisky sour Jack had ordered.

As he waited, Jack glanced around the bustling restaurant. It had been a while since he'd dined out – he usually just grabbed a ready meal for one – but seeing the exquisite food being carried towards other tables, he knew he'd been missing out and vowed to make the effort to get out more.

His drink arrived and he took a sip. Perfect: tart, but with just the right amount of sweetness. He gazed out through a window, his mind drifting back to the past, to the times he'd spent with his father and Edgar and of course Edgar's brother, Arthur, his godfather. Both Arthur and Edgar had been like uncles to him when he was a child. He noticed movement out of the corner of his eye, and turned to see Edgar approaching the table with a crinkled smile.

'There he is,' Edgar greeted him warmly, clapping Jack on the shoulder as he settled in the chair opposite him. 'It's been too long, my boy.'

Jack grinned. 'It's really good to see you. What were the chances of us bumping into each other?'

'Quite high. I do live on the island.' Edgar chuckled, waving the waiter over and ordering a drink. When it arrived he raised his glass. 'To old friends.'

They clinked glasses and then gave the waiter their orders. Jack picked up their conversation from the other day. 'Remember how I was telling you that I've been struggling a bit recently?'

Edgar nodded.

'There's more. I, uh… I dropped my agent quite recently and I ended up writing a rather pointed article about how much I dislike working with agents, which was printed in the nationals.' He glanced at Edgar, whose expression had shifted with interest and surprise. 'The reason I mention this is because my agent was Vivienne Langford.'

Edgar raised an eyebrow. 'Vivienne Langford…'

'I take it by the look on your face that you're not a fan either?'

'Well,' Edgar began, choosing his words carefully, 'Vivienne wasn't exactly loved around here. She ... well, she was married to someone from Puffin Island.'

'Amelia's father,' Jack confirmed.

Edgar nodded. 'Do you know her?'

'Yes. We've actually been kind of dating since I arrived on the island, but I've not yet told her that I've written some quite successful books.'

'And why not?'

'Because I liked the fact she was getting to know me for me, not for what I do for a living.'

'I think you might be overthinking things. Amelia is a lovely, down-to-earth character and values honesty. I'd think about telling her, if I were you, because she'll likely figure it out soon – if she hasn't already. She does own a bookshop, after all.'

'I know. It's just been so nice developing a connection with someone that has nothing to do with my success.'

'You seem to really like her. How do you think things will pan out when you go back to London?'

'That's something I'm not sure about.' Jack had thought about that question a lot in the last twenty-four hours. Even though it was early days with Amelia, he knew he wasn't ready to give her up any time soon. 'Tell me about Vivienne. I understand they got married here?'

Edgar nodded, his expression grim. 'It was a quiet affair, held on the beach here on Puffin Island. Vivienne's idea, of course. She wanted something private, away from prying eyes.'

'That really doesn't sound like the Vivienne I know.'

'She never gave me the impression she was the shy type either.' Edgar paused, his brows furrowing as he frowned. 'In my opinion ... I think Vivienne thought she could avoid questions about her motivations and intentions by keeping the wedding quiet.'

'And what do you think her intentions were?'

'To take his money. Ethan was very affluent as he'd saved wisely and was never one to waste money. Until he met her, of course. I never understood them together. Vivienne was nothing like his first wife.'

'Amelia's mum?'

Edgar nodded. 'Lillian was a lovely, kind, genuine soul. She died of a complication in hospital.'

The waiter appeared at the table with their food and they ordered another couple of drinks.

'Tell me about the wedding.'

'It was ... well, let's just say it wasn't the warmest of weddings. Vivienne had this way of keeping everyone at arm's length so none of us – Ethan's friends – had had time to get to know her. To be honest, I felt it was too soon. What was the rush? Why did they need to get married so quickly after meeting?'

Jack leaned back. 'How did Amelia feel about her?'

Edgar sighed. 'Amelia saw right through her from the start. She's a perceptive young woman, that one. There was always tension between them, and it didn't take long for it to create a rift between Amelia and her father. I observed from a distance, even tried to talk to Ethan about it, but to no avail. Vivienne took over and, for some unknowable reason, Ethan let her.'

'It must have been tough for Amelia,' Jack murmured.

'Tough is putting it mildly,' Edgar replied. 'Amelia adored her father. She was his world, and he was hers. But when Vivienne came along … well, let's just say she wasn't exactly interested in keeping the peace. She seemed to thrive on the tension, the drama. It was as if she enjoyed keeping Amelia on the outside.'

Jack ran a hand through his hair, feeling a surge of frustration on Amelia's behalf. 'And then … the accident.'

'Yes,' Edgar said, his tone grave. 'Amelia was devastated. She lost not only her father but also her best friend. And then there was Vivienne, standing there, inheriting everything.' He shook his head. 'It didn't sit well with a lot of people, myself included.'

Jack felt a knot form in his stomach. 'So Vivienne just swooped in, changed everything, and then…?'

Edgar nodded. 'And then, just like that, she was gone. Sold the yacht, collected her share of the inheritance, closed up the house Ethan left her, and left. And the strange thing is, she doesn't talk about Ethan, not publicly, as far as I know. It's as if he was a chapter of her life she'd rather erase. It all seems very calculated and cold.'

Jack sat there, silent, the weight of Edgar's words settling on him. He could feel the hairs on the back of his neck prickling, a sense of unease creeping into his mind. What exactly had Vivienne been after? And why had Ethan, a man who seemed so grounded, been drawn into her world so easily?

'She was my agent,' he told Edgar, 'and I had no clue about any of this. Not that I'm saying her personal life was any of my business, but you'd think I'd get wind of her getting married.'

Jack's thoughts churned. This was the perfect opportunity to share with Edgar that he'd landed a job at *The Morning Ledger*, writing articles for Vivienne's nephew, a commission that was becoming more dubious by the second. Her personal interest in the piece, evident in her frequent follow-up calls and emails, only deepened the mystery.

And then there was the timing. Who exactly had sent him to Puffin Island – Miles or Vivienne? Her husband's tragic death here made the proposed article feel like a targeted attack, loaded with ulterior motives. Was she seeking to reshape the narrative, perhaps hoping to destroy the island's legacy? Jack couldn't ignore a nagging thought that she might harbour resentment or even a desire for vengeance against the island and its people.

The unsettling idea gripped him. It was clear now that she and Miles were manipulating him, but to what end? For now, though, Jack knew he needed to tread carefully.

Edgar's tone was firm but kind. 'I'm sure I don't have to say this to you of all people,' he continued, his gaze steady on Jack, 'but treat Amelia right. She deserves the world.'

Jack nodded, his expression earnest. 'I know.'

Edgar gave an approving nod. 'Good man.'

He took a sip of his drink, and the two lapsed into a companionable silence, the kind that spoke of mutual respect and understanding. The clinking of cutlery and the murmur of conversation from nearby tables filled the air as they finished their meals.

Jack's thoughts swirled as he processed everything Edgar had shared about Ethan and Vivienne. The weight of it all pressed down on him, yet he also felt reassured. Edgar's openness made it clear he could be trusted. Jack remembered his father advising him that if he was ever in need of help and his godfather wasn't around, Edgar was someone he could turn to.

Jack leaned forward, lowering his voice. 'I've got something I need to share with you. Another reason why I'm here on the island, and it has to do with Vivienne.' He hesitated, choosing his words carefully. 'Miles, her nephew, sent me here to write an article. At first, I thought it was just a simple assignment. But now I'm not so sure. It feels like there's more to it, like they're deliberately trying to make Puffin Island look bad, and I can't figure out what their scheme is, what Vivienne is hoping to achieve.'

Edgar raised a hand, stopping him. 'Before you go any further, think carefully. I'm representing Amelia in her legal battle. I don't want to be put in a position where knowing something could potentially jeopardise the case.'

Jack exhaled sharply, leaning back in his chair as he thought about Edgar's caution. 'If I tell you off the record?'

Edgar's steady gaze didn't waver. 'Off the record, then.'

The room seemed to still as the two men stared at each other. After a moment, Jack nodded, deciding this was a piece of information Edgar needed to hear. 'Miles sent me to write an article about the island, but the way Vivienne has been involved, following up personally with calls and emails, is making me think this isn't just about the island. There's something calculated about it. And given her connection to Ethan and what happened here, I feel like it's all tied together. I just don't know how.'

Edgar's expression grew thoughtful. 'That's troubling,' he said, his voice low. 'In my opinion, Vivienne's not the type to move without a reason. If she's pulling strings, there's a purpose behind it. This might be about more than just an article. You're right to tread carefully.'

Jack asked the question that was preying on his mind. 'Do you think that Vivienne had a hand in Ethan's death?'

'Again, off the record … it's crossed my mind.'

Jack nodded, relieved to have his suspicions shared. He hoped that Edgar would be able to help him piece this puzzle together without putting Amelia at risk.

Edgar leaned back in his chair. 'I don't think Amelia needs to know about this, Jack. She's already dealing with more than enough, and this would only bring her more worry and possibly distrust. She deserves some peace.'

Jack absorbed Edgar's words, his respect for the older man deepening. He was right.

'And I'm sure,' Edgar continued, his tone sharpening slightly, 'I don't need to ask whether you're actually planning to go ahead with that article.'

Jack met Edgar's gaze and nodded. 'You don't. I wouldn't do that to her or to this place. I'll figure out a way to handle it, something that won't harm her or the island.'

Edgar's expression softened, and he gave an approving nod. 'Good man. Amelia deserves someone who'll look out for her, and I'm glad she has that in you. Let's focus on what really matters – helping her get what she's owed and keeping Puffin Island safe from those who don't have its best interests at heart.'

'I'll drink to that.' Jack lifted his glass. Knowing Edgar shared his priorities gave him a renewed sense of determination. He wouldn't let Amelia down, no matter what.

Chapter Twenty-Four

AMELIA

The next morning, after feeding Pawsworth, Amelia swung open the door of the bookshop. The day was as glorious as the one before. As she began to lay out books on the trestle table outside the shop, she couldn't stop smiling, the memory of her date with Jack still vivid in her mind. She'd felt like she was floating all night after he'd dropped her off, and her dreams had been filled with glimpses of that secluded island, the sparkling waterfall and Jack's laughter. It had all been so perfect that she could hardly believe it had happened.

As soon as she'd returned home, she'd texted her friends, unable to keep the excitement to herself. Clemmie, Dilly and Verity had responded with an avalanche of emojis, exclamations and virtual squeals, practically exploding with questions and enthusiasm. She'd given them a somewhat edited version of the day, of course, leaving out certain steamy details.

CLEMMIE

> You do know that according to the book the third date's invitation involves a Cessna plane flying over Zara Quinn's house with a message trailing behind the plane announcing the time and place?

AMELIA

> I'm fully aware.

DILLY

> And it's meant to happen at noon two days after date two

Verity had then suggested they all gather at the shop just in case Jack went through with it, and the others agreed instantly, determined to witness the spectacle if it happened.

By eleven-thirty, they were all there, filling the shop with laughter. Clemmie leaned against a bookcase near the romance section, scrolling through her phone as though determined to be the first to catch a whiff of any news about the impending sky message. Dilly sat cross-legged on the counter, while Verity, the practical one of the group, was stationed by the window, scanning the sky for any sign of an approaching plane.

'You lot should all be at work,' said Amelia, smiling at her friends' enthusiasm.

'We should, but we weren't going to miss this for the world,' replied Dilly. 'It's so romantic.'

'We aren't even sure whether this is going to happen. Flying a plane over Puffin Island seems a little extreme … and who would he know who owns a

The Story Shop

plane?' added Amelia, looking out of the window up at the sky.

'Probably the same person who owns a private island.' Clemmie cocked an eyebrow.

'I think it'll happen,' said Dilly. 'The Northern Lights, hot air balloons, jet skis, private islands and now a plane. I think he's secretly aiming for some kind of world record in over-the-top dates. I'm really chuffed for you, Amelia.'

Amelia laughed as she shelved a stack of newly arrived books.

Just then, Edgar Carmichael, wearing his usual tweed jacket and kind, slightly weary smile, walked into the bookshop.

'Ladies,' he greeted them, a glint of amusement in his eyes at the sight of the small crowd gathered in the shop. 'Am I missing something? Are we waiting for a famous author to appear for a book signing?'

'That's something you need to organise, Amelia; give your little empire some publicity,' Clemmie suggested.

'Good morning, Edgar. Please ignore my friends; they are ... actually it doesn't matter,' Amelia exclaimed, her excitement shifting slightly as she recognised the file that he was holding and realised the nature of his visit. She gestured for him to follow her to the kitchen. 'Is that what I think it is?' she whispered once they were alone.

Edgar nodded. 'A date has been set for the hearing,' he said, his voice calm but determined. 'The judge will pass judgement on whether the terms of your father's last will are valid, and you'll find out if you'll be able to keep the family home.' He handed her the letter.

Amelia took it and glanced over it. 'I'm ready for this.

It's time Vivienne understands that she can't just swoop in and take everything that matters to me.'

Edgar's expression softened. 'I know this hasn't been easy, but we're in a good position. Vivienne's wealth and her other properties will go against her. You aren't in a financial position like Vivienne and your history with the property goes back a lot longer than hers. Ultimately, she doesn't need your family home the way you do.'

Amelia let out a breath she hadn't realised she'd been holding. 'That's what I'm hoping. But...' She hesitated, glancing away, feeling a strange twinge of apprehension. There was something she hadn't shared with Edgar, something personal that she felt was hers alone to protect until the time was right. It wasn't that she didn't trust him – she did – but revealing it now, especially with the legal battle looming, felt like opening herself up in a way she wasn't ready for. What if the judge viewed the information she was withholding as a reason to rule against her?

'Something on your mind?' Edgar asked gently, noticing her hesitation.

She forced a smile, shrugging it off. 'Nothing important. Just nerves, I guess.'

Edgar studied her, his sharp eyes narrowed at her. 'Amelia, whatever it is, you can tell me. Is there anything else I should know?'

She bit her lip. 'No, there's nothing.'

Edgar gave her a long look, but he finally nodded, his expression softening. 'Okay, and trust me, we're in with a good chance.'

As Edgar turned to leave, he chuckled as he passed Clemmie, Dilly and Verity. 'Enjoy your surveillance operation. I don't even want to know what you three are up to.'

Clemmie grinned. 'It's essential work we're doing here.'

Edgar waved as he wandered back down Lighthouse Lane.

'Everything okay?' asked Dilly.

'The court date is set for contesting the will.'

'How are you feeling about that?' asked Verity.

'Nervous and dreading it. If it doesn't go in my favour, the smug look on Vivienne's face…'

'Let's hope the judge has common sense but at this very moment…' Verity looked at her watch. 'We have planes to look out for!'

'I know we joked about it but I really don't think he'll be following the book to the letter,' Amelia protested.

'He sent the flowers at the same time as Asher Knight did,' Dilly pointed out.

As the clock's hands crept closer to noon, they all stood in the doorway of the bookshop looking up at the sky.

'What if he's already flown past and we missed it?' Clemmie asked, her tone half-joking, half-serious.

'Not a chance,' Dilly replied confidently. 'We've been here watching and we'd hear it. There's no way a Cessna could fly over this island without us noticing.'

Amelia tried to keep her composure, but her heart was racing and she couldn't hide the thrill bubbling up inside her. She knew Jack was capable of just about anything, and the idea of him going to such lengths just to surprise her left her a little giddy.

Finally, just as the clock struck twelve, a faint rumbling

sound broke through the air. They all froze, then raced out onto Lighthouse Lane and looked up.

And there it was, a small plane gliding across the clear blue sky, a banner trailing behind it. In bold letters, the message read:

AMELIA, MEET ME AT BLUE WATER BAY TOMORROW AT 8PM – JACK

The girls squealed then erupted into cheers, clapping and laughing. Clemmie was practically jumping up and down while Dilly and Verity exchanged delighted glances, all three as excited as Amelia herself.

'Oh my God,' Clemmie gasped. 'That's ... that's insane! He actually did it!'

Amelia couldn't stop smiling, her heart racing as she stared up at the banner flapping in the breeze. 'I can't believe it.' She laughed, feeling slightly breathless. 'Who even does things like this?'

'Jack, apparently,' Dilly said, grinning. 'And let me tell you, girl, you've got yourself a keeper. We need to know more about this man!'

For a moment, Amelia's heart soared. For the first time in ages, she felt genuinely happy. Carefree, even. The doubts, the court battles, her secrets, none of it mattered in that moment. Right now, she was just a woman standing on the edge of something new and thrilling, watching a sky-written message from a man who made her feel alive. But then her mood suddenly changed.

'I can't go,' she murmured, looking at her three friends in panic.

They stared at her.

'What do you mean, you can't go?'

Amelia walked back into the shop, picked up Pawsworth and cuddled him before placing him back on the counter. 'Because he's going to break my heart. Where is this all going to go?'

'Right up that aisle,' exclaimed Clemmie. 'You've been waiting for someone like this all your life, you can't just give up on it now.'

'His life isn't on Puffin Island. He lives in London.'

'Things change,' reassured Dilly. 'None of us have a crystal ball so there's no point worrying about the future. Live in the now, Amelia. This could be the start of something great if you let it, and let's be honest here, the start of this relationship has been something out of a movie.'

'Something out of a book,' confirmed Amelia. 'Maris Wilde's *The Temptation Bucket List* to be exact!'

'Talking of crystal balls, Cora is holding a psychic night at The Olde Ship Inn. That's going to be so much fun.'

'I'm not being honest,' blurted Amelia.

Clemmie immediately sobered and gestured towards an armchair. Then she shut the door of the shop and turned the sign to 'CLOSED'. Amelia sat down and the three friends did likewise. 'Get talking,' ordered Clemmie. 'What do you mean?'

They watched Amelia closely as she stood up, walked towards the travel section, pulled out a book and placed it on the small table in front of them. 'This is not to be repeated. It stays between the four walls of this bookshop, understand?' She hesitated. 'Jack is Jack Hartwell, and I know he's Jack Hartwell, but he doesn't know that I know.'

Clemmie picked up the book and looked at the name on the cover. 'Your Jack is this Jack?'

'I'm confused,' said Dilly.

'He's not told me who he is and I'm guessing that may be because of his books. It's likely women usually want to get to know him just because he's a famous author and a well-known personality. So I'm worried – am I smitten just because I know who he really is? Like, do I like Jack for being Jack, or because he's Jack Hartwell, one of my favourite writers? I need to tell him I know, but how? And when?'

'Give your head a wobble. You don't need to tell him anything. We know you, Amelia, so we can say without doubt that you like him for him. And when he does get round to telling you, you act surprised,' ordered Verity.

'I don't like being deceitful.' As soon as the words left her mouth, Amelia recognised herself for the hypocrite she was, and she wasn't proud of it. She had a secret and knew that soon she needed to be honest about that too, especially with Edgar, in case Vivienne's solicitor used it to hang her out to dry. It was preying on her mind – she wanted to control when that secret came out, but she might not have a choice. No, she needed to tell Edgar, and soon.

Chapter Twenty-Five

AMELIA

It was late and Amelia had been lying in bed for the past hour. Pawsworth was curled up at the foot of her bed, a comforting, purring presence as she read the last couple of chapters of Ellis Ford's debut novel. Reaching the last page, she set the book down, feeling utterly bereft, as though she'd just said goodbye to a dear friend. It wasn't just that the story had come to an end, it was the writing itself – intimate, raw, and even a little haunting – that lingered, leaving her with that rare ache only the best novels could produce.

She shook her head, marvelling at a debut that definitely did deserve the hype. It read like the work of an established literary giant, and yet Ellis Ford was a complete unknown. She pondered why some books exploded into the world, while others seemed to drift quietly, only to be discovered by those with a knack for finding hidden gems. It was one of the strangest mysteries of the publishing world, a funny old game that seemed less about merit and more about the whims of visibility. She'd lost count of how many times she'd seen books hyped on social media, pushed by influencers whose every post seemed to turn to gold, only to pick up those books and feel very underwhelmed.

Pawsworth stirred, stretching and yawning as Amelia placed Ellis Ford's book on her bedside table. She reached for the remote control. She wasn't usually one to flip the TV on late at night, but tonight was different. Her mind was a storm of emotions; memories of her father tugged at her heart, bittersweet and vivid, while her recent conversation with her friends about Jack's true identity replayed in her head, filling her with both hope and unease. She wished desperately for a crystal ball, some way to glimpse the future, to know how everything was going to turn out, but all she had were questions and the restless stirrings of her own heart.

She hit the power button and the TV screen illuminated her room, drawing Pawsworth's sleepy gaze for a second before he nestled back into her blanket. A familiar theme tune filled the air, signalling the start of *Late Night Conversations*, one of those enduring talk shows that had been on the air for years. The host, Charles Stone, a distinguished man with silver hair, walked on stage, his warm smile setting the tone. Amelia had always admired his interviewing style. He had a way of making his guests feel at ease while drawing out stories that no one else could.

But when Charles began introducing his guest, Amelia froze, her pulse quickening. She could hardly believe her ears. 'Tonight, we're joined by one of the industry's most influential literary agents, a woman whose clients are among the most successful and prolific authors in the world. Please welcome to the studio ... Vivienne Langford.'

Amelia's eyes widened as the camera shifted, showing Vivienne walking onto the stage. She was as immaculate as ever, dressed in a tailored black suit, her hair sleek, shiny and falling down her back. Her expression was cool and composed as she exchanged greetings with Charles, taking her seat opposite him. The last person Amelia expected to see on her television tonight was the woman who'd once belittled her writing and discouraged her father's dreams, yet here she was, sitting in the spotlight, looking every bit the successful agent.

'Vivienne, it's a pleasure to have you here,' Charles began. 'You've been in the industry for over three decades now, and your clients read like a who's who of bestsellers, with combined sales of over forty million books. You're one of the most successful literary agents in the business and still identifying the biggest hits to this day. Tell us, what's the secret to finding the hidden gems?'

Vivienne gave a small smile, the kind that didn't quite reach her eyes. 'Charles, there's no secret, really. It's a combination of instinct and experience. You come to know what resonates with readers, and you're constantly keeping an eye on the trends, but sometimes you also just know a manuscript has that something special, that spark that will make it fly off the shelves.'

Amelia rolled her eyes, a bitter taste in her mouth as she listened. Her father had had that spark, he'd poured his heart and soul into his stories, stories that Vivienne had dismissed without a second thought. Amelia wondered if

Vivienne had ever regretted not giving her father a chance, or if she'd even thought about him at all after his death.

Charles leaned forward. 'And you've represented some extraordinary authors over the years. Anyone you're particularly excited about right now?'

Vivienne's expression softened, and Amelia recognised that familiar gleam in her eye. 'Well, there's always new talent emerging. But there's one debut I'm particularly proud of, one that's been performing exceptionally well since its publication in July – *The Forgotten Portrait* by Ellis Ford.' She smiled, obviously pleased with herself. 'I just knew from the moment I read it that it was special, and of course I was right. In only a couple of months it's taken the book world by storm, selling over two million copies, and I've just negotiated a deal for a TV adaptation.'

'That's just amazing, and I bet Ellis Ford cannot believe his fortune.'

'He won't have a fortune,' Amelia muttered to herself, 'if she has anything to do with it.'

'I think he's very happy with the way things are going,' Vivienne replied.

'And even with all the success, Ellis Ford still wishes to remain out of the spotlight?'

Vivienne nodded. 'I think you find that with a lot of creative geniuses. They write for themselves, not the fame it may bring. They don't crave attention and don't want to be famous either. They want their private life to stay private, and that's why having an agent like myself can be so useful. I can make them successful while also keeping their identity under wraps.'

'I've Googled Ellis Ford myself and there's nothing

anywhere so I'm assuming he's writing under a pseudonym?'

Vivienne smiled. 'I can neither confirm nor deny.'

Charles continued. 'Ellis Ford's work has certainly captivated readers. What do you think it is about this story that's resonated with so many people?'

Vivienne leaned back, a practised confidence in her posture. 'I think it's the authenticity. Readers today crave something real, something that makes them feel deeply. *The Forgotten Portrait* does that. It taps into universal themes of loss, resilience and redemption. And Ellis has a remarkable voice. I knew from the first page that this was something special and it will be brought to the small screen just before Christmas with a star-studded cast.'

'Shall we talk about the one that got away?' added Charles.

Amelia sat up straight, noticing that Vivienne suddenly looked a little uncomfortable.

'Tell us about Maris Wilde. The latest figures'—Charles looked at his notes—'have her sales at over five million. Her latest novel, *The Temptation Bucket List*, is the fastest-selling novel of all time and it's surely only a matter of time before it will hit the big screen. From our research, it appears Maris is an astute businesswoman who has negotiated all the deals herself, leaving authors questioning whether they actually need an agent at all. What are your thoughts on that?'

'Yes, Charles!' Amelia exclaimed out loud, watching Vivienne squirm a little.

There was no denying Charles had put her on the spot. Amelia watched as she took a sip of water. 'Yes, Maris

Wilde slipped through my fingers,' she admitted. 'She should be congratulated for her negotiation skills and the way she has represented her own books within this industry.'

Amelia noticed Vivienne had swerved the question about needing an agent; thankfully, Charles had noticed too. 'And as for agents? With a rapidly changing publishing landscape, and with self-publishing becoming more accessible, are literary agents still really needed?' he pressed.

Vivienne smiled a polished, confident smile, no doubt one she'd perfected over years in the business. She took a moment, as if carefully weighing her words, and then leaned forward, addressing both Charles and the audience.

'Absolutely, Charles. Literary agents are more essential than ever,' she began, her tone measured but passionate. 'There's a common misconception that agents are simply middlemen. But the reality is, we're advocates, champions and mentors for our clients. We're not just finding publishers and securing deals, we're helping authors navigate an industry that's often complicated and, at times, overwhelming.'

Vivienne turned to the audience, holding their gaze. 'Agents bring a level of insight and expertise that goes beyond contracts and negotiations. We have our fingers on the pulse of the market trends, an understanding of what resonates with readers, and relationships with editors and publishers that have taken years to build. When a manuscript crosses my desk, my job is to look at it from every angle, see how it can be marketed, how it fits in the current literary landscape, and what can be done to elevate it from a good book to a great one.'

She paused, letting her words sink in. 'Self-publishing is a wonderful option for many writers, and I have great respect for those who pursue it. But traditional publishing comes with certain advantages, and it's an agent's job to ensure that an author maximises those opportunities. We don't just find a home for a book. We fight for the best possible terms, advocate for quality marketing and publicity, and work to ensure that our authors' work reaches its full potential. An agent is like a compass and a guide in a dense forest. When you have someone by your side who knows the terrain, it's a lot easier to find the right path.'

Amelia shook her head in disbelief.

Vivienne smiled again, a touch warmer this time. 'At the end of the day, an agent isn't just there to make a deal. We're invested in our authors' careers for the long haul. We believe in their voices, in their stories and in their dreams. And to me, that's a partnership worth having.'

Charles nodded, clearly impressed, and a murmur of approval rippled through the audience.

'And as for Maris Wilde ... I wish her every success with her career.'

'So the question is, will you go and watch *The Temptation Bucket List* if it does hit the big screen?'

'Probably not.' She smiled. 'I'll concentrate on my own clients.'

The sound of applause wrapped up the interview and Charles thanked Vivienne for being his guest before the credits rolled.

Amelia felt ... angry. Vivienne had walked into her life and made it unbearable every moment since, and now she was out there thriving, with no mention of the devastation she was causing. Amelia wanted to shout from the rooftops exactly what that woman had done to her family.

Amelia had been biding her time for too long. Her father's work might never see the light of day, but she knew she was holding a trump card. First, though, she had to show it to Edgar, to let him advise her on how to play it with the maximum impact.

Chapter Twenty-Six

JACK

Jack glanced at his reflection, adjusting the sleek black bow tie and running a hand down the front of his jacket. The polished shoes, tailored tuxedo and cufflinks were not his usual attire, but he wanted tonight to be special. He hoped that Amelia would realise tonight's dress code mirrored exactly what was in the book.

Edgar's advice had been playing on his mind and he agreed: he didn't need to keep his identity a secret from Amelia. He knew she was the type of girl to like him for who he was, and he had probably just been over-cautious. Being on Puffin Island was making him think more about his future, and he knew now that he wanted her to be a part of it, which meant total honesty. He checked his watch, feeling a flutter of nerves. Taking one last look in the mirror, he left the B&B and began to walk towards Blue Water Bay.

When he arrived there, he took a moment to admire the scene he'd set. Flickering tealights in small glass jars illuminated a path from the sand to the jetty, leading to The Sea Glass Restaurant. And then he saw her.

Amelia was walking down the beach towards him, her floaty silvery-grey dress swirling around her. She'd understood the dress code perfectly. Her hair cascaded loosely over her shoulders, the wind lifting a few stray curls to frame her face perfectly. As she came closer, Jack's heart raced.

She lifted her hand in a wave and chuckled. 'Not a puffin scrunchie in sight.'

He laughed, taking a step towards her, unable to look away from her smile. 'You look stunning.'

'And you don't look too bad yourself.'

He kissed her softly before offering his hand. As they walked hand in hand along the path of tealights, Jack couldn't resist looking at her again, unable to believe he was lucky enough to have her by his side.

'Did you do all this?' she asked.

'With the help of Sam.'

The lights led them to the entrance of The Sea Glass Restaurant. He gestured for her to step inside, followed her and awaited her reaction.

'Where is everyone? The place is empty.'

Jack grinned.

'Wait ... did you hire out the whole restaurant?' she asked, wide-eyed.

'I'd like to take the credit for that, but...'

'But?'

Jack rubbed the back of his neck, a sheepish smile spreading across his face. 'Well, let's just say I had a little help. It turns out one of Edgar's clients had hired the restaurant for a private event but couldn't make it at the last minute. The booking was non-refundable, so Edgar worked it out with Sam to make sure the reservation didn't go to waste.' He glanced at her, his grin softening.

'Edgar? How do you know Edgar?'

'He's actually a very good friend of my father's, and his brother is my godfather. I bumped into him at the cove after I'd set up the tent for our first date. We had a catch-up over dinner the other night.'

'I can't believe this. What a small world! You actually know Edgar.'

Jack smiled. 'It's funny, isn't it? The way connections work. They say everyone in the world is linked by six degrees of separation, but sometimes it feels like even less. I mean, think about it, how often do we cross paths with people who turn out to be tied to someone we already know?'

'I just can't believe it.'

'When Edgar mentioned this cancelled booking it reinforced what I've learned about the people on this island – that they love to help out ... especially when it comes to true love.'

Amelia blinked, caught off guard by the last two words. 'True love, eh?' she echoed, her voice light but her pulse skipping a beat in her throat.

He held her hand as they walked towards their table. A bottle of champagne was already chilling beside their place settings, and as they sat, a waiter appeared to pour them each a glass.

Amelia looked at him, her eyes sparkling. 'I don't know what to say. It's all... I'm actually speechless.'

They raised their glasses, and Jack met her gaze. 'To tonight,' he said, his voice soft.

They began their meal with a beautifully arranged platter of lobster and oysters. The champagne complemented the meal perfectly, and Jack saw Amelia's face light up with each bite.

'Who knew you had such a flair for romance?' she teased, giving him a playful glance.

Jack laughed, raising an eyebrow. 'There's more to me than meets the eye, Miss Brown.'

'Oh, I'm beginning to see that,' she replied with a warm smile, before taking a sip of champagne. 'And I have to say, I'm impressed ... but...'

'But?' he questioned.

'I know we're mirroring the book and the characters have no clue about each other and their real lives as such. But ... you know everything there is about me. I work in a bookshop and you know about my dad and me ... contesting the will ... yet you're still very much a mystery.'

Jack put down his knife and fork, then reached across the table and took her hand.

'You look very serious,' she said, sounding nervous.

'Amelia,' he began, 'there's something I want to share with you. Something I probably should have told you earlier ... and now I'm going to say it, it seems ridiculous that I didn't tell you the moment I was blown into your beautiful bookshop.'

'Go on,' she said gently.

He held her gaze. 'I don't just work in lifestyle

journalism or whatever it was I said,' he admitted, giving her a small, nervous smile. 'My work is a bit better known than I let on. I'm Jack Hartwell, and you have many of my books on your bookshelves.'

Amelia's eyes widened. 'Wait, not *the* Jack Hartwell? *The* Jack Hartwell?' she repeated.

He chuckled somewhat sheepishly. 'The one and only. I wanted to tell you, but … I was just enjoying the anonymity, you know? I liked being "Jack" to you, without any of the baggage that name might carry.'

'Jack Hartwell, the travel writer, right here on Puffin Island. Now I get why you were so good with all those adventure ideas! I mean, you're practically the king of travel.'

'Oh God, no, I don't do this all the time… Actually, I do this none of the time. That's partly why I wanted to keep myself to myself. I've found when I tell people who I am they change towards me and want to be my new best friend.'

'That's understandable,' said Amelia. 'And is that why you're here? Oh my God…' Her smile slipped.

'What is it?' he asked, noticing her sudden look of alarm.

'All this, all your romantic gestures, it's just for a book, isn't it? It's not real, is it? You're just writing about these experiences and using them to inspire your next story. It's just research.'

'Absolutely not,' Jack replied, hoping to instantly squash her doubts. 'I was blown into that bookshop for a reason and I believe that reason was to meet you. But … it is true that I've been struggling with my last book, the final one in my contract. My ideas just weren't flowing, and sales of my other books have been dropping in recent years. That's part of the reason I came to Puffin Island – I was hoping to find some inspiration. But please believe me when I tell you that everything we've experienced is real.'

She squeezed his hand. 'That's a relief. And how is that inspiration going?'

'The temptation bucket list has made things a lot more interesting, and meeting you has been like finding a fresh page in a worn-out book.'

'I see what you did there.'

'You're the best thing that's happened to me in a long time and I mean that.'

'That's one of the loveliest things anyone's ever said to me, Jack.'

He paused. The next words needed to be said. 'There's one more thing I need to be honest about, though,' he added, meeting her gaze. 'We also have someone in common…'

She looked at him quizzically.

'Vivienne Langford was my agent. Until recently.'

Amelia visibly stiffened. 'How do you know I know Vivienne Langford? I never mentioned her name,' she asked, sounding uneasy.

'I did some online sleuthing after you told me about your father's accident. I was just curious, I suppose, and that's when I saw her name. I was surprised to learn she was married to your father, because I didn't know she had been married at all, and she usually isn't one for keeping things private.'

'And what's your story with Vivienne?'

Jack leaned back in his chair, considering for a moment before answering. 'I sacked her.'

Amelia raised an eyebrow. 'She would not have liked that.'

'She didn't,' Jack admitted.

'How did you meet her?'

Jack exhaled. 'It started with an enthusiastic young writer with huge dreams attending the London Book Fair, clutching a manuscript that he'd poured his heart and soul into. I'd organised a meeting with her and emailed my manuscript beforehand. Vivienne is … well, she's not easily impressed. She told me straightaway that my work didn't stand out from the crowd but added that I should keep her posted if I received any offers. It wasn't exactly encouraging, but it was something.'

'So what happened next?' Amelia asked, leaning in slightly, intrigued.

'I kept sending my manuscript to publishers and finally got an offer. I was thrilled, of course, and posted about it on social media. That's when she reached out to me, congratulating me and saying she'd love to have me on board at the agency. She offered to look over the contract with the publisher. It seemed perfect at the time.'

'But it wasn't?'

Jack shook his head. 'No, it wasn't. What I didn't realise was that while most publishers' contracts are standard, agency contracts aren't. She'd made some … adjustments. The version I signed gave her rights to my books indefinitely. She'd stitched me up.'

'That's awful,' Amelia murmured. 'How did you find out?'

'She had been doing nothing to earn her commission for a long while so I decided to part ways, and that's when clauses in her contract came back to haunt me. She'd made sure her agency held onto the rights in perpetuity, which complicated everything. It was a mess. I had no choice but to terminate our agreement and fight to regain control over my work.'

Amelia's eyes widened. 'That must have been a nightmare.'

'It was,' Jack said grimly. 'But it was a lesson learned. Always read the fine print. And Vivienne? In my eyes she's a crook who, despite what she might claim in TV interviews, cares nothing for the author, only herself.'

'Did you have any friends in the industry you could turn to?'

Jack shook his head. 'Not at all. You interact almost exclusively over social media. Support those with the same publisher. On the whole, being an author in London is a lonely existence. People have their own lives and families to focus on.'

'So why stay there?' Amelia asked cautiously. 'If we're being honest tonight, Jack, I need you to know that I don't like the thought of you going back to London and us never seeing one another again.'

'That's not going to happen, because of course you're going to see me again,' he reassured her. 'Puffin Island seems to have worked its magic on me, and I'm convinced I was sent here for a reason.'

'You were *sent* here?'

'Just a figure of speech.' Edgar was right, there was no

need to fuel the fire and share with Amelia why he'd actually ended up on Puffin Island. Amelia meant more to him than earning a bit of extra cash writing an article he didn't agree with, so there was no way he was going through with it. He reached across the table and took her hand in his. 'I want to explore what this is, and I promise I'm not going to disappear.'

'Good, I'm glad to hear it,' she replied. 'And why do you want to see me again?' she teased.

'Because you're a breath of fresh air, and different from anyone I've ever met. What I love about you is that you do what makes you happy. You love books, so you open a bookshop. You love puffins, so you wear those cute fluffy puffin jumpers. And you surround yourself with the right kind of people, people who lift you up, who want to see you winning at life. When I go back to London, we'll work this out, if we both want to.'

'We will. I feel the same and all this'—she glanced around the restaurant—'is just perfect. Spending time with you is perfect.'

'Dessert?'

Dinner over, they walked hand in hand along the jetty, savouring the warm night air and the sounds of the sea, neither wanting the evening to end.

When they reached the sandy shore, Jack tilted her face towards his. 'This was another best night I've had in ... well, I don't even know how long,' he said softly.

'Me too,' she replied, looking into his eyes.

Jack leaned in, capturing her lips in a kiss that was gentle, yet filled with the depth of everything he felt, a kiss that spoke of possibilities yet to come.

When they finally pulled apart, Amelia smiled up at him. 'So, what's next on the adventure list, Mr Hartwell?'

Jack slipped an arm around her shoulders as they strolled back towards Lighthouse Lane. 'Well, Miss Brown,' he said with a teasing grin, 'it seems we might just have to find out together. In the book, Asher and Zara's final date takes place at that coastal cabin. Remember? They write letters to each other by candlelight, sharing secrets no one else in the world knows.' His gaze softened as he added, 'So, Amelia Brown, what secrets are you hiding?'

Feeling her heart race, Amelia looked up at him. 'What secrets could I possibly have?'

Their steps fell in sync as they walked towards the bookshop, the gentle rhythm a quiet reminder of the connection between them. When they reached the door, they both paused.

Amelia pointed to the door. 'Do you want to come in?' Jack hesitated, his expression softening. 'I do, but I'm not going to,' he said.

Disappointment flickered across her face, and he caught it immediately. With a gentle squeeze of her hand, he continued, 'I want to do this properly. I want to date you, drop you at home, and spend the rest of the night looking forward to the next time I see you. I want this to be perfect.'

Amelia's smile returned, warm and full of understanding. 'Sounds good,' she whispered.

Before she could say more, he leaned in and kissed her tenderly, his lips brushing hers with a quiet promise of all the things to come.

He watched her close the bookshop door, the soft click of the latch echoing in the quiet night. It had taken everything in his power not to follow her through that door, but he wanted to do this right.

As he walked back down Lighthouse Lane, something Amelia had said to him earlier that evening came back to him. What was keeping him in London? He turned the question over again and again, only to arrive at the same answer: absolutely nothing.

Chapter Twenty-Seven

AMELIA

The Olde Ship Inn was buzzing with the kind of excitement that only small-town events could bring. Fairy lights were strung along the old wooden beams, and tables were crammed together to make room for tonight's attraction: a psychic night with Madam Zelda. *The woman who knows all, sees all*, according to her flyer, which looked as if it had been hand-drawn by an enthusiastic child. Still, her name had managed to drum up a fair crowd.

Amelia arrived with Clemmie, Dilly and Verity, who were all chatting animatedly about what kind of visions Zelda might see tonight.

'Oh, I'm sure she's very skilled in, uh … generalised statements,' Clemmie said with a smirk as they squeezed into a corner table next to her grandmother Betty, Dilly's aunt Annie, and Becca from the Cosy Kettle.

Dilly rolled her eyes. 'She'll probably take one look at my palms and tell me I'm about to come into a windfall, just like the last psychic at the summer fair.'

They laughed as Dan, one of the pub landlords, leaned over their table, grinning. 'You ladies ready for the most mind-blowing night of your lives?'

Amelia laughed, taking a sip of her drink. 'Dan, if she tells us one of us is about to meet a tall, dark stranger, I'm holding you responsible.'

Dan winked then tapped the side of his nose. 'Well, keep your wits about you. Rumour has it that Madam Zelda is the real deal. She told my mum her favourite colour once, and I swear she was spot-on.'

With the stage set, Madam Zelda entered with a flourish, looking as if she'd stepped out of a carnival fortune-teller's booth. She was dressed in a flowing purple gown that shimmered in the dim pub light, and draped in far too many scarves and beads. Her dark hair, shot through with silver, was barely visible beneath an enormous, glittering purple turban adorned with a single iridescent feather that bounced and swayed as she moved. Her eyes were lined with a heavy layer of kohl, giving her a mysterious look, and her lips were painted a deep, dramatic crimson. Gold rings gleamed on almost every finger, and around her neck and from her ears hung an assortment of charms, pendants and dangling earrings that chimed faintly whenever she turned her head.

In her hand, Madam Zelda held a glass orb that she insisted was a genuine crystal conduit to the other side (although Amelia whispered to her friends it looked suspiciously like a paperweight), and she waved it around as she spoke, claiming it helped her tune into the spirits' whispers.

Perched on the makeshift stage, she was a showwoman of the highest order.

'Good evening, spirits and souls of Blue Water Bay! I'm Madam Zelda, gifted with visions from beyond the veil. I see all, I know all, and tonight, I'm here to reveal the secrets within your souls!'

'Watch out, Granny, I bet you have a few secrets!' Clemmie nudged her grandmother who playfully pushed her away.

'Tonight, I'll be reading auras and connecting with energies. Spirits are already speaking to me!' She closed her eyes dramatically and took a deep breath, waving her hands in little circles. 'Yes, the spirits are very active here tonight. They're telling me … they're telling me'—she opened one eye, peeking at the audience before she continued—'that someone here has recently changed their washing-up liquid?'

Amelia stifled a giggle as an older woman in the front row gasped. 'Oh, that's me! I changed from lemon to lavender just last week!'

Madam Zelda gave her an approving nod. 'The spirits thank you. Lavender is much more conducive to positive energies.'

She closed her eyes again, her face scrunched up as if she were trying to pick up a faint radio signal. 'And now … someone else is facing a very big decision. Yes, it's life-changing. The spirits say you're not sure, but you should trust your instincts!'

This time, it was Clemmie's grandmother, Betty, who let out a loud exclamation. 'That's me! I couldn't decide whether to get the cottage re-roofed or just patched up.'

Madam Zelda's eyes sparkled. 'The spirits say ... you should re-roof it. Patch jobs never last!'

Betty, clearly delighted, nodded with satisfaction, glancing around with a grin. 'I always knew I had the spirits looking out for me!'

'Now,' Madam Zelda announced, holding her hands high. 'I'm sensing a love triangle in the room ... a very complicated one.'

There was a collective intake of breath. Everyone knew Puffin Island was not immune to a little small-town gossip.

'Who?' whispered Dilly.

'Shh...' muttered Clemmie.

'I'm seeing ... yes, I'm seeing ... two souls in conflict!' Madam Zelda declared dramatically. 'He has a huge sack.'

'Oo-er, that seems a little too much information!' Verity giggled.

'Someone has been skiving off their job and sharing delights at number thirty-nine. I can see the number and a lady with long blonde hair, a blue nightie and ... I can't repeat what else I can see.' She raised her eyebrows then her finger jabbed towards a table in the back corner where Alf, the local postman, was sitting, cringing with a look of absolute terror as she continued. 'Alf, the spirits say your wife knows but she doesn't mind as secretly she has been waiting for you to leave her for years. She would like the house and the dog, but you can keep your mother.'

The room erupted into laughter as Alf turned bright red, hiding his face behind his pint glass.

Amelia was doubled over in laughter. 'Poor Alf,' she exclaimed.

'Everyone has known about his affair for years; it's why

our post never arrives until late afternoon on a Friday!' added Clemmie.

As Madam Zelda moved around the room, calling out predictions with outlandish theatrics, everyone was thoroughly entertained by her increasingly bizarre statements, from 'You'll soon cross paths with a very large seagull' to 'Avoid the bakery this Wednesday, the spirits sense a burnt batch of scones!'

'I do not burn my scones,' shouted Betty in a dismissive tone.

'Maybe not but sometimes on a Friday you travel across to Sea's End first thing and buy up their bread so you don't have to bake your own.'

'Betty!' exclaimed Amelia.

Betty looked sheepish and swigged back a glass of Guinness and black. 'I do not!' she protested. 'Maybe once, when I had a hangover.'

Then Madam Zelda stilled, the smile fading as she closed her eyes once more, her voice dropping to a whisper.

'There is ... something else tonight. Something serious.'

The room fell silent, and Amelia felt a shiver of suspense. Madam Zelda's eyes opened.

'One among you is carrying ... a secret. A secret that has been hidden for too long. It's a weight on your soul, a revenge secret, and very soon this secret will be revealed.'

A murmur ran through the crowd, but Madam Zelda's gaze was unflinching as it fixed upon Amelia. Amelia could feel the eyes of her friends turn towards her and gave an awkward laugh.

Clemmie nudged her, 'What's the big secret, Amelia? Spill it!'

Amelia's pulse was racing. She began to shake her head.

Madam Zelda didn't seem satisfied. She raised a hand, palm outward, and closed her eyes, swaying as if catching the wisps of some otherworldly vision. 'It's strong ... a powerful secret, and as I said, it will be unravelled soon. There's no stopping it now.'

The silence thickened, and Amelia forced a laugh, trying to shake off the eerie feeling creeping up her spine. 'Maybe she means I've secretly been keeping a stash of chocolate biscuits behind the till.'

The crowd chuckled, but Madam Zelda remained solemn. 'The spirits have spoken, and they do not joke. Keep this in mind, my dear,' she said, her gaze locked on Amelia.

The rest of the evening passed in high spirits, with Madam Zelda making increasingly bizarre predictions. When she got to Clemmie, she gasped theatrically and declared, 'You, my dear, will find your true love ... when you least expect it. I see a palace and a garden party.'

'You're going to marry a prince!' quipped Dilly.

'There are no available princes left!' Clemmie rolled her eyes then grinned. She turned to Zelda. 'Can you tell me more?'

Madam Zelda nodded wisely. 'A past scandal makes the present stronger.'

Clemmie raised her eyebrows.

Then it was Verity's turn, and Madam Zelda waved her hands with great flair. 'You, my dear, are destined for great things in the realm of ... of...' She paused, looking around as if waiting for inspiration to strike... 'Dogs, lots of them! But not just any dogs, no, they're part of something larger. I see a restaurant on the water, a haven for dog lovers, where patrons can dine with their furry companions. and maybe even a dog-friendly menu.'

Verity laughed, shaking her head. 'Could you imagine me suggesting to Sam that he turns The Sea Glass Restaurant into a dog café? He'd be horrified!'

As the night wound down they all spilled out of the pub discussing Madam Zelda's wild declarations and grand gestures. Clemmie nudged Amelia, her eyes twinkling. 'So, what's the big secret, eh?'

Amelia rolled her eyes. 'Surely you don't believe what Madam Zelda says?'

Verity chuckled, throwing an arm around Amelia's shoulders. 'Well, apparently, it's all coming out soon anyway! So brace yourself!'

They all dissolved into laughter as they walked back along the cobbled streets, the fresh sea air blowing away any lingering tension. Amelia tried to dismiss Madam Zelda's serious expression, the intensity in her eyes when she'd looked at her. After all, it was just for show, a funny, ridiculous performance meant to entertain. Yet a tiny part of Amelia couldn't help wondering what lay ahead for her. The court date was fast approaching and before it came she'd need to seek Edgar's guidance on whether to share her secret with the court.

Chapter Twenty-Eight
JACK

Jack sat at his desk in the bedroom at the B&B, the early morning light filtering through the curtains. When he'd first arrived at Puffin Island, he hadn't expected that writing in his journal would turn into the most natural, effortless process of storytelling he'd done in years. What began as personal musings, reflecting on the island's quiet beauty and his unexpected feelings for Amelia, was starting to turn into a fully-fledged manuscript, a novel that felt raw, unfiltered, deeply personal and something he could be truly proud of.

This wasn't the structured writing he was used to in his travel fiction. It was different, something closer to his heart, an exploration of love, vulnerability and the charm of life in a small town where he was made to feel at home.

Opening up his laptop, he found an email from Miles that had landed at six a.m. Jack knew he was itching for a draft of the article, but he couldn't tell Miles just yet that he'd changed his mind, because first he wanted to run something past his editor, Laura.

They had been through several successful books together, but this one felt different and he was eager to hear her thoughts. He opened a new message. He attached the manuscript, then wrote a brief note, trying to keep it casual.

Subject: New Pages from Puffin Island

Hi Laura,

I've been keeping a bit of a personal journal since I got here, and it's accidentally turned into … well, a novel. It's a little different from my usual, so I'm not sure it's what you'd expect. I'd love for you to take a look and let me know your honest thoughts.

No rush, and feel free to tell me if I'm crazy for thinking there's a book here.

Cheers,
Jack

With a final deep breath, Jack pressed send, his heart racing with excitement and nerves. As the email made its way to Laura's inbox, an unexpected sense of calm descended upon him. Even if it wasn't what she was expecting, he'd rediscovered something he'd feared he'd lost – his love of writing. Now, all he could do was wait.

He grabbed his coat and decided to take a walk along the cliff tops and feel the bracing sea breeze. As he watched seabirds dip and dive, his mind drifted to Amelia and their next date, which he wanted to make truly spectacular. Of course he was going to try to mirror the time and delivery of the next invitation from the Maris Wilde book, but he might need a helping hand.

After his walk he grabbed some lunch from Beachcomber Bakery and headed back to the B&B, hoping that Laura had replied to his email. As soon as he took his coat off, he opened up his laptop and was pleased to find her response waiting for him.

Taking a deep breath, he clicked it open and began to read.

Subject: RE: New Pages from Puffin Island

Jack!

I'm absolutely, entirely blown away. This is phenomenal, there's no other way to put it. This story has heart, humour, and, above all, romance. It's layered and real, and it feels like the best thing you've ever written. The way you capture the island and its people and your central characters, Jack and Amelia … they're magnetic. They leap off the page, and I couldn't stop reading!

I think we have something truly special here, Jack. I already have ideas for the cover, something modern yet timeless, maybe with a view of Puffin Island and a hint of romance. I can see this book cover on billboards, buses, even as a stunning display in Piccadilly Circus. This is the kind of story people are craving. Passion!

Let's meet soon to discuss the next steps. For now, keep writing! And Jack, this is going to be big.

Warmly,
Laura

Jack's heart pounded as he read her words, a huge smile spreading across his face. She loved it! More than that, she saw something in it he hadn't dared to believe possible. For the first time in months, he felt that old spark ignite, and then his thoughts turned to Amelia. Technically, he was writing their story, and he wondered if she minded. Of course, he could change the characters' names if she wanted. He only hoped the ending was as happy as he anticipated.

Whirling with excitement, he knew there was no better way to celebrate than by planning his next date with Amelia. She deserved the most memorable date he could dream up. And in his mind, that involved an unusual, magical touch, a message delivered in the most romantic way possible. And he knew just the man to help.

Once again grabbing his coat, Jack headed over to Cliff Top Cottage in search of Pete. Pete was a local legend for his uncanny ways of diagnosing and treating the island's feathered and furry friends, and Jack had a plan that he hoped Pete could help him bring to life. As he approached the quaint stone cottage, set against a backdrop of sweeping cliffs and wildflowers, he saw Pete tending to his garden, a gentle-looking dove perched comfortably on his shoulder. Jack grinned, thinking how perfectly he had timed this.

'Pete!' he called out, waving as he walked up the gravel path. 'Got a minute?'

Pete looked up, a friendly smile spreading across his face. 'Jack! Come on over. What can I do for you?'

'I need a bit of help with something ... romantic, and I think you may be just the man who can help me.'

Pete brushed some soil off his hands. 'Romantic, huh? Does this have anything to do with a certain bookshop owner?'

Jack laughed, rubbing the back of his neck. 'It might. You see, I've been following this romantic bucket list, it's in a book...'

'Which book?'

'Maris Wilde's *The Temptation Bucket List*.'

Pete raised his eyebrows. 'I've heard about that book, isn't it meant to be...'

'A little raunchy, yes, but I'm focusing more on the emotional connection side.' Jack felt himself blush a little. 'I want to invite Amelia to a special date. I thought ... maybe you could help me deliver the invitation in a memorable way.'

Pete tilted his head, intrigued. 'What did you have in mind?'

Jack gestured to the dove that was now perched on a nearby bird table. 'Would it be possible to train a dove to deliver the invitation? I want it to fly over to her at the bookshop. Nothing says romance like an old-fashioned message by dove, don't you think?'

Pete's eyes twinkled. 'Would it be possible?' He shook his head. 'My doves are the best you'll find. This here's Lottie. She's one of my finest, and she loves a good adventure. I think she'd be perfect for the job.' Pete clicked his fingers and Lottie immediately flew to him and nestled on his hand.

'Wow, that was like magic.'

'Have you written the invitation?'

Jack shook his head. 'But I've brought the stuff with me. The invitation needs to be received at approximately one o'clock, if that's possible?'

'Absolutely possible. Write your invitation. Lottie's clever.'

Pete led Jack to a small wooden table, where Jack sat down, took out a small scroll and began to write his invitation. Once finished, he rolled up the scroll and tied it securely with a ribbon, then handed it to Pete, who attached it gently to Lottie's leg. Pete stroked the dove's feathers, whispering something soothing before placing her in a box. He checked his watch. 'We'd better be on our way.' He grabbed his keys and walked towards his van, giving Jack a reassuring nod as he headed off to the bookshop.

Jack watched as Pete's car disappeared down the dirt track, transporting the small white messenger that was about to carry his words straight to the woman who had captured his heart.

Chapter Twenty-Nine
AMELIA

Amelia was in the middle of sorting a new shipment of books, her mind only half on the task at hand as she caught herself daydreaming about Jack. Then, suddenly, Clemmie and Dilly burst through the door.

'Lunch!' Clemmie held up a white paper bag. 'Sandwiches and flapjacks.'

'We thought we'd come and keep you company,' added Dilly. 'I've told Max he needs to up his game with all these romantic dates going on in your life.'

'You've just given birth to twins, you live in the lighthouse, the most romantic building on the island, and Max runs around after you all day every day,' Amelia reminded her friend.

'That he does, but it's still good to keep him on his toes.'

They settled into the armchairs, unpacking their lunch with eager anticipation.

'According to the book, the next invitation should arrive at one o'clock,' stated Dilly.

'Honestly, I can't concentrate.' Clemmie grinned, catching Amelia's eye. 'I wonder what he has planned for you this time.'

'I know it's a date writing letters to each other in a cabin, but I'm not sure how Jack will deliver this invitation.'

'We won't have long to wait. I have a feeling something exciting's about to happen.'

Amelia felt the familiar mix of anticipation and nerves bubbling in her stomach. Ever since Jack had started mirroring Maris Wilde's famous bucket list and organising the most romantic dates, she'd started to believe in the magic of romance again. And now here she was, surrounded by friends who were just as eager as she was to see what he'd planned next.

'What's that noise?' asked Clemmie.

'Probably the pipes playing up again,' replied Amelia.

'That's not pipes.'

There was a gentle but persistent tapping on the shop window. Amelia looked up, startled.

'Oh my … surely not!' she exclaimed.

There, perched outside the window, was a small white dove, its eyes bright and curious. A tiny scroll was tied to its leg with a delicate red ribbon.

'Amelia!' Clemmie gasped, bringing her hands to her heart. 'He's sent a dove!'

Amelia hurried to the door, gently opened it and allowed the dove to flutter onto her wrist. She untied the scroll, her heart pounding as she carefully unrolled the small piece of parchment.

In Jack's handwriting, the note read:

For our next adventure, a journey anew,
A little surprise is waiting for you.
Tomorrow evening, where the stars meet the sea,
In a cabin that's nestled for just you and me.
We'll sit by candlelight, letters to share,
With whispers and laughter filling the air.
A step back in time, just you and me,
In a place where love and magic run free.
At seven, a carriage with horses will stand,
To bring you to me, to a place we had planned.
Wear what you like, what feels right for the night,
A touch of fairy tale magic in sight.

Jack x

She read it twice, feeling her heart race as her two friends gathered around her to read over her shoulder.

'Is this guy actually real?' Clemmie's eyes were wide. 'He sends doves and writes poetry. Is there anything he can't do?'

'Writing letters by candlelight in a cabin? This man is something else,' Dilly agreed, her eyes sparkling.

'We're going to make sure you look perfect tomorrow. Don't you worry about that!'

They watched as the dove cooed and then took off.

The poem still in Amelia's hand, the three of them screamed and hugged each other.

That evening, Amelia lay awake, tossing and turning as the hours crept by. Despite her excitement about the date, there were several things she couldn't stop thinking about. One of them was the mysterious letters by candlelight that had been mentioned in the book by Maris Wilde. In the book, the two lovers each wrote down a secret they'd never shared with anyone, sealed it in an envelope and entrusted it to the other. They also had to include a note stating whether they wished to continue seeing each other or part ways, and the envelopes were to remain unopened for forty-eight hours.

Madam Zelda's reading was also on her mind, as it had struck uncomfortably close to home. Amelia had thought she'd done a convincing job of brushing off the fortune-teller's insinuations, but what if Zelda had seen through her? Surely she couldn't have discovered her secret?

The other matter weighing on her mind was the court case. It loomed large, coming just forty-eight hours after her planned date with Jack – right around the time the letters were meant to be opened, in fact. Part of Amelia wondered if the courtroom was the right place to reveal the truth. Getting even simply wasn't her style, nor was causing anyone public humiliation, but this situation was different. Vivienne was trying to claim her inheritance, and Amelia knew that the truth would strike a nerve that Vivienne wouldn't forget in a hurry.

The next morning, Amelia was up early and eagerly swinging open the bookshop door to start the day. The moment she flipped the sign to 'OPEN', a steady stream of customers began flowing in. Books practically flew off the shelves and Amelia smiled when a couple of tourists purchased books by Jack Hartwell.

Between serving the customers, she reorganised the display table twice, dusted shelves that didn't need dusting and even flicked through a few new arrivals, but her mind kept drifting back to the evening ahead. She still hadn't decided what to wear. Jack had told her to dress comfy, which left her in a whirlwind of possibilities, but her mind kept coming back to the book. Just like the heroine, Zara, Amelia had a mischievous idea brewing. If Jack wanted comfy, then comfy she was going to be. She'd show up in her brand-new puffin pyjamas, with bright teal cuffs and little puffins dotting the fabric. She grinned at the thought, imagining his reaction. She stared at the clock for the umpteenth time that day, relieved to see it was – finally – nearly time to close. She felt the excitement rising and just as she was about to lock the door it burst open.

'The three musketeers have arrived … again!' Clemmie exclaimed as she was followed through the door by Dilly and Verity.

'You would think we were all still at high school. You can't keep turning up every time I have a date.'

'We can, we're invested in this fairytale love affair, and because my life is boring as hell at the moment, I'm living yours with you,' retorted Clemmie.

Amelia held up her new pyjamas. 'He said comfy so this is what I'm going with.'

All three friends looked horrified. 'You can't wear those,' exclaimed Clemmie.

'I can! I love lounging around in my PJs, book in hand, and he specifically said to come comfy.'

'Talking of books...' said Verity.

'We *are* in a bookshop.' Amelia chuckled.

'I saw Vivienne on Charles Stone's chat show. Did you see it?'

'I did.' Amelia took a breath. 'And I finished the Ellis Ford book seconds before it came on air. It pains me to say it, but it was brilliant.'

'I couldn't put it down. I finished it in the early hours of this morning,' said Dilly. 'The twins slept through but I'm still waking up before dawn. It's just a shame Vivienne is going to profit from it. But she won't be full of herself in forty-eight hours' time. There is no way on this earth the judge will rule in her favour.'

'I don't want to think about it, but I hope you're right,' said Amelia. She knew she still needed to have that chat with Edgar, and it troubled her. But that was going to have to wait until tomorrow.

'Are you really wearing those?' asked Dilly.

'I am! This is me.'

'Well, if you're sticking to those pyjamas we need to make the rest of you look stunning.' Dilly guided Amelia up the stairs to the dressing table in her bedroom. Verity popped the cork on a bottle of prosecco and Clemmie stood in the corner texting, before asking Alexa to play Heart Radio. 'Just like the good old days.'

After an hour of chatting, a few curls and a dab of makeup that made her eyes sparkle, Amelia slipped into her PJs along with her puffin slippers.

'I can't believe this is real,' she murmured.

'And we can't believe you're wearing those!' Clemmie shook her head. 'I'm hoping at least you have something sexy underneath them.'

'I can't tell you that!'

'I think he's head over heels for you. Only a man who was truly smitten would put this much effort into making you feel special.' Dilly placed her hands dramatically on her heart. 'Oh my gosh, listen to that!'

The rhythmic sound of hooves echoed on the cobbled street, drawing everyone to the window. Amelia's heart leaped as she peered outside. There, in front of the bookshop, stood a majestic black horse, its glossy coat gleaming. It was harnessed to an elegant carriage adorned with twinkling fairy lights that shimmered like stars. The scene was pure magic.

Clemmie squeezed Amelia's hand, her voice filled with awe. 'It's enchanting! There's your chariot, princess!'

Amelia giggled, her cheeks flushed with excitement. 'I suppose this is my cue, then.' She gave each of them a tight hug, whispering her thanks before hurrying down the stairs. Taking a deep breath, she stepped out of the bookshop and onto the lane.

A small crowd had begun to gather to see what all the fuss was about.

The coachman, dressed impeccably in a dark coat and top hat, gave her a gentlemanly nod, smiled and said, 'Miss Amelia, your carriage awaits.' He extended his hand to help her into the carriage. His lips twitched in amusement as he noticed her pyjamas and slippers.

As soon as she settled into the plush seat, he handed her a delicate flute of fizz and tucked a soft woollen blanket over her lap. The small yet thoughtful gestures made her heart flutter; she could hardly believe this was real.

The carriage began to move, the rhythmic clatter of hooves echoing on the cobblestones, and Amelia leaned out slightly to wave to her friends gathered outside the bookshop. They waved back enthusiastically, cheering and clapping as if they were proud parents at a graduation. Their warmth and joy only amplified her own, and she found herself grinning so wide her cheeks hurt.

Amelia had never ridden in a carriage before, and the experience felt surreal. With the twinkling fairy lights casting a soft glow and the gentle swaying of the carriage, she felt like royalty.

As they made their way down Lighthouse Lane, the scenery shifted. The carriage followed a winding path that led to the beach. On the other side, fields rolled lazily, dotted with grazing sheep and wildflowers swaying in the breeze. She sipped her champagne as the carriage continued its leisurely pace towards the next bay. Each moment felt like a page out of a storybook, one she never wanted to close.

When the horse came to a halt outside a secluded cabin, nestled amongst pine trees, Amelia felt her heart quicken. The little building exuded a charming rustic appeal with its weathered wooden exterior, sharpened by a touch of elegance. Warm golden light spilled from the windows, illuminating the surrounding trees, while a thin wisp of smoke curled lazily from the chimney into the crisp evening air. Standing at the door, looking effortlessly handsome, was Jack.

Amelia burst out laughing the moment she saw him –

grinning from ear to ear, dressed in his very own pair of puffin pyjamas. The sight was both absurd and endearing, and the sheer joy on his face as he took in her appearance made her heart skip a beat.

'Look at those pyjamas!' she exclaimed, as he helped her down from the carriage. 'What impeccable taste you have. And you've even got the slippers!'

Jack chuckled. 'You can thank Clemmie for that! She gave me the heads up. But honestly, Amelia, you look like an absolute dream.'

Hand in hand, they walked into the cabin, where candles glowed softly in every corner. A little table set for two waited by the window. A log fire was roaring. It was intimate, cosy and timeless. Amelia's eyes roamed the room, taking in the stack of beautiful stationery and fountain pens he'd placed on the coffee table for them to write their letters, then she spotted a spectacular bookshelf that seemed to be full of first editions.

'This place is magnificent. Look at this bookshelf.' She gazed at the titles. 'This is something else. I know from local gossip that this place has something to do with Edgar, but I've never actually been inside.'

'Yes, it belongs to Edgar's family. Pick a book from the shelf.' Jack sat down on the comfy settee in front of the fire and placed his drink on a nearby coffee table.

'Imagine this place at Christmas, the snow on the cliffs, the waves rolling in.' A gentle knock at the door made Amelia pause. 'Who's that?'

'Why don't you go and take a look?' Jack smiled.

'What have you planned now?' Her eyes barely left his as she walked towards the door.

When she opened it, her jaw nearly dropped. Standing on the doorstep was a man in a chef's jacket, holding a neatly packed leather case of knives and a tote of fresh ingredients. He smiled politely, his eyes twinkling. 'Good evening,' he said. 'Miss Amelia Brown?'

'Yes.'

'I'm here to cook your dinner,' the chef said with a warm smile, stepping forward confidently. Amelia blinked, glancing back at Jack in amazement. 'You … you've hired a chef?'

Jack's grin widened. 'Well, I wanted to make tonight memorable. Thought we could do dinner right.' He gestured to the chef, his voice carrying a note of pride. 'Amelia, meet Chef Luca Moretti. I met him a few years ago while researching one of my books. He was running a tiny trattoria on the Amalfi Coast at the time. We got talking, and I ended up introducing him to a contact at my publisher's. Now he's working on his first cookbook.' Jack glanced at Luca, his smile turning fond. 'This is his way of saying thanks.'

Luca gave a small, theatrical bow. 'It is my honour to cook for you tonight. Trust me, signorina, you will not be disappointed.' His Italian accent was rich and melodic.

Amelia stepped aside to let him in, her cheeks warming with a delighted blush. She hadn't anticipated anything quite this extravagant.

The small kitchen quickly came alive under Luca's skilful hands. He unpacked his supplies with practised precision, spreading an array of fresh ingredients across the counter: thick bunches of fragrant herbs tied with twine, cuts of meat wrapped in crisp brown paper, and an assortment of seasonal vegetables that glistened in the soft light. The bottles of olive oil and wine looked like they'd come from an Italian vineyard.

Amelia couldn't take her eyes off the transformation. She watched in awe as Luca moved effortlessly, his hands deftly arranging the ingredients, his presence exuding a quiet confidence. The cabin kitchen felt so alive, and for a moment it was as though they'd been transported to a bustling Italian villa.

Noticing her fascination, Jack grinned. 'Luca's actually travelling to Scotland to visit his family, so the timing worked out perfectly for him to stop by.'

Luca soon filled the cabin with mouth-watering aromas as he prepared their first course, and Amelia and Jack settled at the laid table overlooking the perfect backdrop of the ocean. To begin, Luca presented them with a delicate appetiser of crisp bruschetta topped with heirloom tomatoes, fresh basil and a drizzle of balsamic glaze. They each took a bite, savouring the bright, fresh flavours. Amelia's eyes sparkled as she looked at Jack.

'This food is incredible. All this, the cabin, the setting … you.'

'What can I say? Fancy dinners in pyjamas have a certain charm, don't you think?'

They chatted happily, their laughter mingling with the crackle of the fire, until the chef returned with their next course, a creamy butternut squash soup with a hint of cinnamon, topped with a dollop of crème fraiche and crispy sage leaves. Each spoonful was warm and rich, the perfect comfort food for a night by the fire. Jack watched her reaction with a grin.

'What do you think?' he asked, raising a brow.

'I'll definitely be stocking the cookbook!'

As they finished the soup, Luca brought out a small bottle of a deep crimson wine and poured them each a glass. Amelia took a sip, savouring its rich, fruity notes. She couldn't stop looking at Jack. Somehow this night seemed even more special than the other dates. She recognised the look in his eyes, and knew he was falling for her just as much as she was falling for him.

It wasn't long before Luca presented the main courses. For Amelia, a beautifully seared salmon, garnished with roasted fennel and a lemon-herb sauce. And for Jack, a tender filet mignon, topped with a red wine reduction and accompanied by garlic mashed potatoes and sautéed asparagus. The smell alone was heavenly, and Amelia felt as if she was in some world-class restaurant rather than in a rustic cabin and cosy pyjamas.

They exclaimed over the contrasting flavours as they tried each other's dishes. 'Who knew fine dining could look like this?' Jack said, taking another bite of steak.

'Sitting in front of a fire eating a five-star meal with a man dressed in puffin pyjamas ... it's every girl's dream!'

Then Luca unveiled a show-stopping dessert, a molten chocolate lava cake for Jack and a vanilla-bean panna cotta with a raspberry coulis for Amelia. She let out a little sigh of joy at the first spoonful, the creamy panna cotta melting on her tongue, perfectly complemented by the tangy fruit coulis. Jack was watching her, smiling as he enjoyed his cake, the rich chocolate spilling onto his plate in a warm, velvety pool.

As soon as the last dishes had been served, Luca wiped down the kitchen before neatly packing all his equipment back into his leather case. In no time at all, every plate, glass and utensil had been cleaned and stowed away, and they both thanked Luca as he left the cottage, calling over his shoulder to Jack that they would catch up soon. As the door clicked shut behind him, Amelia's heart swelled with happiness.

Jack's face relaxed in the flickering firelight, and without thinking, she wrapped her arms around him, standing on tiptoe as she leaned in to kiss him. She'd been waiting to do that all night. When they pulled apart, Jack took her hand, his eyes full of warmth. 'Ready for the next part of the night?' he asked.

She knew exactly what he meant and nodded. They settled down on the rug either side of the coffee table, the logs kicking out a lovely warmth, and casting soft light across their faces, glasses of wine at their sides. Amelia's heart raced as Jack handed her a sheet of cream-coloured paper, a fountain pen and an envelope. She could feel the weight of the moment as she took them, marvelling at the surreal beauty of it all, the two of them here, together, in this small cabin, sharing something so intimate, something that no one else knew about them.

'Remember, no judgements, right?' Jack said, his tone light but his eyes serious. 'Whatever we write here ... it stays between us.'

Amelia nodded, her heart fluttering as their eyes met. 'No judgements,' she agreed. 'Only honesty.'

They sat for a moment holding each other's gazes, and then they both looked down, their pens poised over the paper. Amelia took a deep breath, felt the slight scratch as the pen touched the smooth page, and began to write.

When she had finished, she set her pen down, folded the paper carefully and slipped it into the envelope. Pressing it shut, she sealed away a piece of herself. The words she'd written were intimate and raw, a truth she'd never shared with anyone at the time, for fear of failure, and the thought of revealing her secret still made her heart race. She glanced at Jack, who had just finished his own letter and was sealing it with a quiet, almost reverent care. When he looked up at her, they traded letters in silence, each holding the other's envelope for a moment.

Amelia's pulse quickened, glad at the decision she had made. Tonight she'd written down her secret and shared it with Jack. In a short time he'd become someone she trusted more deeply than anyone. He had never questioned her ambitions, never made her feel small. She'd opened up to him in ways she'd never thought possible, and he'd reciprocated with nothing but warmth and support. She still felt vestiges of fear, but there was something about Jack that made her believe the timing was right.

Chapter Thirty

JACK

After dropping Amelia off at the bookshop just before midnight, Jack walked back through the quiet streets towards the B&B. The evening had unfolded with a sense of enchantment he hadn't felt in years. When he first came to Puffin Island, it had been with a malicious intention, but now his loyalty lay elsewhere. Amelia meant so much more to him than any job ever could, no matter how desperate he was for the money. Despite Edgar's advice that she didn't need to know, he'd confessed everything in the letter, both that secret and another.

As soon as he reached the B&B, he quietly headed towards his room and propped Amelia's letter on the desk. He couldn't open it for another forty-eight hours.

Taking off his coat, he smiled down at his puffin pyjamas then sat down at the desk, opened his laptop and began to write, knowing for certain now that these journal entries were going to come together as a novel.

Puffin Island isn't at all what I was expecting when sent here to write an article. I was supposed to be here to expose and highlight the rot and the apparent decay of the island as a tourist destination, and to detail the small-minded people that lived here. But I'm starting to wonder – no, I know – that the only rot was in the assignment itself, and it really isn't worth the money. It's taken me only a short time to see this place's charm, and I'm not sure how anyone could ever want to write anything to hurt it.

Meeting Amelia was unexpected. She's as much a part of this place as the waves and the puffins themselves, and to harm this island would be to harm her. Vivienne knew what she was doing. If I write a bad article, the resulting backlash could devastate this place. More than a few people would suffer, Amelia included, and I'm not prepared to let that happen. It's strange, this evening, sitting with her, I felt the walls I'd built around myself beginning to soften and that's thanks to how wonderful, genuine and loyal she is.

She asked me something tonight that I wasn't expecting. After we exchanged our letters – personal confessions, each penned by candlelight like in the book The Temptation Bucket List – she asked me to attend her upcoming court date. She's going up against Vivienne and fighting for her inheritance. She wants me there, by her side, and I've told her I'll come. But now I'm questioning what effect will this have on Amelia, as knowing Vivienne as I do, she won't take kindly to my involvement, and the fallout could be brutal. I don't want to create any more upset for Amelia.

Jack closed the laptop and thought back to their

conversation while snuggled in each other's arms in front of the fire. Amelia had opened up to him, revealing that she feared losing everything, and even though she was determined to face Vivienne in court she dreaded the smug look on Vivienne's face if the judge didn't rule in Amelia's favour. Jack had held her as she'd bared her soul, and her vulnerability had drawn him even closer to her.

Unable to sleep, he decided to head downstairs and grab a drink from the B&B's small honesty bar in the communal living room. He was unsurprised to find that he was the only one there at this time of night. He poured himself a measure of whisky and moved over to the window seat. As he sat down, his gaze lingered on the dark, silent street outside.

The whisky warmed his throat, but it did little to ease the knot in his chest. His mind drifted back to that first meeting with Vivienne, which had never sat right with him. As he took another sip, he noticed a car – a cab – creeping down the street, the headlights slicing through the dark. The cab passed by the window and Jack caught a glimpse of the passenger in the back seat. He sat up straight and stared. His pulse quickened.

Vivienne had arrived.

He leaned forward and watched the cab wind to the end of the narrow street, heading in the direction of Dune House. Jack watched until the taillights disappeared around a bend. His stomach had churned at just the sight of her. He knew she was here for the court date, but no doubt Miles would have her checking up on the article while she was here.

He threw back the rest of the whisky, the heat settling uneasily in his chest.

He had one advantage that meant he was a step ahead. He knew she was here now, so all he had to do was stay out of her way.

Chapter Thirty-One
AMELIA

Amelia woke to sunlight streaming through her window, warming her face. She lay there, still smiling at the memories of last night. Jack had outdone himself with that date, the candlelit cabin, the private chef, the handwritten letters exchanged by candlelight. It had been, without question, one of the most beautiful nights of her life. As she replayed every romantic detail, she reached for her phone, lying silent and charging on her bedside cabinet.

She laughed to find that the girls' text group was already alive with questions about her date.

CLEMMIE
OMG. I NEED details! I can't believe you haven't said a word yet. How was the date?

DILLY
She's all LOVED up!

VERITY

Do you think he's whisked her off to New York? Maybe she's not answering because she's on a plane. We need to check at 9am if the bookshop is open!

AMELIA

Patience, ladies! I've only just woke up! It was incredible. I have to tell you EVERYTHING! Sorry for the shouty capitals but it was amazing!

Within a second everyone had read her message. She could see they were all typing at once.

CLEMMIE

Spill! And don't leave out the juicy stuff!

AMELIA

We both had puffin pyjamas on, which I believe was down to you, Clemmie!

CLEMMIE

You're welcome!

AMELIA

Oh, and there was wine. And not just any wine. A bottle of something French, something expensive. I don't even know what it was, but it tasted like pure luxury, and we had a private chef in the cabin.

DILLY

You lucky woman! Tell us about the food, was it really Michelin-star-worthy?

The Story Shop

AMELIA
> It was unreal, and the dessert! Heavenly. Oh, and Jack arranged for us to write letters by candlelight. Actual, honest-to-goodness love letters.

VERITY
> Oh, he's a keeper! When's the wedding?

AMELIA
> Ha ha!

DILLY
> Are you going to share what you wrote?

AMELIA
> Not yet! Just like in the Maris Wilde book we have to wait forty-eight hours before opening the letters. Honestly, I'm nervous to read his … terrified, in fact!

CLEMMIE
> And what was your secret?

AMELIA
> It's a secret!

Her phone buzzed with heart emojis and Amelia stretched out in bed, savouring the happiness that bubbled up every time she thought about Jack. It was hard to believe someone so thoughtful, so perfect, had just walked into her bookshop at random.

After a shower she wandered down the stairs to the shop, picked up the local newspaper from the mat and grabbed the delivery of more copies of Ellis Ford's book. She'd drop Edgar's copy off at his office at lunchtime.

All morning, the bookshop was busy with customers, each bringing their own stories, quirks and questions. Amelia loved these interactions, the quick chats about the weather, the longer conversations about book recommendations, and the occasional heartfelt exchanges with tourists who shared snippets of their lives. Time went quickly and before she knew it, it was time to close the shop and head towards Edgar's office.

She knocked on his door and heard Edgar's chair scrape on the wooden floor before his footsteps headed her way. The door swung open, but instead of welcoming her with his usual smile, Edgar looked very serious.

'Amelia.' He stepped aside and she walked into his office. 'Is there something you need to tell me?'

Her heart skipped a beat. He couldn't know ... could he? She hesitated, her mind racing, but before she could speak, Edgar's stern expression broke into a wide smile.

'I heard all about Madame Zelda's reading,' he teased, crossing his arms. 'You're the talk of the town, Amelia. Seems everyone wants to know what you're hiding.'

Relief flooded her and she laughed, rolling her eyes. 'You scared me there for a moment, Edgar! I thought I was in trouble.'

He chuckled, shaking his head. 'Only with the town gossips, it seems.' He motioned for her to sit as he moved around his desk, pulling out a stack of files. 'I was just about to go over your file one last time. Have you got ten minutes?'

'I have,' she replied, placing Ellis Ford's book on his desk. 'It's arrived and a brilliant read.'

'Looks good.' He picked it up and flicked through the

pages, looking through the spectacles that were perched on the edge of his nose. 'I can start this tonight,' he said before putting the book down and opening the file.

Edgar slipped seamlessly into business mode and they talked through the will and the points he would present to the judge to contest it. Edgar worked through each point methodically, his razor-sharp mind picking apart every detail, every argument, every angle. Then the discussion turned to Amelia's finances. She didn't have much, beyond her business and the flat above the shop, unlike Vivienne, who had a number of properties even before she'd stolen Amelia's childhood home.

'Did you see her on the Charles Stone show?' Edgar asked.

'I did, and every time she lands on her feet I fume. I don't think I've ever disliked a person so much in my life.' For a moment Amelia fell silent. She wasn't one to feel animosity; she firmly believed in fairness and doing the right thing, the exact opposite of how Vivienne operated. 'I can't bear to look at her face if she wins, she is going to be so smug.'

'We still have a good chance of winning this,' Edgar said reassuringly.

Amelia fell silent for a moment, and then reached into her bag and pulled out a sheet of paper. She unfolded it slowly, taking a deep breath before sliding it across the desk towards Edgar. Without looking up, she spoke quietly, her voice tinged with regret. 'I owe you an apology, Edgar. I've kept this from you, from everyone. I wasn't sure when was the right time to tell you, But I'm worried this might come to light in court and I don't want us to be caught out.' She paused. 'This all started when my relationship with my father was falling apart because of Vivienne. I kept it quiet, expecting nothing would come of it, that it would all fade away. But then everything happened, just days after my father died, and I ... I just kept quiet, trying to figure out what to do. And time kept ticking, and then it just felt easier to keep quiet until I could control my emotions and grief and see how it all panned out.'

Edgar raised an eyebrow. 'Was Madame Zelda right? Have you been keeping secrets?' he quipped, his voice light, though his gaze was intense.

He picked up the paper, his eyes flicking between it and Amelia for a moment before he began to read. As he scanned the document, his expression changed and his mouth fell open in shock. He adjusted his glasses on the bridge of his nose before looking up at Amelia, eyes wide. 'Bloody hell! How have you managed to keep this quiet?'

Chapter Thirty-Two

JACK

When Jack woke up the next morning, the image of Vivienne sitting in the back of the cab lingered in his mind. He got up and made a strong cup of tea and picked up Ethan's notebook, which was still lying on his desk. He stared at it, contemplating his next move.

Jack knew that trying to return the notebook now carried the risk of running into Vivienne, as where else could she be staying than at Dune House? The thought of an encounter with her sent a wave of unease through him. It would be too risky, too complicated. Deciding it was safer to keep the notebook hidden, he slipped it into his rucksack then opened up his laptop.

Over the past few days, Jack had poured every spare moment into his writing. The diary entries he'd initially composed were evolving, transforming into a novel he was becoming proud of. It was the most personal and raw story he'd ever attempted. His editor had gushed about its potential and he felt it, too. Every line, every paragraph, seemed to capture not just his creative vision, but a deeper emotional undercurrent too. Puffin Island was a pleasure to write about, its rugged cliffs and endless ocean providing the perfect backdrop. He'd written successful novels before, but something about this felt different. This story, he sensed, had the potential to stand out as his best work.

However, even though his writer's block seemed to have lifted, his tax bill still loomed. Jack considered his options. Perhaps he could offer his expertise to others, mentoring debut authors and guiding them through the labyrinth of writing a novel. Or host writing groups online. Helping fledgling writers to stay motivated could be both a way to share his passion and a source of income. It was definitely something to think about.

On the desk also sat a copy of Maris Wilde's book, the pages a little worn from his constant thumbing, and Amelia's unopened envelope. The temptation to tear it open was nearly overwhelming, and more than once he'd pressed his fingers against the paper, trying to make out a word or two which of course was impossible given the high quality of the paper and envelope.

In the book the couple had agreed they would reunite at the clocktower, and after they'd read the letters, they would decide whether to be together or leave the relationship behind. But the ending to his own fairytale was already clear in his mind: he wanted to embark on a life journey with Amelia.

They had agreed to meet in Puffin Island's park by the floral clock face made up of thousands of bedding plants.

Grabbing his coat, Jack stepped out of the front door of the B&B and walked down the lane. The day was mild, with a light breeze, and as he paused at the bottom of the jetty leading to The Sea Glass Restaurant, he slid his phone out of his pocket and dialled Edgar's number.

'Edgar, it's Jack,' he said as soon as the other man picked up. 'I wanted to return the key for the cabin and run something by you. Are you at the office?'

'Yes, come by,' Edgar replied, his voice warm and welcoming. 'I could do with a break so I'll put the kettle on.'

Jack tucked his phone back into his pocket and headed towards Anchor Way, his mind preoccupied with thoughts of Amelia. Though their time together had been short, he couldn't deny the connection he felt with her, nor did he want to. She'd entered his life out of the blue, and now, it seemed, she was always on his mind.

As he passed Betty and Clemmie's tearoom, he spotted a familiar figure strolling along the cobbled street, the very person he'd hoped to avoid – Vivienne. As always, she was impeccably dressed, her long trench coat billowing as she moved with practised elegance. Instinctively, he stepped back into the doorway of a nearby shop, wanting to remain out of sight. The last thing he needed was any sort of conversation with her. He watched keenly from his hiding place, his attention sharpening as he noticed something strange.

As Vivienne passed the tearoom, she waved at Betty, who was serving a couple seated in the garden. Normally upbeat and chatty, Betty seemed to stiffen when she caught sight of Vivienne. Her posture straightened, and she quickly turned away, her eyes fixed on her teapot as she poured, deliberately ignoring the other woman's presence. Jack's gaze followed Vivienne as she continued down the lane, making her way towards Blue Water Bay. She neared the jetty, where Sam was standing at the end, writing the restaurant's specials for the day on the blackboard. He looked up and saw her and turned back to his chalkboard without a word, pointedly ignoring her as she passed by. Jack watched as everyone she passed refused to acknowledge her. Their silence was unmistakable: they were taking a stand for Amelia.

Once Vivienne was well away, Jack carried on to Edgar's office and knocked on the door. He was greeted with a wide smile. 'Jack! Come in, come in.' He gestured for him to sit down on the worn leather armchair by the window, and placed a freshly brewed pot of tea on the table between them.

'Vivienne's on the island,' Jack told him.

Edgar nodded as if he'd been expecting the news. 'Yes, I expected she'd be arriving soon for the court case. No doubt she's installed herself back at Dune House,' he replied.

'And it's clear the islanders aren't exactly thrilled about her arrival. I just saw Betty and Sam give her the cold shoulder as she walked by.'

'Can't say I blame them,' Edgar said, handing Jack a mug of tea. 'Vivienne hasn't exactly won anyone over here. This island looks after its own, and Amelia, she's one of us.'

Jack took a sip of his tea. 'That's what I wanted to talk to you about, actually,' he began, choosing his words carefully. 'I hadn't planned on staying here long, only long enough to write the article I'm no longer going to write, but things have changed.' He slid the key to the cabin across the table. 'Thank you for this. It's a wonderful place.'

'You're welcome – but what's changed?'

'Amelia's important to me, Edgar. It may sound impulsive, but I want to stay, see what it could be.'

'You've taken quite a shine to her, haven't you?' he said. 'She's a very special girl.'

'I'd like to rent the cabin from you, if that's possible. It's the perfect writing retreat and would allow me to stay on the island.'

Edgar smile. 'I think we can arrange that.' He slid the key back across the table towards Jack.

'That's brilliant news.'

'We can sort out the rent once you're settled.'

'Thanks, Edgar.'

Edgar took a sip of tea, leaning back in his chair. 'You know, if you're planning to stay a while, it might be worth looking into some work around here, especially if the book sales aren't doing as well as expected.'

'I've been thinking about that. I was wondering if there might be any interest in a writing workshop or some kind of mentorship programme for new writers. I could help people with their novels, guide them through the process. It's something I'd enjoy, and it'd help keep me afloat.'

A thoughtful look crossed Edgar's face. 'Well, now, that's an idea. You would be best speaking with Dilly, as she runs the community gallery here. Her partner, Max, teaches art classes there, mostly for beginners, and the space allows local college kids and community members to display and sell their own work. Max's classes have done well so far, and I imagine there'd be a fair few people interested in a writing class. Dilly's got a good eye for these things though, she'd know best if there's a demand.'

Jack's face lit up at the suggestion. 'That's a brilliant idea. I'll pay her a visit, see if there's any interest.'

Edgar nodded approvingly. 'Good, good. And if you need anything, you know where to find me. We're a tight-knit bunch here, Jack. We look out for our own and good folk like yourself are always welcome.'

They sat in comfortable silence for a moment, sipping their tea as the sounds of the village drifted through the open window. Jack felt a quiet sense of belonging that he hadn't felt in a long time. Here, on Puffin Island, he'd found a place where he could truly be himself.

'How do you think Amelia is holding up? She's asked me to go to the court with her.'

'She's strong, she'll get through this.'

'I suppose there being a will makes it difficult.'

'A will that wasn't drafted by me. I'd been his solicitor for as long as I've been qualified. Far too many decades for me to admit to.'

'The will wasn't drafted by you?' Jack repeated.

'No, but I'm guessing the reason Ethan didn't bring it to me was because he knew I would have tried to talk him out of it.'

Jack leaned forward slightly. 'What do you think Amelia's chances are?'

'Good, but you never know how these things are going to play out. She's going to need all the support she can get, especially if Vivienne somehow manages to walk away with everything.'

'I'll be there. Thank you again for this.' He picked up the key as he stood. 'I didn't expect to feel so at home here, but I can't imagine being anywhere else now.'

Edgar's eyes crinkled with a smile. 'That's the magic of Puffin Island. It has a way of finding people who need it just as much as it needs them.'

Jack nodded. 'You're right there.'

'You get yourself moved into the cabin and I'll see you at court. There are a few more things I need to do this afternoon to prepare.'

'I will,' Jack replied, pocketing the key, grateful that he'd found a place to start anew and pour himself into his writing, while staying close to Amelia. It was a win-win situation.

'I'll see you tomorrow.'

As Jack left Edgar's office he wandered towards the lighthouse, planning to speak to Dilly about the potential writing classes. Walking back past the tearoom, he caught a glimpse of Betty through the window, bustling around with her usual cheer. She looked up, spotted him and gave him a warm smile and a wave. Being welcomed by Betty felt like being knighted by royalty, like being accepted into an exclusive circle.

Edgar was right, this place was truly something special.

Chapter Thirty-Three

AMELIA

Amelia hadn't slept a wink. The anticipation of the court case had kept her awake, leaving her staring at the dark ceiling well into the early morning hours, her mind churning and her stomach an anxious ball of nerves. Normally, her morning routine was simple: she'd wrap herself in her favourite oversized jumper adorned with a puffin and slip into her baggy trousers before feeding Pawsworth and opening the bookshop. But today was different. Today, she needed to present a different version of herself, one that looked confident and resilient, even if she didn't feel it inside.

As she pulled back her curtains, she looked up at the sky. The weather thankfully looked okay, though maybe a little dull, but it was better than rain. She opened her wardrobe door and slid the hangers back and forth on the rail. She glanced over various tops, jumpers and cardigans, knowing she couldn't wear her usual attire, and finally plumped for a charcoal-grey suit. It looked smart and she paired it with a soft cream blouse and a favourite pair of ballet pumps.

Satisfied, she took a deep breath, trying to steady her nerves. She wandered downstairs and glanced at Pawsworth, who sat patiently by his bowl, watching her with keen eyes. After she'd fed him, she noticed Jack's letter propped up on the counter where she'd left it last night. She slipped it into a drawer, looking forward to opening it once the court day was over.

The cab was due at any moment but as Amelia peered through the window onto Lighthouse Lane she spotted it already waiting by the kerb, with Jack sitting inside. Grabbing her bag, she locked the door and took a deep breath.

As she stepped onto the pavement, Jack got out of the cab and opened the door for her. He kissed her cheek and gave her a loving smile. 'Good morning, how're you feeling? Silly question, I know.'

'Nervous. I just want it over and done with. That woman has got a nerve, but I've got to do my very best to stay composed,' she replied, sliding into the back seat of the cab, trying to muster up a smile.

'You look great, by the way,' he said softly. 'Professional. Strong.'

'Thank you,' Amelia replied. 'I didn't sleep well,' she admitted.

Jack reached over and gave her hand a squeeze. 'Whatever happens, you're not alone. I'm here, and Edgar is too. And the whole of Puffin Island is in your corner.'

They set off along the road that led to the causeway. The island was quiet and as they travelled across the causeway, the sea shimmered with the light of the rising sun. The tide was low, revealing sandbanks and rocky patches along the shoreline.

The cab weaved around the town of Sea's End before turning left towards the courthouse, a stately old building at the edge of the town square, made of dark stone with a large arched entrance and tall windows that loomed over them like watchful eyes. It had a solemn, almost timeless air to it, and Amelia briefly wondered how many people had passed through its doors seeking justice or closure.

As they pulled up to the kerb, Amelia spotted Edgar waiting on the courthouse steps, his familiar figure standing tall and composed. He was dressed in a dark suit, crisp and formal, with a briefcase in one hand and a calm, determined expression on his face. His silver hair caught the light, and his piercing gaze softened when he saw them approach. He raised a hand to greet them as they stepped out of the cab and climbed the broad stone steps.

'Good morning, Amelia,' he greeted her with a kind smile, his eyes warm and full of encouragement. 'Are you ready?'

'As ready as I'll ever be,' she replied, her voice wavering slightly despite her best efforts to sound confident.

'Remember, you're not alone in this,' he said, placing a hand on her shoulder. 'We'll go through everything together. Just follow my lead, and focus on speaking your truth. I need to go inside but if you want to take a moment you've got some time before you need to come inside.'

She nodded. 'I'll stay here for a sec. I feel like some fresh air.'

Edgar nodded and entered the courthouse.

Jack turned towards her, taking both of his hands in hers. He didn't say anything; he didn't need to.

'I need to nip to the bathroom ... probably nerves,' Amelia said. 'Can you wait here?'

'Of course,' Jack replied. 'Take your time.'

As Amelia made her way inside, weaving through the crowd in the lobby, she felt a knot in her stomach that she couldn't dispel. She was on edge. Despite the distance between her and her father at the end of his life, she still couldn't believe he would ever have wanted to put her through this. Vivienne, without a doubt, was the one responsible for the breakdown of their relationship.

After a freshen up and a few deep breaths to calm herself Amelia stared at her reflection, silently willing herself to stay strong. Then she turned and headed back towards the courthouse steps where she'd left Jack. She spotted him through the open glass doors ... but he wasn't alone. Standing beside him was Vivienne. Amelia's pulse quickened, and she froze in her tracks, lingering on the other side of the door, unsure what to do next.

Vivienne stood with an air of confidence, her expression intense. Amelia knew she'd once been Jack's agent, and it was likely that, as she'd walked up the steps past him, he'd felt he couldn't ignore her. But that didn't mean Amelia was eager to speak to her, and she stayed out of sight, but close enough to overhear their conversation. A tiny part of her felt a little guilty for eavesdropping, but something about Vivienne's body language and the tension in Jack's face told her this was a conversation she needed to hear.

'So, how's the article coming along?' asked Vivienne,

tilting her head, eyeing up Jack. 'Have you managed to dig up anything juicy on the residents of Puffin Island?'

Amelia's breath caught in her throat, her heart pounding with sudden dread. *Article? Digging up anything juicy?* A sick feeling settled in her stomach as she carried on listening.

'I'm ... still working on it,' he said, his voice low.

'Oh, I'm sure you are and I'm sure it'll be good. Miles is hoping this will be the beginning of a long, successful working relationship,' Vivienne continued, her voice smooth but carrying an edge. 'Having you on board at *The Morning Ledger* will be good for both of you. You've got potential, Jack. And you took my advice, you met with Amelia, wined her, dined her. You're playing your part well, aren't you?' Her smile widened, as if savouring some unspoken victory. 'I can't wait to see what you've come up with. I'm sure whatever you've written will shed a ... unique light on the residents of Puffin Island. This place, this little paradise... They all think they're so above the rest of us, don't they? It'll be interesting to see how they react when the truth comes out. Let's just hope you've really dug deep.' Vivienne's smile widened.

Amelia's thoughts reeled. The idea that Jack could be working for Vivienne, digging into her life and the lives of everyone she cared about, made her feel sick. She'd trusted him with so much.

Vivienne leaned in slightly, her voice lowered to a more conspiratorial tone. 'I'm glad you've taken such a particular interest in Amelia. Considering the case today, I imagine she needed a friend to open up to.'

Amelia's blood ran cold. She felt like her world was crumbling.

Vivienne's gaze turned calculating, almost patronising, as she continued. 'Don't go soft on me, Jack. I brought you in because you know how to get people to trust you, to open up. That's what makes your writing so compelling, remember? And let's not forget, you need the money.'

Amelia felt her world tilt. He was doing this for money? The warmth she'd felt from Jack, the tenderness, the genuine moments they had shared, the feelings he'd given her, convincing her that she was in the first flush of love … it was all a lie. Her throat tightened as the hurt and anger bubbled up inside her. She felt like a fool for letting her guard down, for believing he could be someone she could trust, someone who cared about her. The realisation that he'd been working for Vivienne, likely from the moment he arrived on the island, hit her like a punch to the gut.

'Remember, Jack, I'm doing you a favour here. Miles gave you this opportunity on my recommendation. Don't waste it.'

'I know, Vivienne,' Jack replied, his voice resigned. The words were like a slap across Amelia's face.

A flood of anger and hurt surged up inside her, and she couldn't stay quiet anymore.

Without another thought, she stepped forward, her heart pounding in her chest. 'I've heard enough,' she said, her voice cutting through the air.

Jack froze, his eyes wide with shock, while Vivienne's lips curled into a smug smile. Amelia stood there, trembling but resolute. She wasn't going to let them get away with it.

'I overheard everything,' she said, her voice growing

steadier with each word. 'You've been lying to me, Jack. All this time you've been working for Vivienne, digging up secrets about me, about my family. For an article. You're just using me, aren't you?'

'Amelia, darling, you really don't understand what's going on here,' Vivienne said. 'Jack's doing what he needs to do. What he's good at. It's just a job, nothing personal.'

The venom in Vivienne's voice stung, but Amelia wasn't about to back down. 'You're disgusting,' she spat. 'And you, Jack, I trusted you. I let you in. And now I know it was all for nothing. You've been lying to me this whole time.'

Jack looked at her, guilt flashing across his face, but Vivienne continued to look smug, as if she were above it all.

'Amelia, I—' Jack started, but she held up a hand, cutting him off.

'Don't say a word, Jack,' she snapped, her voice hard. 'I don't want to hear it. I know enough. And as for you, Vivienne... Why? Why my father? Why me?'

Vivienne raised an eyebrow, a smirk playing on her lips. 'Why? Because I saw the chance to make him into the man he should have been. Do you think your father would have amounted to anything more than a grieving recluse if it weren't for me? He was stuck in the past, talking endlessly about your mother, your family. It was pathetic.' She shook her head pityingly. 'I was the one who got him to live again, to try new things, to look beyond the shadow of his perfect little first family.'

Amelia's breath hitched, her voice trembling with anger. 'You were jealous. Of my mother. Of us. That's what this is about, isn't it? You couldn't stand that you were never enough for him!'

Vivienne's smirk twisted into a sneer. 'Enough for him? I was the only one who challenged him to be better, to let go of that baggage. And do you know what he told me? That I was the first person to make him feel alive since losing your mother.' Her eyes glinted with malice. 'And you? You were just a weight around his neck, dragging him down. He might not have admitted it out loud, but I could see it. Every time he talked about you, it was with guilt and regret, not pride.'

Amelia felt the words hit her like a physical blow, but she stood her ground. 'That's a lie. He loved me.'

Vivienne gave a cold laugh. 'Maybe he did. In his own way. But love didn't stop him needing me to pull him out of the pit he'd thrown himself into. And don't think I didn't notice how you looked at me, Amelia. Always blaming me for taking him away, when really I was the one keeping him from drowning in his own misery.'

Amelia's hands clenched into fists, her voice steady but seething with rage. 'And that's why you're trying to take the house? Because you feel you saved him, and now you deserve everything he left behind?'

Vivienne's expression hardened, her voice icy. 'Yes, I deserve it. After everything I did for him, for us, I deserve more than endless grief from some sentimental brat who tried to keep him in the past because she herself can't let go of the past. That house isn't just bricks and mortar, Amelia. It's proof that I mattered to him. That I made a difference.'

Jack shifted uncomfortably beside her.

Amelia didn't take her eyes off Vivienne. 'You didn't save him,' Amelia said quietly, her voice trembling with controlled fury. 'You manipulated him. You isolated him.

You wanted to erase us from his life so you could have him all to yourself. But no matter how hard you tried, you never had what we had.' Amelia drew breath. 'That day on the yacht, what really happened, Vivienne? I don't believe it was an accident.'

'Don't be foolish. The authorities ruled it an accident, so that's what we should all assume it was.'

Amelia's mind was racing. The suspicion she'd buried since her father's death roared to the surface, but she forced herself to stay calm. 'You ... you're admitting you had something to do with it?' She stared deep into Vivienne's eyes.

Vivienne's mask of confidence slipped for a moment before she regained her composure. 'Believe what you want, Amelia. It doesn't change anything. I earned my place, and I'll fight for what's mine.'

Amelia's eyes burnt with unshed tears.

Jack looked between the two women, his face pale, the tension crackling in the air making him visibly uncomfortable. 'Amelia, I—'

She shot him a glare, silencing him.

Without another word, Amelia turned and walked back into the courthouse, her heart pounding. Behind her, Jack called out her name, but she didn't stop. She couldn't. She wouldn't let either of them see how badly they had hurt her. She had more important things to focus on now. Namely fighting for what was hers.

'Where's Jack?' asked Edgar, doing a double-take when he saw her expression. 'And are you okay? You look kind of ... shaken.'

'He's gone and I don't want to talk about it,' stated Amelia, livid that she'd been taken for a fool.

Edgar raised both eyebrows.

'Not now, Edgar. Sorry, I don't mean to be abrupt,' she apologised quickly, 'but I really don't want to talk about it.'

They sat in a quiet corner of the courthouse hallway, the buzz of murmured voices and the shuffle of hurried footsteps filling the space around her, but she barely registered any of it. Her thoughts were all over the place. How could he have done this to her? She blinked back the tears, knowing she somehow needed to get through the next couple of hours even though this was the last place she wanted to be.

'Try not to worry too much, Amelia,' Edgar said, leaning slightly towards her. His voice was low.

Amelia managed a faint smile.

Just as he finished speaking, a court official approached them, clipboard in hand, wearing an unreadable expression. 'Mr. Edgar Carmichael?' he asked, glancing at Edgar before his gaze shifted briefly to Amelia. 'We need you in the judge's chambers for a moment.'

Edgar gave Amelia a reassuring look. 'I'll just be a minute,' he said softly before standing and following the official down the corridor.

Amelia's heart began to pound a little harder as she watched him disappear around the corner. What seemed like hours but was probably only a few minutes passed and Edgar reappeared. His face was calm, but there was a hint of disappointment in his eyes.

'Amelia...' He paused, as if searching for the right words, and then exhaled. 'The case has been postponed.

The judge needs additional information as there was an issue with some of the documents submitted by the other side. They'll need more time to review everything before proceeding.'

'Postponed? I just wanted it over with. Now it's all being dragged out even longer.'

'I know. I'm sorry, Amelia. This is often the way of the legal system ... slow, bureaucratic. I know you're ready for a resolution, and I promise it'll come, even if it takes a little more time than we'd like.'

She nodded, trying to hold back the disappointment.

'Let's head back. There's nothing more to do here today.' He motioned towards the courthouse doors and Amelia followed Edgar through the bustling lobby, weaving past clusters of people deep in conversation. As they stepped outside, Edgar gestured towards a cab waiting by the kerb and without a word they moved towards it and climbed inside.

As the driver pulled away, Amelia leaned back against her seat and glanced at the courtyard. Her eyes locked with Vivienne's. Amelia didn't flinch. She held Vivienne's gaze, refusing to look away, letting her see that she wasn't intimidated by her. Not anymore. If today had taught Amelia anything, it was that she was stronger than she knew.

Chapter Thirty-Four
JACK

Jack was fuming, his mind churning with thoughts of Vivienne and the mess she'd pulled him into. This was all her doing, Miles clearly having been just her pawn. He clenched his fists, regretting every moment he'd spent keeping secret why he'd originally turned up on Puffin Island. As soon as he'd learned that Miles was Vivienne's nephew and that Vivienne was Amelia's stepmother, he should have walked away from the article, refused to be involved and come clean with Amelia, sparing her the pain of discovering the truth from anyone else. He could kick himself for not telling her. He would have loved to be standing by her side, united against Vivienne, the two of them putting her in her place.

Hindsight, as they say, is a wonderful thing. But the damage was done, and he could still see the disbelief and pain etched across Amelia's face when she'd confronted him. Even now, it cut him to his core.

Back at the B&B, he let himself into his room. He

collapsed onto the bed, staring at the ceiling, his thoughts consumed by Amelia. He could still see her face, the look of shock and betrayal that had broken his heart in an instant. She'd been right to walk away, right to shut him out when he'd tried to explain. Amelia had come to mean everything to him, and now, because of Vivienne, she was standing in a courtroom with her heart aching, probably thinking he'd done her wrong.

Needing to clear his head, Jack changed out of his suit and into something more casual. Then he opened his rucksack and took out Ethan Brown's notebook, the one he'd taken from Dune House. With everyone in court, now seemed like a good time to put it back where it belonged.

Notebook in hand, he set off for Dune House, his steps steady but his mind far from calm. He couldn't get rid of the irritation bubbling inside him. When he reached the sandy shoreline, memories flooded back to him ... the tent pitched under the clear night sky, the two of them wrapped in each other's arms, sharing stories and laughter. They'd watched the Northern Lights that night, the colours shimmering across the sky, and he remembered how Amelia's eyes had sparkled as she looked up, captivated. And that kiss... That night had felt like the start of something real, something more than the fleeting relationships he'd known before.

Making his way across the sand, he slipped around the side of Dune House, glancing about to ensure that there was no one on the beach to spot him, then made his way to the shed. He opened the filing cabinet and suddenly sensed someone was watching him. With his heart hammering against his chest, he spun around and came face to face with Amelia. She was standing only inches away, her face a mix of anger and betrayal. 'What are you doing here?'

Amelia's eyes narrowed, her gaze steely. 'I think I should be asking you the same question.' She took a step forward, reached out and firmly pulled the notebook from his hand. 'You've been caught in the act. What are you doing with this?' she demanded. 'As if you haven't already betrayed me enough, now you're stealing things from my father's house? Tell me, Jack, what exactly are you and Vivienne up to now? I should just call the police, have you arrested for trespassing … theft…'

'Amelia,' he began, 'it's not what you think.'

'That's the second time I've heard you say that today,' she retorted.

Jack swallowed. 'This has nothing to do with Vivienne,' he began, his words falling flat, his sincerity sounding hollow even to his own ears.

Amelia raised her hand, cutting him off with a look of unyielding finality. 'Even now, you're defending her? You're unbelievable,' she said, her voice trembling with anger. 'I don't want to hear it, Jack. No more lies, no more excuses. I don't trust a single word you say. And to think I believed you were different. What a fool I was.' She took a step back. 'Just go, Jack. Go back to wherever you came from.'

He stood there, reeling from the way she'd shut him out completely. He was in two minds to try one last time, to explain that his intentions were good, that he was falling in love with her, most probably *had* fallen, and that he wanted to protect her from Vivienne's schemes. But her body language was leaving no room for argument.

Jack nodded slowly. He turned towards the door then stopped.

'With you being here, does that mean you won today?'

'Why don't you ask Vivienne. Go!' she shouted, her voice sharp and trembling.

He looked at her one last time, searching for a glimmer of the warmth he'd become so used to, but there was nothing. His stomach twisted as he turned and walked out the door, his footsteps heavy and slow as he left her standing there, clutching the notebook. He'd messed up. Again.

Outside, the sea breeze hit him, the sound of the waves crashing against the rocks below drowning his footsteps as he walked down the winding path. He stopped, looking out over the water, the vast expanse of the ocean stretching towards the horizon. He had come here, yes, sent by Miles – by Vivienne really – but he knew his own morals would never have let him write that article. Instead, he'd found inspiration for his next novel, and he'd found Amelia. And now, in one bitter twist, he'd lost it all.

When Jack arrived back at the B&B, he headed straight for the honesty bar in the lounge, bypassing the friendly faces of guests to whom he would normally offer a warm smile. Not now. For now, he needed to be alone. Grabbing a heavy tumbler, he poured himself a generous measure of whisky, the amber liquid catching the warm light as he lifted it to his lips. He took a slow, steadying sip, feeling the heat trickle down his throat, and let out a long sigh, hoping it might ease the knot in his chest.

As he stood there, his gaze drifted to the little lending library tucked in the corner. The shelves were packed with books left for others by holidaymakers who'd finished reading them. He scanned the shelves, and his eyes landed on a shiny new copy of Ellis Ford's novel. He'd planned to order through Amelia's bookshop but that wasn't an option anymore. He took it from the shelf and climbed the stairs to his room, whisky glass in one hand and the book in the other. Once inside, he shut the door, settled on his bed and opened the book, hoping that the fictional world would drown out his thoughts, even if only for a while. He took another sip of whisky and turned to the first page. The dedication shouldn't have taken him by surprise. Even in the comfort of the B&B's bedroom, it appeared he couldn't escape Vivienne.

For Vivienne, my agent. Without all your hard work and belief in me, this would have never been possible.

He began reading, wondering if this book was going to live up to the hype. Almost immediately, something started to feel off. He couldn't place it at first and kept reading, an unsettling familiarity growing as he turned each page. He began skimming the middle chapters, realising he'd definitely read this story before, or at least something hauntingly similar. Jack's heart thumped harder as he flipped to the final chapter and skimmed it. He couldn't quite believe it. He *had* read this before. And recently.

His mind was racing as his eyes flicked to Amelia's letter, still propped up on the desk where he'd left it, unread amidst the chaos of the last couple of hours.

With a sudden urgency, he grabbed the envelope, tearing it open as his pulse thundered in his ears. Her neat handwriting blurred slightly as his eyes darted across the page. The more he read, the more his mouth fell open in shock. Her secret … it was staggering, almost too much to comprehend, but it was also just the tip of the iceberg. This was bigger than he could ever have imagined. As the enormity of it sank in, he leaped off the bed clutching both the book and letter and shoved them into his bag. Bounding down the stairs two at a time, he bolted out the door and headed straight for Edgar's office. As he rounded the corner near Betty's tearoom, he spotted Edgar outside, deep in conversation with Betty, who was balancing a tray of pastries in one hand.

'Edgar!' Jack called out, his voice carrying a note of desperation. 'Quick, I need you!'

Both Edgar and Betty turned, startled by his urgency. Jack didn't slow down, his steps eating up the distance between them.

Edgar's brow furrowed in concern as he took in Jack's frantic expression. Immediately, he crossed the street and fell into step with him. 'What's the matter? Where are we going?'

'The bookshop.'

Chapter Thirty-Five

AMELIA

As soon as Amelia stepped back into the bookshop she placed her father's notebook on the counter and scooped up Pawsworth. Tears began to spill down her cheeks. The enormity of what Jack had done had shattered her heart into tiny pieces. How could she have been so blind? He had made her feel like she was the only girl in the world, and then everything – the glances, the quiet moments, the laughter, the kisses – all of it turned out to be a lie. Jack hadn't come to Puffin Island to escape his troubles or find inspiration. He was here for a story, a juicy scoop for Vivienne and her nephew's newspaper. Worse still, he'd wormed his way into Amelia's life and made her fall for him. It hurt more than she ever could have thought possible.

Placing Pawsworth on the counter, Amelia marched over to her laptop, an idea brewing in her mind. She typed in 'Vivienne Langford, newspaper, editor' and hit search with a force fuelled by anger. The first link that appeared was a profile of Miles Thornton, newly appointed editor of *The Morning Ledger*. The article was short and celebratory, describing Miles's new position at the newspaper, with an accompanying photograph of Vivienne looking proud of her nephew as they stood outside the office of the newspaper. But what caught Amelia's attention was the link to 'Meet Our Team', just below the photograph. She hesitated for a moment, then clicked. Her eyes scanned down the page, skipping over faces and names until she froze. There he was, staring back at her: Jack Hartwell. Alongside a glossy author photo was a brief paragraph saying he had been hired as a freelance journalist writing topical travel articles and in-depth local profiles. It was all there, the truth she hadn't wanted to believe, glaring at her from her laptop screen. It had all been nothing more than a game to him.

'Bastard!' she shouted, the word echoing through the empty shop. Startled at her outburst, Pawsworth looked up with wide eyes.

'Shit. Double shit,' she muttered, remembering her letter. She closed her eyes and did everything in her power not to scream. It had been a trick, a calculated ploy to pull her close enough to get the story he wanted, and she'd played right into his hands and told him everything.

Deciding she couldn't bear to open the shop today, she scribbled a quick note and stuck it to the window.

Closed for personal reasons. Apologies for any inconvenience.

After turning the 'CLOSED' sign on the door, she poured herself a large glass of red wine, the deep ruby colour matching her mood, and took a long, slow swallow before she went upstairs and ran a bath, pouring in her favourite lavender bubble bath. As the steam began to rise, she got undressed and slipped under the water.

Thud … thud … thud …

'Go away,' she muttered. 'I'm closed for the day.'

But the banging didn't stop.

'Urghhh!' She climbed out of the bath and quickly dried herself, pulling on a pair of joggers and a T-shirt. Whoever it was wasn't going away. Muttering to herself she padded back down the stairs and walked to the shop door. Looking back at her through the glass were Jack and Edgar. Just what she didn't need. Amelia opened the door. 'What's going on?' she demanded, her tone sharp as she crossed her arms over her chest. Edgar offered a nonchalant shrug, clearly not eager to get involved. That left Jack standing awkwardly in the doorway, a book clutched in his hand, looking like he was bracing himself for a storm. Amelia's sharp gaze flicked between the two of them before settling on Jack. 'This better be good,' she said, her voice low and firm. 'Because, honestly, the last thing I want is to see you here in my shop.' Edgar couldn't help raising an eyebrow at her directness.

Jack lifted the book slightly, the movement hesitant but determined. 'I'm going to say this as fast as I can,' he began, speaking quickly, 'and Edgar can back me up, because I confided in him a while ago about the real reason I came to Puffin Island.'

Amelia's eyes narrowed as his words sunk in. 'Oh, this just gets better,' she snapped, interrupting him mid-sentence. Her attention shifted to Edgar, disbelief etched across her face. 'So, you knew all along? And neither of you thought it was worth mentioning to me?'

Edgar looked mildly uncomfortable, but before he could answer, Jack held up his hands in a placating gesture.

'Amelia, please,' Jack said. 'I think I've discovered something that will expose Vivienne for who she is.'

'You've got exactly one minute,' she said, her voice clipped. 'Make it count.'

She ushered them inside and closed the door behind them.

'Edgar knew I was never going to write that article, I was just playing along, stringing Miles and Vivienne along for as long as I could. I didn't want them sending someone else to the island to do it. But that's not why we're here.'

'I'm not entirely sure why we're here, to be honest,' Edgar interjected, his tone edged with mild exasperation as he adjusted his glasses. He glanced between Jack and Amelia, clearly wary of what he was about to be dragged into.

Jack shot him a brief, apologetic look before turning back to Amelia. 'Just hear me out. This is important.' Jack held up Ellis Ford's book. 'This book, I picked it up from the B&B just now, started reading it, and I knew I'd read it before.'

'You can't have read it before, he's a debut author,' stated Amelia.

'But I have. Amelia, I know this is going to sound unbelievable, but let me explain.' He took a deep breath, his gaze steady on Amelia. 'When I was setting up the tent on the beach for our date, I noticed Dune House was empty. At the time, I had no idea it had anything to do with you, or that Vivienne was your stepmother. I didn't connect the dots until much later. It was just a beautiful, empty house that intrigued me, so I walked over and poked around a bit. I know I shouldn't have and I'm sorry. But that's not important. What's important is that while I was there, I came across a notebook – your father's notebook.' He swallowed hard, guilt evident in his eyes. 'And … I slipped it into my bag and took it with me.'

Edgar looked alarmed but, seeing that Amelia was about to lay into Jack, he put his hand on her arm. 'Let's hear him out, Amelia. If this notebook can shed any light on what's been happening, it's worth looking at.'

'I'm not proud of myself for what I did, but I admit I read it.' Jack paused, his eyes upon the notebook resting on the counter. 'It's not just a notebook,' he continued. 'It's a handwritten novel, and it's one of the best works I've ever read. Pure genius. Your father was a brilliant writer. Open it. Go on, open it.'

Amelia opened the notebook. 'I don't understand what's going on here.'

Jack placed the Ellis Ford book next to it. 'The words in that notebook are the same words as in Ellis Ford's book. Your father is Ellis Ford.'

Amelia blinked at him, her disbelief evident. 'Don't be ridiculous,' she scoffed. 'I would have known if he was. He would have told me.'

'Read it,' Jack urged, stepping back to give her space.

Both Edgar and Amelia leaned over the notebook. Edgar adjusted his glasses as Amelia hesitated before opening to the first page. Her eyes skimmed the familiar handwriting, and then her movements became frantic as she flipped through page after page, recognising the book she'd only just finished reading.

Jack crossed his arms. 'My guess, and I'd stake my life on it, is that Vivienne is hiding behind a fake name to mask her involvement. She's stolen your father's work and concocted this story about him not wanting fame. She's profiting off his genius, and this notebook proves it.'

Edgar's expression darkened as he examined the pages. 'Amelia,' he said quietly, pointing to the date on the first page, 'this is absolutely your father's handwriting. There's no mistaking it.'

Amelia's hands trembled as she gripped the notebook, her mind racing to piece everything together.

Jack leaned closer, his voice gentler now. 'You see. It's all here. Vivienne didn't just steal his house, Amelia. She stole his legacy.'

'After my mother passed away, he stopped sharing any of his writing with me,' Amelia said, her voice thick with emotion. 'It was a huge step for him to go to London and share his work with anyone. That must have been when Vivienne started scheming. She saw his talent but crushed his ambition, content to bide her time and profit off my father in more ways than one. She was never interested in my father's love.' She paused, swallowing hard. 'I was right all along. There *must* have been more to his accident.' Her voice cracked as she looked at Jack and Edgar. 'And this … this is…'

'Fraud, copyright infringement. You're right, Amelia, I think there's a good case here to open an investigation into your father's death,' Edgar interjected firmly.

'What are we going to do about it?' Amelia asked.

The Story Shop

'Hang her out to dry,' Edgar replied with a sharp nod.

Amelia turned to Jack, her expression softening. 'Jack, thank you.'

'You deserve the truth. Your father deserves the truth. And for what it's worth, I'm sorry for all the ways I've messed this up.'

She stepped closer and took his hand, her eyes locked on his. 'Promise me, Jack,' she said quietly, 'promise me you won't ever hurt Puffin Island. This place means everything to me. The people, the history, the stories … it's home.'

'I promise. I'd never do anything to harm this place. It's become … it's become more than just a place to me, too. It means a lot to me. *You* mean a lot to me.'

The tension between them melted into something warmer, something deeper. Without thinking, Amelia leaned in, wrapping her arms around him in a spontaneous hug. Then, on impulse, she tilted her head up and kissed him softly on the lips.

When they broke apart, Jack grinned, a flicker of his usual charm returning.

'You're amazing,' Amelia murmured, her cheeks flushed.

'I have my moments. So … does this mean I'm forgiven?'

Amelia smiled. 'Yes,' she said simply.

From the corner of her eye, she noticed Edgar stepping outside, already on the phone. His voice carried back through the door. 'I can't wait to see Vivienne get her comeuppance,' he was saying.

'It's been a long time coming,' Amelia agreed, her gaze shifting back to Jack.

'But there's something else we need to talk about,' Jack said, his expression turning serious again as his eyes met hers.

'And what's that?'

'Your letter,' he said pointedly. 'I think you have some explaining to do.'

Amelia smirked, a playful look flickering across her face. 'Then we'd better meet later at the clock as planned,' she said, teasingly drawing out the moment. 'I'll tell all!'

'You're going to make me wait that long?' Jack asked, his tone half-joking, half-pleading.

'I am. For now,' she replied, stepping backwards, 'there's a bath with my name on it, and I, too, have a letter to read!'

Chapter Thirty-Six

JACK

Jack strolled towards the floral clock, Amelia's letter clutched tightly in his hand. His mind raced. How had she managed to keep such a remarkable secret under wraps? It wasn't just the revelation itself that astonished him, but also the strength it must have taken to keep it a secret. He needed to know everything. He looked up and his heart skipped a beat as he spotted her stepping through the gate on the far side of the park. The evening sun was still warm, and when their eyes met, she broke into a radiant grin that sent a rush of even greater warmth through him.

As soon as she was close enough, he reached out and wrapped his arms tightly around her waist. Lifting her effortlessly, he spun her around, lowered her back down and planted a kiss on her lips.

'Amelia Brown, you are a dark horse!' He exhaled and raked his hand through his hair. 'You need to explain yourself!'

Amelia's cheeks flushed as she bit her lip, her eyes sparkling with what looked like both pride and trepidation. And no wonder. She'd spent the past year keeping this to herself.

Jack opened the letter, his expression shifting from amazement to utter incredulity.

'*You* are Maris Wilde?' he said, his voice rising as he paced in front of her. '*The* Maris Wilde, bestselling author of *The Temptation Bucket List*? The one whose books are flying off the shelves faster than I can drink cups of coffee? How do you just … sit on that kind of secret?'

Amelia let out a laugh, though it trembled with emotion. 'You have no idea the lengths I went to, keeping it under wraps. I haven't even told Clemmie yet! She's going to kill me when she finds out!'

Jack stopped pacing and turned to face her, his grin wide. 'This is unbelievable. You should be so proud of yourself! And all those steamy, swoon-worthy scenes that have readers hooked were written right here, on this quiet little island, while you ran your bookshop like nothing was happening?'

Amelia's grin was wide. 'Exactly that!'

Jack shook his head, still trying to process it all. 'Amelia, you're one of the most successful romance authors in the business, and yet you're here, quietly working away in your little bookshop, like it's the most normal thing in the world. Do you even realise how insane this is? How did all this happen? I want to hear everything.'

They sat on a nearby bench. 'It wasn't easy,' she admitted. 'When I first started writing, I didn't think anyone would take me seriously. When I showed Vivienne my manuscript, she said that it was 'like a bad GCSE project' and I'd never make it. That was like a red rag to a bull. I was going to do anything it took to prove her wrong. I decided to cut out the agent and just submit my manuscript directly to publishers, via their websites. I couldn't believe it when multiple publishers came back, offering me contracts. I was amazed, honestly. I ended up signing a three-book deal, but chose to do so under a pseudonym because the timing was ... complicated. My father and I were in a bad place, and I was also terrified of rejection, of looking foolish if the books didn't sell.'

She paused. 'This way, no one would know it was me. I never expected the success I'd find. *The Temptation Bucket List* was the third book of the deal, and I have a meeting in a couple of weeks to discuss a new contract. It's surreal.' She paused for a moment, a soft laugh escaping her lips. 'I can't tell you how pleased I was to hear that Vivienne's only regret is not signing Maris Wilde.'

'But you said you were determined to get published without an agent. Did you actually send the manuscript to her?'

'I did, but only to see if she'd have different feedback when she didn't know I was the one who had written the book. She came back with exactly what she said to you: "Get back in touch if you land a contract."'

'You're a *mastermind*. This is incredible!'

'It's just a shame my dad didn't see my success ... or his own. I guess I was scared initially, scared to own my success in case it all fell apart and came to nothing. And then scared to tell anyone the truth in case it changed the way they treated me.'

Jack reached for her hand. 'But it didn't fall apart. You're a phenomenon. Millions of people love your work. And I'm standing here, completely floored by what you've accomplished.' He laughed. 'You're going to have to prepare yourself for Clemmie's reaction because when she finds out she's been living next to Maris Wilde this whole time, you're not going to hear the end of it!'

'She is going to squeal!'

Jack was still shaking his head in disbelief. 'It's unbelievable, talk about talent in your family… But what I really want to know is how your imagination ran that wild and went to those places? *The Temptation Bucket List* had *me* blushing. It was so…'

'Raunchy?' she finished his sentence. 'You know what they say, it's always the quiet ones!'

Chapter Thirty-Seven
AMELIA

The next morning, Clemmie burst into the bookshop, wide-eyed and breathless. 'Where on earth have you been? You've gone completely AWOL! I have no idea what's happened with the court case.'

Amelia looked up from her coffee, smiling at her friend's frantic energy. 'Oh, I've got so much to tell you, and honestly, I don't even know where to begin. It all sounds like something straight out of a novel, but I promise you, every word is true.'

Clemmie pulled up a stool and sat across from Amelia at the counter. 'Start talking.'

'Well, for one, Edgar has notified the police, and hopefully Vivienne will be arrested very soon.'

Clemmie leaned forward. 'What's she done?'

Amelia's lips twisted into a frown. 'We believe she's committed fraud. Impersonated my dad.'

Clemmie's eyebrows shot up. She looked incredulous … and curious. 'Wait … what do you mean?'

Without saying a word, Amelia reached under the counter and slid a copy of Ellis Ford's novel across to Clemmie. 'I couldn't be prouder of my dad,' she said. 'I just wish he was here to see it.'

Clemmie blinked in confusion, staring at the book. 'Are you saying ... Ellis Ford is your dad?'

Amelia nodded, her smile growing. 'Yep. My dad wrote this. Jack found the original handwritten manuscript gathering dust at Dune House. Turns out Vivienne stole my dad's work, invented a fictional debut author and has been pocketing all the profits.'

Clemmie's hand froze over the book, the magnitude of what Amelia had just told her sinking in. 'No way. She really did all that?'

'It's a lot to take in.'

Clemmie's mouth dropped open as she processed it all. 'This is ... unbelievable. I mean, it's thrilling, horrifying and ... yes, a lot to take in.'

'There's more,' Amelia said, her eyes shining with excitement. 'Edgar called me this morning. Vivienne's finally agreed to hand over my inheritance.'

Clemmie's eyes widened. 'Dune House... It's yours?'

Amelia nodded and smiled. 'Back where it belongs.'

Clemmie let out a delighted squeal, jumped up and wrapped Amelia in a tight hug. 'Oh, Amelia! This is incredible!'

Amelia laughed, pulling back just enough to see her friend's face. 'Though I'm sure Vivienne didn't do it out of the goodness of her heart. More than likely, she's hoping this might paint her in a better light when she has to face these new charges.' She reached down beside the till and picked up a hefty set of keys, which she jangled. 'All mine.'

'Do you think this was the manuscript your dad showed her when they first met? The one she said was unrepresentable?'

'Very possibly,' Amelia replied, nodding thoughtfully. 'But now, with these keys, I have access to his study, and who knows what other hidden gems I might find there. He wrote so many things I haven't even seen.'

'You might uncover some more literary treasures!'

'I've got a meeting with the publisher soon because the Ellis Ford contracts are no longer valid now they know Vivienne must have forged all the signatures. And … there's a movie deal on the table to consider.'

Clemmie's eyes widened, her voice full of disbelief. 'A movie deal? This is huge!'

Amelia nodded. When she spoke, she sounded both excited and cautious. 'It is. But there's still a lot to work through. And…' She hesitated before adding, 'Edgar is going to suggest to the police that they reopen the case and look into my father's death in light of new evidence.'

Clemmie's expression shifted to one of shock. 'You think she had something to do with it?'

'I think that's a huge possibility, but only time will tell.'

Clemmie sat in stunned silence for a moment before murmuring. 'I don't know what to say. This is all so … much! I hope they lock up Vivienne and throw away the key.'

Amelia scrunched up her face. 'There's more.'

Clemmie's eyes widened. 'How can there possibly be more?'

'And I'm not entirely sure how you're going to react to what I'm about to tell you…'

Clemmie leaned in, her face turning serious. 'Please don't tell me that you and Jack have run off and got married without a word to me! That's exactly what happens in *The Temptation Bucket List*, and I swear, if you got married without me, I'll be furious.'

Amelia burst out laughing, shaking her head. 'It's not quite that dramatic,' she replied.

With a secretive smile, Amelia walked over to the display table and picked up a copy of *The Temptation Bucket List*. Flipping to the dedication, she turned it towards Clemmie and pointed to the words *Patience is the sharpest weapon*.

'I'm not quite sure what you're trying to tell me … but Maris Wilde was certainly onto something with that line.'

'Someone was onto something, but it wasn't Maris Wilde. More like Amelia Brown.'

Clemmie tilted her head, a puzzled look crossing her face.

Amelia held her gaze, allowing the words to hang in the air, letting them sink in.

Finally, realisation struck, and Clemmie's eyes widened. 'NO … no way. You can't be! Wait. *You're* Maris Wilde? No … don't be ridiculous…'

Amelia smiled.

'No way! You're telling me that my best friend, quiet, bookshop-owning, puffin-mad Amelia, is the mind behind Maris Wilde and all those spicy romance novels?'

Amelia extended her hand formally. 'Pleased to meet you,' she said, suppressing a laugh.

Clemmie stared at her for a second, still in shock, before letting out a shriek as she launched herself forward to hug Amelia. 'My best friend, the published writer! You've been sitting on this secret all this time? Amelia, this is incredible! The bestseller lists, the millions of readers ... are you going to tell the rest of the world?'

Amelia hugged her back. 'Yes, I think it's time to come clean.'

'I can't take this in. Oh my God, are you actually being serious?' Clemmie's eyes were wide, her jaw practically on the floor.

Amelia laughed. 'I am.'

Clemmie let out another joyful shriek, looking at her with a mix of pride and awe. 'Maris Wilde? Why Maris Wilde? Where has that name come from?'

'I used a different name just in case it ultimately amounted to nothing, and the books flopped. Maris means "of the sea", which fits perfectly with the coastal setting and the charm of Puffin Island, and Wilde, well ... maybe there was a hint of rebellion there.'

'That last book was definitely wild! But seriously, why didn't you tell me?'

'I sent the manuscript off on a whim, not expecting it to go anywhere. Then, when things got so bad with my dad, I was consumed with sadness, and I know it sounds daft but it became something just for me, something I could hold on to while everything else seemed to be falling apart around me. Do you forgive me?'

Clemmie threw her arms around her again. 'Of course I do. You're something else, Amelia Brown! And to think, my best friend writes ... filth!' She grinned wickedly. 'I have to ask, how on earth did you come up with some of those activities in *The Temptation Bucket List*?'

Amelia smirked, folding her arms. 'I can neither confirm nor deny my sources of inspiration!'

They both burst out laughing.

'Two successful authors in the family,' Clemmie marvelled, shaking her head. 'Wait until everyone finds out Maris Wilde and Ellis Ford are both from Puffin Island. Your little bookshop is going to be the most visited place in the country.'

Amelia's cheeks flushed with pride. 'Let's hope so!'

Clemmie's eyes sparkled. 'And Jack … does he know you're Maris?'

'Yes! I think he was a bit stunned when he learned I'm Maris Wilde.'

'I bet! Him and me both!' Clemmie clapped her hands. 'We need to make a big reveal out of this. How about the pub tonight? You'll have to tell everyone! Especially before the newspapers get hold of it.'

Amelia laughed, nodding. 'I'm always up for a night at the pub.'

'Perfect. I'll see you later. I cannot wait to see everyone's faces! I still don't know how you kept this a secret for so long.'

Amelia waved as Clemmie left the shop. Her smile lingered as she reached into the drawer of the desk and pulled out Jack's letter to reread it yet again.

He had confessed everything, the truth about being sent to Puffin Island to write an article intended to tarnish the place's reputation, and how he'd wrestled with the assignment and ultimately decided not to write it. And then decided to stay. But it was the final line that made her pulse quicken more than anything else he'd written.

This surely is no secret, but ... I'm falling in love with you, Amelia Brown.

Her heart swelled with happiness, her pulse racing for all the right reasons.

Chapter Thirty-Eight

Six months later

It was a Sunday afternoon, and Amelia and Jack were nestled in their little world, sharing a cosy escape in the cabin overlooking the sea. A picnic was laid out on the carpet in the centre of the room, with cushions and blankets strewn around. An open bottle of wine sat beside a spread of cheese and crackers. The log fire crackled warmly, while the TV played quietly in the background.

'Do you miss London?' asked Amelia, snuggling into his chest.

'Absolutely not. I always felt lonely there and here I have a brand-new family. Everyone on Puffin Island has welcomed me with open arms. And, of course, you're here, so it's exactly where I want to be.'

Life had changed in ways Amelia could never have imagined. When the news broke that Maris Wilde was not only a Puffin Island native but also Amelia Brown, and that her father was the celebrated but reclusive author Ellis Ford, the island had practically exploded with pride. Once the national papers caught wind of the story, reporters flocked to Puffin Island, all eager to catch a glimpse of the small-town bookshop that had become something of a legend. Visitors poured in from everywhere, filling the shop daily with fans hoping to meet Amelia, who greeted each one with a smile and a story. It was a whirlwind, but at her core Amelia felt the same as always. She was still just a girl who loved books, her bookshop and her beautiful life by the sea.

Today, though, Amelia noticed Jack was acting a bit ... off. Every few minutes, his gaze would drift away from her, towards the door, and he seemed nervous.

'Jack,' she said, arching an eyebrow, 'why are you acting so strange? You're a little ... jumpy, maybe?' She laughed lightly, watching as his gaze darted towards the front door for about the tenth time.

Just then, there was a knock. Jack sprang up energetically and dashed to the door, his eyes flickering with excitement. Amelia caught the muffled sound of the delivery driver's voice.

'A special delivery for Jack Hartwell. Signature required.'

'Oh, so you were expecting something.' Amelia's eyes narrowed playfully as Jack returned with a box in his hands wrapped with a pink satin bow.

With a nervous smile, Jack held out the box towards her. 'Actually, it's for you.'

'For me?' Amelia tilted her head, studying his face. 'Why do you look so nervous?'

Jack ran a hand through his hair, a hint of red colouring

his cheeks. 'Well ... you know how we promised no more secrets after Vivienne? I've got a confession to make. I've been keeping a tiny one from you. Or, maybe ... it's not so tiny.' He took a deep breath. 'I'm honestly a bit nervous about how you're going to react.'

Amelia's heart skipped a beat. 'I'm intrigued,' she replied, her gaze fixed on him as she reached for the package. 'Now, give me that box.'

'Okay, but before you open it,' he began, 'I need to say that this seemed like a good idea at the time, and now I'm beginning to worry it's ... well, maybe not.'

She looked up at him. 'There's only one way to find out.' She smiled, untying the ribbon. Lifting the lid, she pulled back the layers of tissue paper to reveal the book beneath. 'Oh my gosh, it's your new book!'

Jack nodded, his own grin spreading wide. 'The very first copy, and I want you to have it.'

'You're giving it to me? Even though you've been so secretive while you were writing it, not letting me take even the tiniest peek?'

'I am,' he said softly.

Amelia's finger ran over the title embossed in gold: *The Bucket List of Us*. Then she turned to the front page. She read a few paragraphs, then stopped, her eyes widening as she looked back at him with dawning realisation. 'You've written about us,' she murmured, lifting one hand to her heart. 'Jack, this is beautiful. It's ... it's our story.'

'When I first came to Puffin Island, I started writing a diary. I was trying to make sense of everything, I guess. From that first moment when I was blown through the door of your bookshop in that wild storm and saw you standing there, I was captivated. I don't think I ever believed in love at first sight until that very moment.' Jack laughed softly. 'I tried to fight it, told myself it was just the charm of the island, the magic of the bookshop … but you had me instantly. That bookish jumper and those puffin scrunchies…' He laughed. 'This story – our story – it's everything I never knew I needed until I met you.'

She clutched the book to her chest. 'I'll treasure this more than you know.'

'But do you mind that I've written about us? I know I should have checked first.'

She shook her head. 'I think it's beautiful. Something to show the children.' She nudged his elbow with hers. 'Asher Knight and Zara Quinn were already on their first baby by now,' she teased.

'I don't think we'll be showing the children Maris Wilde's book until they're much older.' Jack grinned, a mischievous glint in his eyes. 'No offence! I have to say, though, my bucket list wasn't nearly as bold as yours. I mean, we never quite got around to the sensual body painting … or that private outdoor shower.' He gave her a playful wink.

Amelia raised an eyebrow, her eyes sparkling with mischief. 'Well, there's no time like the present,' she said, leaning in close. 'I'm game if you are.'

'Oh, now you're talking,' Jack replied, pulling her against him and pressing his lips to hers. When he finally pulled back, his face lit up with excitement. 'And I have more news. My editor loved *The Bucket List of Us* and offered me a new contract. A five-book deal!'

'Jack, that's incredible!' Amelia squealed, throwing her

arms around him. 'With the writing courses you're teaching at Dilly's gallery, you'll be the busiest man on Puffin Island!'

He laughed, holding her close. 'This is the life, isn't it? How could anyone ever speak ill of this place?' They both gazed out of the window at the rugged beauty of the sea stretching to the horizon.

Just then Jack's phone rang and he glanced down, surprised. 'It's my editor … calling on a Sunday?'

Amelia nudged him. 'Well, there's only one way to find out what it's about – answer it! Go on!'

Jack picked up, a little confused. 'Hey, Laura, you shouldn't be working today… What's up?'

He listened in silence, his eyes widening at her every word. When he finally hung up, he turned to Amelia, a look of disbelief on his face.

'Well?' she asked. 'Come on, don't leave me hanging!'

Jack took a step back, a grin spreading across his face as he reached for her hands and pulled her to her feet. 'I can barely believe it,' he said, his voice full of excitement. 'The book only came out at midnight and it's flown straight to the top of the charts. We need champagne, I'm a number one *Sunday Times* Bestseller!'

Amelia's mouth fell open, and then she erupted in a cheer. 'That's … that's amazing! Number one! Oh, Jack…'

He laughed, his own excitement spilling over. 'Number one! Can you believe it?'

Amelia stopped mid-step, pointing at the TV. 'Look! They're talking about Puffin Island!' Amelia and Jack's eyes fixed on the screen as Jack turned up the volume.

The newsreader's tone was lively, brimming with excitement. 'In tonight's top story, Hollywood comes to town! Puffin Island will soon be hosting some of Tinseltown's finest, as production begins on *The Forgotten Portrait*, the internationally bestselling novel by the late Ellis Ford, aka Ethan Brown, a beloved local resident of Puffin Island whose brilliant writing was hidden in plain sight. The revelation of Brown's identity follows the shocking scandal involving Vivienne Langford, Brown's former partner and literary agent. Langford fraudulently claimed authorship of Brown's novel and collected royalties under the alias of Ellis Ford. Her deceit was uncovered after Brown's original handwritten manuscript came to light, proving the truth. Langford is now serving a prison sentence for fraud, and a new investigation is underway into the suspicious circumstances surrounding Ethan Brown's untimely death.'

Jack squeezed Amelia's hand, his warmth grounding her in the moment.

'They said his real name,' she whispered, tears shimmering in her eyes. 'Ethan Brown. He would have been so proud.'

Jack smiled, his voice full of admiration as he said, 'From now on his work will have his real name on the cover and that's all thanks to you.'

The newsreader continued.

'Ellis's daughter, Amelia Brown, who has written three novels under the pen name Maris Wilde, is no stranger to literary fame herself. Known for her sensational bestseller *The Temptation Bucket List*, Amelia has captivated millions with her words. Her recent bookshop signing caused a media storm on Puffin Island. But today it's her partner, author Jack Hartwell, who is making headlines by hitting the number one spot on *The Sunday Times* Bestseller list with his newest book, *The Bucket List of Us*, a novel inspired by his time on the island and his love for Amelia. In a remarkable twist, Amelia's latest novel and Ethan Brown's bestseller join Jack's book in the top three spots on the national charts, making it a family affair!

'The trio has made literary history with their achievements, and with Puffin Island soon to host a major film production, we can only imagine how the fame and charm of the small community will continue to grow. Stay tuned as we bring more updates on casting, production and the excitement to come! This is truly one for the books.'

Jack's grin widened, his eyes gleaming with mischief. 'It is truly one for the books,' he repeated. 'There's champagne in the fridge, and if you look under the tissue paper in that box, there's one more present waiting for you.'

Amelia tilted her head, intrigued, and started rummaging through the box. Her laughter bubbled up as she pulled out a set of body paints and held them up. 'Really, Jack?'

He leaned closer, his voice low and teasing. 'We have a temptation bucket list to finish, remember? But first, champagne!'

Amelia shook her head, still laughing as Jack popped the cork, the sound mingling with the crackling of the fire. Their cosy cabin by the sea was full of love, laughter and possibilities, and she realised once and for all that her greatest adventure wasn't to be found in the pages of a book – it was here, unfolding in real life, right in front of her.

Acknowledgments

Every book is a journey, and the magic of Puffin Island would not have come to life without the support, encouragement, and love of some truly wonderful people.

First and foremost, to Charlotte Ledger, the best boss anyone could ask for. Your unwavering belief in me is nothing short of magical. I'm so grateful for you and everyone behind the scenes at One More Chapter – thank you for turning my stories into books, you make dreams come true.

To my amazing editor, Laura McCallen – your insight, care, and dedication are like the perfect lighthouse guiding my words safely to shore. Your edits have the precision of a puffin navigating stormy seas, and your passion ensures every story finds its perfect home, much like the book shop nestled in the cosy corner of Puffin Island. You make every book the best it can be, and I'm so lucky to have you as my wing-woman.

A heartfelt thank-you to Tony Russell, my brilliant copy editor, for catching every detail and polishing every sentence to ensure the stories truly shine.

Thank you to my children, Emily, Jack, Ruby, and Tilly, you are the light of my life and my greatest inspiration even if you haven't read any of my books!

To my writing partners in crime, Nellie and Cooper, my

loyal dogs who are always by my side, offering comfort and company through the long hours. While your contributions to storylines are non-existent, your ability to demand walks at the most inconvenient times is unparalleled – and I wouldn't have it any other way.

Much love to Anita Redfern, my best friend and absolute rockstar cheerleader – I can't fault you and I'm so lucky to have you by my side. Thank you for always being there!

A massive thank you to Julie Wetherill, my dear friend, gin partner, swim partner, and travel companion – who keeps me on the straight and narrow every day. We've explored so many incredible places together (with a few more adventures planned this year!), and you've even managed to read all my books, which makes you a certified legend in my eyes. I'm endlessly grateful for your friendship and your unwavering support, whether we're plotting our next trip or sharing many memes in the early hours of the morning!

Thank you to Bella Osborne, my gorgeous author friend who's always just a phone call away. Your humour is so brilliantly funny it makes me laugh out loud every time I receive a text. I can't wait for our trip to see the puffins this year – it's bound to be another adventure filled with laughter, prosecco and great memories!

And huge love to the readers who choose my books to read and help spread the word, the bloggers who champion them, the bookshops that place them on shelves, and the libraries that make them accessible to all – thank you for your passion and support. My books wouldn't exist without each and every one of you.

I've truly enjoyed writing the story of Amelia Brown and Jack Hartwell. The idea of The Temptation Bucket List came to me one evening while I was lucky enough to witness the Northern Lights and thinking about how life can be full of unexpected, magical moments – much like love itself. I really do believe in love at first sight, and that true love is one of the most enchanting and life-changing experiences we can have. I hope their story has brought a little bit of that magic into your world, just as writing it has for me.

Warm wishes,

Christie x

ONE MORE CHAPTER

YOUR NUMBER ONE STOP FOR PAGETURNING BOOKS

The author and One More Chapter would like to thank everyone who contributed to the publication of this story...

Analytics
James Brackin
Abigail Fryer

Audio
Fionnuala Barrett
Ciara Briggs

Contracts
Laura Amos
Laura Evans

Design
Lucy Bennett
Fiona Greenway
Liane Payne
Dean Russell

Digital Sales
Laura Daley
Lydia Grainge
Hannah Lismore

eCommerce
Laura Carpenter
Madeline ODonovan
Charlotte Stevens
Christina Storey
Jo Surman
Rachel Ward

Editorial
Janet Marie Adkins
Kara Daniel
Charlotte Ledger
Laura McCallen
Ajebowale Roberts
Jennie Rothwell
Tony Russell
Sofia Salazar Studer
Helen Williams

Harper360
Jennifer Dee
Emily Gerbner
Ariana Juarez
Jean Marie Kelly
emma sullivan
Sophia Wilhelm

International Sales
Peter Borcsok
Ruth Burrow
Colleen Simpson
Ben Wright

Inventory
Sarah Callaghan
Kirsty Norman

Marketing & Publicity
Chloe Cummings
Grace Edwards

Operations
Melissa Okusanya
Hannah Stamp

Production
Denis Manson
Simon Moore
Francesca Tuzzeo

Rights
Helena Font Brillas
Ashton Mucha
Zoe Shine
Aisling Smyth
Lucy Vanderbilt

Trade Marketing
Ben Hurd
Eleanor Slater

The HarperCollins Distribution Team

The HarperCollins Finance & Royalties Team

The HarperCollins Legal Team

The HarperCollins Technology Team

UK Sales
Isabel Coburn
Jay Cochrane
Sabina Lewis
Holly Martin
Harriet Williams
Leah Woods

And every other essential link in the chain from delivery drivers to booksellers to librarians and beyond!

Verity Callaway is running away.

The plan is simple: hop in her reliable camper van and cross the Channel, headed for a rendezvous with her best friend in Amsterdam to kick off six months of travel. But when Verity stumbles across a decades-old postcard while preparing her cottage for its temporary tenants, her life takes an unexpected turn, and she finds herself on a ferry to Puffin Island instead.

Verity's childhood was filled with tales of adventures set on the picturesque island, but she'd always thought her beloved granny had made it all up. Now, knowing the stories and the setting were real, Verity is determined to find the postcard's sender and uncover the secrets of her grandmother's past … even if it means setting off a sequence of events that will change not just her own life, but also that of the sleepy island's close-knit community…

Available now in paperback, eBook and audio!

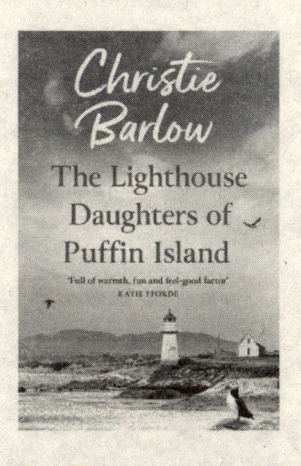

Can she weather the storm?

Having narrowly avoided losing everything to her romance scammer ex, artist Delilah Waters is done with men and focused entirely on her quest to buy Puffin Island's magical lighthouse. It's a crucial piece of her own family's history and the perfect space to turn into her home. But then Max Harrington walks through her door.

Her feelings for her former art teacher might have been forbidden at the time, but now he's back, and single, and there's no denying that the attraction is mutual! But when something seems too good to be true, it normally is, and Dilly soon makes a shocking discovery that changes everything…

Available in paperback, eBook and audio!

**Next, prepare to fall in love with the
Love Heart Lane series!**

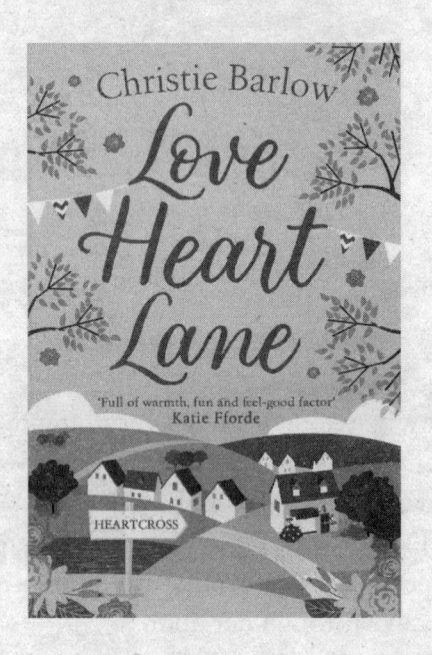

Christie Barlow

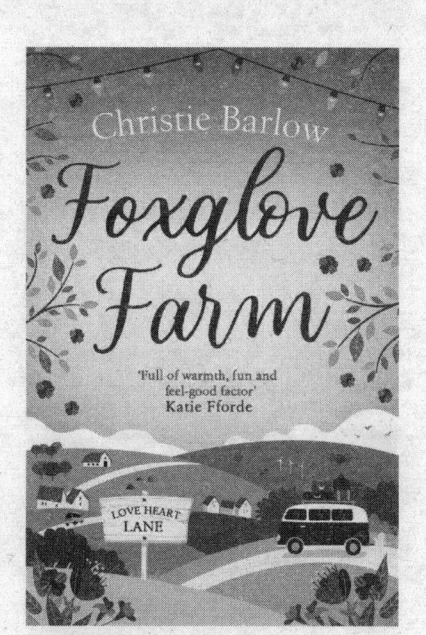

Foxglove Farm

'Full of warmth, fun and feel-good factor'
Katie Fforde

LOVE HEART LANE

Christie Barlow

Clover Cottage

'Full of warmth, fun and feel-good factor'
Katie Fforde

LOVE HEART LANE

Christie Barlow

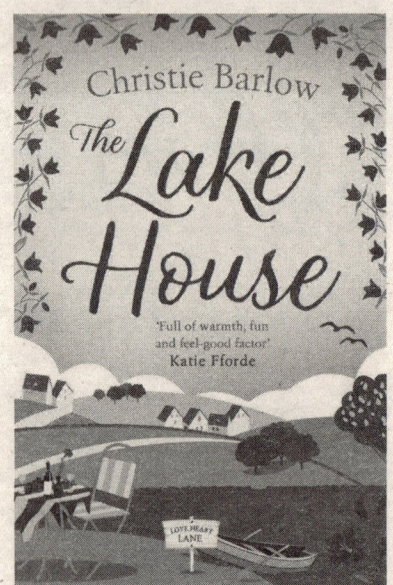

Starcross Manor

'Full of warmth, fun and feel-good factor'
Katie Fforde

Christie Barlow

The Lake House

'Full of warmth, fun and feel-good factor'
Katie Fforde

Christie Barlow
Primrose Park

'Full of warmth, fun and feel-good factor'
Katie Fforde

Christie Barlow
Heartcross Castle

'Full of warmth, fun and feel-good factor'
Katie Fforde

Christie Barlow
The New Doctor at Peony Practice

'Full of warmth, fun and feel-good factor'
Katie Fforde

Christie Barlow
New Beginnings at the Old Bakehouse

'Full of warmth, fun and feel-good factor'
Katie Fforde

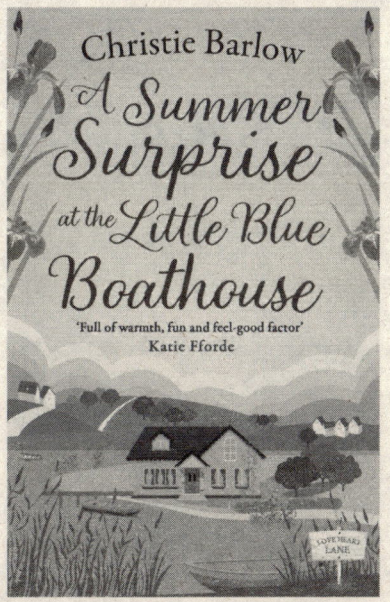

Christie Barlow
The Hidden Secrets of Bumblebee Cottage

Christie Barlow
A Summer Surprise at the Little Blue Boathouse

'Full of warmth, fun and feel-good factor'
Katie Fforde

Christie Barlow

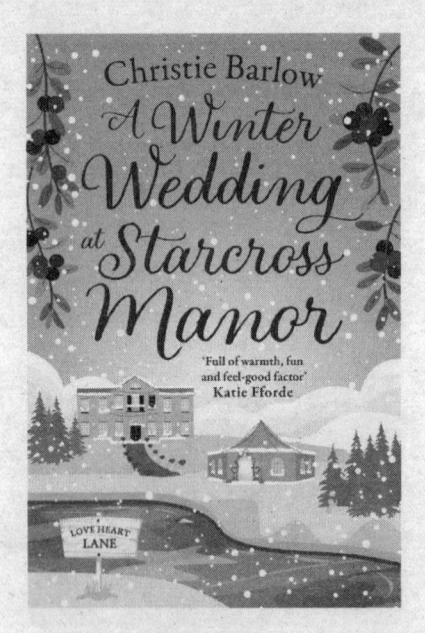

A Winter Wedding at Starcross Manor

'Full of warmth, fun and feel-good factor'
Katie Fforde

LOVE HEART LANE

Christie Barlow

THE LIBRARY ON LOVE HEART LANE

Take a Book

LOVE HEART LANE

ONE MORE CHAPTER

YOUR NUMBER ONE STOP FOR PAGETURNING BOOKS

One More Chapter is an award-winning global division of HarperCollins.

Subscribe to our newsletter to get our latest eBook deals and stay up to date with all our new releases!

signup.harpercollins.co.uk/join/signup-omc

Meet the team at
www.onemorechapter.com

Follow us!

- @OneMoreChapter_
- @onemorechapterhc
- @onemorechapterhc
- @onemorechapterhc

Do you write unputdownable fiction?
We love to hear from new voices.
Find out how to submit your novel at
www.onemorechapter.com/submissions